The True and Outstanding
Adventures of the Hunt Sisters

The True and Outstanding Adventures of the Hunt Sisters

A Novel

Elisabeth Robinson

Little, Brown and Company
Boston   New York   London

This is a work of fiction. The author did work briefly on a film project of *Don Quixote* in which John Cleese and Robin Williams were involved, but the movie was never made. This is where fact ends and fiction begins. The dialogue and every scene and situation are fictitious, including those in which celebrities appear. Except for the celebrities, all of the characters, from the protagonist and her family to the medical and film professionals, who appear in this book are inventions, and any resemblance to anyone living or dead is coincidental.

Grateful acknowledgment is made to

New Directions Publishing Corp., for permission to reprint an excerpt from "The Dead Woman," by Pablo Neruda, from *The Captain's Verses*, copyright © 1972 by Pablo Neruda and Donald D. Walsh. Reprinted by permission of New Directions Publishing Corp.

Scribner, an imprint of Simon & Schuster Adult Publishing Group, for permission to reprint an excerpt from "The Cradle Song," by W. B. Yeats, from *The Collected Works of W. B. Yeats, Volume I: The Poems, Revised,* edited by Richard J. Finneran (New York: Scribner, 1997).

Bruce Springsteen, for lyrics from "Thunder Road," by Bruce Springsteen. Copyright © 1975 by Bruce Springsteen. All rights reserved. Reprinted by permission. And for lyrics from "No Surrender," by Bruce Springsteen. Copyright © 1984 by Bruce Springsteen. All rights reserved. Reprinted by permission.

ISBN 0-316-73502-7

Designed by Interrobang Design Studio

Printed in the United States of America

For Laurie

Hope is itself a species of happiness,
and perhaps the chief happiness this world affords.

— SAMUEL JOHNSON

The True and Outstanding
Adventures of the Hunt Sisters

August 25, 1971
August 26, 1971
August 27, 1971

Dear sister,

My name is Olivia Hunt. I am your sister. You are inside mom. Jim is our brother. He's OK for a boy.

I had a dream about you. I was in the canoe. My hair was in a braid but it was a snake too. You came out of the lake. You crawled up my snake braid. You got in the canoe. You look like me. The canoe tipped over but we could talk under water.

Me and Jim are up here at Aunt Louise's. It's pretty nice. We go swimming. We pick blueberries. We play in the woods. I get to name you if you're a girl. Dad said Let's call her Martini. Mom said That's terrible. I don't like that name. I like the name Madeline. It's my favorite book. I'll read it to you sometime.

Other fun stuff we can do:

1. Play in the treefort.
2. Play dress up in the attic.
3. Pretend we are princesses. I have a crown. Dad will buy you one. You can't touch mine. Dad buys you whatever you want.
4. Pretend we are brides.
5. Lots of other fun stuff.

I like writing this letter. It's like you're here. Only you're invisible.

I love you already,
Olivia

August 28, 1998
35,000 feet over Nevada

Tina Burns
188 Westborne Park Road
Portland, Oregon 97211

Dear Tina,

I was sitting at home yesterday (where else?) working on the fourth draft of my suicide note when I got the call. I resented the interruption and nearly didn't answer the phone. I was having a hard time getting the tone right and, as we've discussed, tone is everything in correspondence. This seems especially true when it comes to your very, very, *very* last words. (But I now wonder: *is* a suicide note correspondence?) The first draft was too angry, especially toward Michael, whom in fact I do not resent for dumping me. Why would I? He was doing me a favor, putting me out of my misery, which is what living with him was like. No, the raging anger and hate hate hate were misdirected in this draft; they were really meant for my former boss, the president of Universal Pictures, Mr. Josh Miller.

As you may recall from our previous discussions, this guy is a real asshole. You remember — the one whose lip curls up to the right when he speaks in his irregular British accent, which he can't seem to shake since his junior year abroad twenty years ago. Whose pride and joy is not his five-year-old son but his custom-made butter yellow Rolls-Royce. Josh, whose fleshy face resembles a rhino's — beady wide-set eyes blinking between a mother of a snout, or maybe it's the personality that makes one think of a dangerous, stupid beast — and whose tongue I found down my throat at the company Christmas party? (I know, I should have sued him as you advised, but I was afraid of being blacklisted.) It was Josh Miller — of the Hollywood Miller dynasty — who after three years as my boss still looked at me with a face that said: *Who let her in?* Who stuck me on that *Babe* rip-off *Lloyd the Hamster* and then fired me the day it tanked, as I repeatedly warned him it would. Clearly, Josh was the true villain in my life story and deserved all the hate in my soon-to-expire heart, not dear Michael. But I couldn't give that windbag the satisfaction of knowing he drove me to suicide, could I? After further analysis, I realized that of course there were *other* people I deeply deeply hated too. So, yesterday afternoon, as the super pounded the eviction notice into my hollow apartment door, I committed to another draft.

Now, I love my mother. We all love our mothers, don't we? Dad, too, okay; somehow. But let's be honest here. You and I both know they destroyed any chances I had in this world. Don't say "therapy" to me, Tina; you know Dr. Schteinlegger did his very best for two years before throwing up his professional hands. I know these dear people from whose clueless loins I sprang have everything to do with why I'm a complete failure, but that sounded so common. Who doesn't blame their parents? That draft was full of clichés and self-pity, and if it's one thing I'm not, it's self-pitying.

Finally, the stewardess brings me my goddamn Bloody Mary. She actually said, Drink it slow because this is your last one. I've had three, big deal. Have I been unruly? I asked nicely. Her cat-ass lips puckered as she lurched away. (The indignity of coach. What better proof of my fall from grace? And now the smell of baking chocolate chip cookies wafts down from first class to torment me, to remind me of all I've lost. . . .)

You may be wondering *why* I had decided to end my life. I got ahead of myself with the suicide note problem. Well, it's all about majesty, Tina.

My career was in the toilet. Hollywood graciously let me, some nobody shiksa from Shawnee Falls, Ohio, into the magic kingdom, and I blew it. Three years at Universal and the only movie I made was a hamster picture that grossed less than we spent on catering. Then I'm on the street, without a hit or enough friends to dine out on. A script of *Don Quixote* I'd optioned with my last ten grand had just been passed on by every studio in town. I had no love, thanks to Michael's mysterious departure, and what were the chances of my meeting someone truly wonderful and marrying him and conceiving a child before my last egg dropped? About the same odds of my father winning the Ohio Mega Millions Lotto. So, no family to live for. No career. No cash. No hope.

What's more, I'm not the blonde I used to be. Highlights weren't cutting it; I needed about three processes every eight weeks or I'd be found out, and, perhaps the final straw (pardon the pun), a new stubborn pubicky hair had sprouted over the right corner of my mouth, a truly horrendous harbinger of a mustache soon to follow. A mustache! Things were bleak *before* that phone call and I don't think that's an exaggeration. I don't think you can say I was being *negative* here. (A *mustache!*) Jimmy Stewart had a helluva lot more to live for when he tried to off himself in *It's a Wonderful Life*. What's incredible is that given how utterly pathetic most people's lives are, more people don't do it.

I'd kill for a cigarette. When you're strapped into a twenty-ton tin can miles above the earth, surrounded by stinking humanity, and you're flying to the scene of the crime, aka your childhood home, you simply *need* a cigarette. Here's another good reason to die. You can't smoke anywhere anymore. The Reign of Virtue is winning, Tina. You watch. You're going to wake up one day and find they've taken *all* the fun out of living.

I know what you're thinking. Sure. Eventually I might have gotten another midlevel, unsatisfying job, and a midlevel, unsatisfying marriage to go with it; with the help of science, maybe even some midlevel, unsatisfying kids, too, who, when I was a retired and unfulfilled midlevel film executive, would hate me for being neither famous nor a good parent — sure, all this could be mine, but the question is, where was the majesty? Some people feel it when they make a stock market killing, get a promotion, or see their kid make a touchdown, some when they win an Oscar, run a marathon, and if you're one of those lucky bastards, you might even feel the majesty one morning when you see the sun rise, or a butterfly land on a sunflower, blah, blah, blah. Knowing myself as well as I do, I knew majesty would not be found in the life that was yawning before me, and that's when it hit me like one of those embroidered pillows: if you can't live a majestic life, die a majestic death.

Ideally this would be in the line of nonprofit duty in Africa or India. Gunned down by guerrillas while spooning rice into a starving but gorgeous brown child's mouth. Or something more (seemingly) spontaneous and heroic: after I pulled Steven Spielberg's drowning child or perhaps a chihuahua out of the flooded Los Angeles River, my body would be swept to sea. That'd be majestic. Or I could rid the world of some scum — take out some white supremacists, a corrupt cop or pedophile — before turning the handgun on myself. I'd like to do something noble, but I was feeling too desperate to organize that kind of opportunity. Just killing myself would be simpler and quicker, and I enjoyed imagining all my friends and enemies reading about my death and feeling real sorry for what they'd done or not done as the case may be. The only thing stopping me was the note, which is why I was still alive when the phone rang yesterday and changed my plans.

Olivia? It's your father. He always identifies himself, even after all these years as my father. He was hammered. I nearly hung up on him.

Oh, god . . . honey . . . It's your sister. He was weeping, too.

What? What happened?

Maddie's got . . .

All your life you try to imagine what bad news sounds like, but when you actually hear bad news, it simply makes no sense; it's like being told the definition of a black hole by a physicist, directions by a local, the evidence of God by a priest. First you say,

What?

Then, after it's repeated to you —

It's leukemia.

— you say:

No.

Olivia

August 29, 1998
Shawnee Falls, Ohio

Dear Tina,

Thanks for calling today. Sorry I couldn't talk. I'm writing this in my childhood bed, under the canopy of purple flowers. Maddie wouldn't let my mother remodel our room, so it remains eerily untouched, like one of those museum alcoves with roped-off chairs. I should be in Tony's varsity jacket talking to you on the phone, or on my way over to get high in your backyard. Too bad you moved. Getting high with you sounds just perfect right now, I'm so wired.

To answer your question, how's it going? I guess I'll begin with Maddie, who seems, well, herself: a big-bosomed, big-smiled, big-haired girl who watches soaps and sitcoms and who gets all indignant if you don't defend the retarded, the poor, stray dogs, or let her spice the spaghetti sauce. At dinner last night she jumped all over me when I wondered why an animal's right to life should trump my right to, say, beef, or fur, especially when the animal wouldn't even *have* a life if not for my desire for it to be dead one day. Her jaw jutted out; I backed down quicker than I normally would. Other than that it was your usual Hunt family get-together. Could have been Christmas, only tenser. The dining table was covered with a white cloth and napkins, the good crystal and Grandma's gilded china, and in the center, an autumnal nosegay of rusty mums and bachelor's buttons. My mother was cooking her heart out, and with the steamed-up windows, the bubbling pots and sizzling pans, the TV blaring from the family room, it felt festive, which was probably Eleanor's intention, to make the best of the situation by bringing out the very best.

Jim and his family got in from New York the day before. I think Jim and Sarah must have told Nell and Sophie some heavy stuff was going down, because they look like droopy-eared puppies braced for a blow. Kids understand way too much. Sarah is on the verge of tears, but around my parents she always is, and Jim is Jim: cheerfully, enviably oblivious, or so he appears.

When I arrived, Mad and Bobby were already here. She was slouched in Ed's La-Z-Boy watching a *Frasier* rerun, Bobby on the couch, and Ed was in the garage in his *old* La-Z-Boy, polishing off a predinner six-pack with Jim. It was just like any other family get-together, except I noticed Maddie didn't meet me at the door like she always does; she didn't hop across the cold deck in her stocking feet, she didn't open my car door and reach in to be the first to hug me, she wasn't even waving from the kitchen door, she just stayed sunk down in Ed's chair and said without looking at me, Hey, Liv. I wanted to hug her. She seemed closed off, so I didn't. I said, Hey, Madster. What're you watching? Like it was just your average Friday. I wish I'd just squeezed into the La-Z-Boy with her for a minute. But that would have been weird and I guess I wanted things to be normal.

All through dinner I watched her face. I'm not sure what I was looking for. A sign of how she was taking it, I guess. Or maybe I wanted to give her a sign, like we'd do as kids with our eyes, a silent exchange across the table: a tilt of the head meant Jim's lying, a blink meant Mom's falling for it, and sometimes with just a perfectly timed glance we could make each other burst out laughing. But last night there were no signals or knowing smiles, and her eyes never looked into mine; our secret language didn't have words for this.

We ate. Our forks clanked against our plates. We talked about the lasagna, the neighbors, the cold front and the gubernatorial election, and we didn't talk about this thing that has happened. Or is happening. Bobby didn't say a word. He didn't look the way I remembered him — the sturdy, handsome strawberry blond I'd cast as a fireman or a baseball player — he looked subdued, somehow, tentative. After dinner he took Maddie home, and the minute my mom heard their car door thud shut she collapsed at the cluttered kitchen table and buried her face in a dish towel, her shoulders shaking with silent sobs. I put my arm around her. She seemed short. I thought, *Must take my calcium.* The towel absorbed her words, but I knew what she was saying, and what she wanted to hear.

It's going to be okay, Mom. It's not like it used to be, I said. Cancer is curable now. It's not like the old days.

I can't handle this, she said.

Come on. It's going to be fine. She'll do some chemo and be home in a few weeks. She's young and strong.

Oh honey, you don't understand. . . .

People do it all the time now, and then get back to completely normal lives, I said. I was prepared for this conversation because I'd just had it with Ed in the Lamplighter at the airport. He met me at the gate, his skin splotchy and his eyes bloodshot; he looked like the one with a disease. We walked to the nearest bar. Fortunately it was only a hundred feet away. He'd already made himself known to the undelightful Ukrainian barmaid. Two more, he signaled with his knobby fingers. And what do you want, honey? he asked me. Ed was drinking double Johnnie Walker Black with a chaser of the same; the man has the thirst of Tantalus.

He swallowed half the tumbler and the amber liquid released his tears before the glass was back on the table. His face curled into itself as he cried, not even trying to be discreet, just openly sobbing there at the table, surrounded by people who weren't sobbing, people who were trying to have a nice quiet drink while waiting for their flights or for their loved ones to arrive. He didn't give a damn. It wasn't that shocking. I'd seen him cry before, after he'd passed through the milder levels of intoxication of Verbose, Bellicose, and Morose, before reaching Lachrymose, when like clockwork he'd mention his poor dead mother, and we'd know the end was near, Comatose was next, Dad would be nodding off very soon.

. . . and she's going to lose all her beautiful hair, he cried.

This seemed like a strange thing to be worried about at a time like this, but Maddie does have incredible hair and I guess it's been a source of paternal pride for Ed all these years. I've always wondered where she got that luscious brown hair and why the hell I didn't. I read somewhere that men subconsciously seek healthy hair and good teeth in mates: maybe *this* is why I'm still single. Ugly girls, fat ones, bitchy ones, if they have good hair they can bag some hair-loving guy. Check it out, Tina, you'll see I'm right. Anyway, I told him don't worry, her hair will grow back. She was young, everything would be fine, cancer was no big deal anymore, the medical establishment had made huge strides, hadn't he seen all the ads on TV? He hung on my every word, like Eleanor was doing at the kitchen table as she carefully folded and refolded the blue striped towel into smaller and smaller squares.

She'll be all right, I said again.

Well. I hope so, she said begrudgingly, like only a fool would do that, like it was a goddamned imposition or something to hope. She's so negative it makes me want to slap her, Tina. She went back to the sink and resumed scrubbing the crusty lasagna pan. At least she would get that pan in line. I needed a smoke.

It was cool out, and the musty smell of fall, of dried leaves and earth, said that something was over, that it was time to put away the summer dresses, that soon it would be dark before dinner, that another season had passed; one whiff and I was melancholy as hell. Ed was watching the Indians game in the garage, a cigarette and a Bud hanging limply at his side. He said, Hi, honey. Sometimes the way he says honey I know he means it; there's true affection in the sweetness of the word: he's happy to see me. He keeps this little black-and-white TV set on a shelf tucked between drippy paint cans and green plastic jugs of rose fertilizer and coffee cans heavy with rusty nails and screws. Why do men keep old nails and screws? Have you ever seen a man use an *old* screw? If they did, they'd have no reason to go to the hardware store ever again. Ed used to go every Saturday morning like it was his house of worship, and he'd always take Jim. One Saturday when Jim was sick, my mom suggested he take me instead. Ed looked at me and sighed, She doesn't want to go to the hardware store, Eleanor. My mom said, Sure you do, don't you? I shrugged, not wanting to appear desperate. He said, She's not even dressed. I saw her give him a look and then he said, Okay, well, hurry up.

In the Caddy I sat next to him on the blue leather bench seat. He smelled good in the morning: a little Brut aftershave, a little tobacco, a little bourbon seeping through his pores, the way I imagine Gary Cooper and Humphrey Bogart must have smelled. He reached across my lap to push in the lighter, and again when it popped out. I watched him guide the tip of the cigarette into the chrome cylinder. Loops of smoke hung in front of my face like empty dialogue balloons in a comic strip. We didn't speak. He kept his eyes on the road, his left hand loosely on the wheel. I imagined he and Jim talked when they were together. I tried to think of something interesting to say. I worried that the entire trip would be made in silence and I wouldn't be invited again because I wasn't as fun as Jim. Finally I said, I can play a sonata now, Dad.

He probably didn't hear me. The car stopped and he shoved the gear arm up into park. I'd failed and felt miserable as he opened his door and I slid out after him.

But when he nodded at the beehived cashier and she said, Morning, Ed, I felt better. Proud, I suppose. People knew him; he was known. We walked down the sloped rows crowded with crowbars and screwdrivers, nuts and bolts, walls jammed with hammers and rods, tubing and rope, my hand in his huge dry hand, and I was happy because it was exotic, the smell of rubber and motor oil and paint and steel and men, the men in baggy gray jumpsuits with their names in red cursive letters over their pen-filled pockets, and the men in paint-spotted khakis studying all that strange gear.

You want something? he asked.

You couldn't go near a store without Ed making you buy something. That's okay, I said.

Go ahead. Pick something out.

I looked at the Peg-Board covered with tiny plastic bags holding screws and washers. On the shelf along the floor were bins of wire brushes and steel wool. Farther down the aisle was rope, twine, and chains on huge spools. Pick something out? It wasn't going to be easy. And money worried my mother, so I felt crummy spending it, even though my father always insisted. He saw a friend and they lit cigarettes and started talking. The paint-mixing machine was shaking a gallon of paint, the frantic clicking making me more fretful: Ed might be generous, but he was also impatient, and if I didn't find something to buy soon, I would fail this second test of the morning. Then I found it.

What do you want that for? he asked.

For a goldfish. It was a small glass bowl.

You don't have a goldfish.

If I get the bowl then maybe I'll get a fish.

He pinched my nose with his tobacco-rough fingers. Okay, missy. Whatever you want. He always had a lot of cash, neatly folded in numerical order in a soft leather billfold. He'd flip through the crisp bills, peel out a few, and slap them on the counter like they made a winning hand: full house! The cashier leaned over the counter to get a look at me. She winked. Who's this? Tell Barb your name, he said. Her hair was a swirl of yellow cotton candy. She was the kind of woman my mother didn't like, so out of loyalty I refused to smile. She dangled a green lollipop at me like it was a big deal.

We went to the pet store and I was paralyzed by the infinity of goldfish — there were millions of them swarming in tanks that lined the dark humid rows. I tried to fix on one, the prettiest one, the biggest, the one that would make Jim most jealous. My dad said, Oh, come on, they're all the same, and then with that little white net he trapped one. He added a ceramic treasure chest and a bag of turquoise pebbles and said, Your mother's going to be mad. She hates fish.

Maybe we shouldn't do it, I said, in the grip of another test.

I thought you wanted a fish.

On the way home he pulled into The Alibi. I'll only be a minute, he said as he closed the door. I gotta raise the roof.

I wasn't familiar with the euphemism. He went inside. I sat up on my knees to watch. I kept my eyes glued to the roof of the building. He was a big man, enormous to me, so I believed he could raise the roof over his head with his bare hands. But it didn't move. I got bored watching it. I also got concerned that my fish was suffocating in that Baggie. I decided to let a little air in. I untwisted the wire. The bag sagged open and the water spilled all over my lap and the goldfish fell down the crack between the seats. I stuck my hand in the crack and felt the tip of my finger push the wet slippery fish farther away. On the blue carpeted floor I reached under the seat, but my arm was too short; I could only see the fish flipping in the shadows. I started bawling. I cried so hard I fell asleep and the next thing I knew the world was upside down as my father carried me up the porch stairs and inside our house.

I don't know why I just told you all that. It's funny what you remember. It's nearly two A.M. This letter has finally tired me out. You, too, I bet. My hand is definitely ready for sleep. And I haven't even asked you how things are with you. I assume you'd tell me if you were pregnant, so I guess you're not yet. I bet if you start *dreading* that you're pregnant, the way we used to every month, instead of hoping you are, then you will be. That's the way life works, isn't it?

It's so quiet I believe I am the only person awake in all of Ohio. The streetlight hums. A dog barks a mile away. My father snores on the other side of this flowered wall. The silence is safe. You don't feel this sound in L.A. When the quiet does come, very late, or at those odd intervals in the day when for a moment there are no motorcycles and no horns and you think you might have gone temporarily deaf, it is not soothing, because you know it's only a pause before a crashing minor chord: in a second, a siren will slice through the silence, reminding you that terrible things are happening somewhere, still.

Wishing you were here,
Olivia

August 31, 1998
Shawnee Falls, Ohio

Johnny Ray Dickerman
6507 Woodrow Wilson
Los Angeles, California 90068

Via fax

Re: *Don Quixote* rewrite

Dear Johnny,

As discussed, here are my notes for the script meeting with Harris Thursday. Sorry I can't be there myself; it looks like I'll have to stay here a little longer than I expected.

Now Johnny, I need you to do me a favor. Harris only agreed to do another free rewrite on two conditions: one, *you* want the work done, and two, it's specific, not a page-one overhaul. So in the *highly* unlikely event that you actually approve of the following suggestions, I'm asking you to please make sure Harris believes they're coming from you. Perhaps I needn't have even asked.

The other thing is, my notes are based on feedback I got from the studios, not what I believe myself. There comes a point when you have to listen to what the market is telling you, Johnny, and I think we've reached that point. Without at least some of these changes, I'm not going to waste my time or risk my credibility (what's left of it) by going to more financiers.

Okay, the biggest problem with the script is it's too dark and depressing. Yes, it's a tragic-comedy, but we're emphasizing the tragic too much. It's a big downer. And before you close that Texas-sized mind of yours, remember that this four-hundred-year-old novel has been interpreted many ways, by many genuises, but even Orson Welles couldn't get his version made because it was so, well, *genius,* no one could understand it. I don't want that to happen to you. Don't start whistling "The Impossible Dream." I am not, as you've suggested a hundred times, trying to turn this into *Man of La Mancha,* okay? Just listen.

If we change the ending (and lay the groundwork for it in the beginning, since the ending begins in the beginning), I should be able to raise $60 million and you will still make the movie you've been dreaming of. And it's down to three little changes:

1. Quixote *wins* the duel with the Knight of the Moon. He can win accidently, by some odd cleverness, so it won't be unrealistic, but he must win or the audience will be too disappointed. It's the big climax, it's Quixote's shining hour, the tournament he's been questing for, and to lose it is too depressing. If it's all an illusion (as some will argue), why would he create such a gloomy final illusion for himself?

2. He dies in his bed because he's an old man — who lived his dream and now *can* die — *not* because his dreams have been crushed or "reality" has killed him. And we merely *underline* that

Sancho has got his spirit now, Quixote lives on in him (blah, blah, blah).

3. Finally, and most important, Quixote *does not renounce* his dream on his deathbed. We've watched this old farmer, so inspired by tales of chivalry and knights to go out and act like one, searching for wrongs to right and battles to fight, believing windmills are giants, a horse trough is a baptismal font, an ugly farm girl is a beautiful princess, etc., etc.; he endures torture and ridicule for this dream of his — he can't, at the end, say he was wrong and he shouldn't have done it! People will demand their money back, Johnny. In fact, we'll never get to make the movie the audience would then storm out of. Hollywood is about wish fulfillment. The guy has to be a hero. He has to die triumphant, which means he can't say it was all for nothing.

4. (I know I said three.) We need five more laughs. Just five. Physical or verbal, Harris can do either in his sleep, don't let him whine to you about this. *Five more laughs.* Because five spoonfuls of sugar will help the medicine go down.

JD, you know I love our version. A penniless idealist lives his dream only to have it mercilessly crushed by reality, by the unfeeling establishment; the masses always kill the individual because he's a threat to the status quo. I love your Marxian interpretation of Dulcinea as unattainable wealth. I love the ruthlessness, the unflinching unsentimentality of your take. It's fierce and grim. Hell, it's true: life sucks and then you die, etc. It's genius, Johnny. But that's a low-budget indie movie — not a $60 million Hollywood Christmas release. The ending has to be up. *You know this.*

Please consider these changes before you meet with Harris on Thursday. They shouldn't take him much time. I wish I could be there, but I'll be in Ohio till Monday. Give me a call here once you've looked these over.

On my knees,
Olivia

September 1, 1998
Shawnee Falls, Ohio

Dear Tina,

It was great talking to you today. A relief to actually hear your voice. Do you realize it was twenty-five years ago this fall that you were in front of Mrs. Zumhagen's class trying to remember the capital of Colorado when I mouthed "Denver" and we became instant friends? Twenty-five years. Well, happy anniversary, Burns.

Here's the folder I mentioned. It was nice of you to offer, but you really don't have to read this grim stuff. I downloaded it from *Best Bets for Leukemia* and made copies for everyone. As you will see, acute lymphocytic leukemia (appropriately acronymed ALL) is not the best leukemia in the world, but it's not the worst. Since they caught it early, and she's healthy and strong, her odds are actually very good: "60 percent to 80 percent attain complete remission." (She's always been in the top twentieth percentile.) It's pretty technical, so I highlighted the most important facts for us to keep in mind. I don't know if anyone will read this stuff, but they should. Especially my dad. Last night I was helping him carry the garbage out to the street. When we finished he said, I have something to show you. I followed him to the backyard where the rock garden slopes down to the lower level. He lifted a rock, and there in a neat little hole was a Maxwell House coffee can, the plastic lid secured with silver duct tape. He ripped off the tape. Inside was a roll of cash.

Gee, thanks. How'd you know? I said.

It's not for you. There's thirty-five grand out here.

Where?

All over.

So you *have* been winning the lottery all these years. . . .

Hell, no. This was just a little deal I did. Don't tell anyone. Especially your mother.

Okay.

I'm going to buy a place in Florida with it. A good deal's come up on a condo down there. It's right on the beach. You know I was planning on retiring in January.

As he squatted to slip the can back into its hole his knees cracked sharply like dry wood. When he stood up he said, But what do you think? I mean, now —?

His hazel eyes are hooded: I've been looked at by these eyes for thirty years, but when he looked at me last night, even in the darkness I could see something in my father's eyes I'd never seen before in my life; he was helpless. He didn't know what was going on and he was asking me to tell him. Not about the money or the condo but about what was happening to Maddie, and, more, to him; he was begging, *what the hell is happening?* He was confused and afraid, like a man on a dark street who's forgotten his name and where he lives: utterly lost. Helpless.

I ignored it, Tina. What the hell, he's my father; I'm not ready for him to be helpless. I pretended I didn't see it. I turned back to the house and told him I thought he should wait awhile before buying the condo, before retiring to Florida. And to read the folder on leukemia I'd left for him on the kitchen table.

This morning I had breakfast at Maddie's. She made blueberry pancakes. When we finished we went out to plant tulips. It was a perfect fall day, warm and clear and bright, the sky as blue as can be; it was so beautiful and gay it felt like a mistake. Shouldn't the world be gloomy? If this were a movie, it would have been: we would reschedule this scene for a suitably ominous afternoon; or, if the budget were lower, we'd bring in a rain machine and a wind machine to whip up some shitty weather. We'd make the sky suit the script. As it was, though, Maddie and I sat in the garden, digging holes in the damp black dirt, and buried the bulbs with our questions.

It's a little early to be doing this, she said. They could come up in February. But if I wait till I come home it'll be too late.

I could do it for you.

No, I want to. I love the smell, don't you?

Of what?

The earth. Dirt.

Yeah. It's great.

You miss having a garden?

I miss having a gardener. Javier was really . . . talented.

You didn't —

Maddie, come on. I only thought about it, okay? It was hard not to when he took off his shirt and the sweat —

Have you told Michael? About me?

No.

Why don't you call him?

What for?

Don't you miss him?

. . . No.

She looked at me. Maddie still has a baby face, round and open with wide-set brown eyes; she looks like she's always looked, like a ten-year-old kid who, in this case, had one on you. She frowned and looked at the holes I'd dug. Deeper, she said, or the squirrels will dig them up.

Tomorrow she goes to Mercy.

More later,
Olivia

— ◆ —

September 2, 1998
Shawnee Falls, Ohio

Michael Klein
State Rd. 75, No. 811
Dixon, New Mexico 87527

Dear Klein,

Maddie thought I should give you a call. I didn't tell her I don't have your number. I hope you're well. That work is going well. What are you painting these days? Still working on that faceless men series? I was fired from Universal — maybe you heard. Yeah, that prick Miller. Big surprise, huh? It's actually a good thing. Because I'm going to make the kind of movies I want and he's going to rot in hell for eternity, so everything worked out for the best. I miss you.

I'm sitting in Mercy's fourth-floor waiting room waiting. The carpet is the color of mold, with worn-out scars cut by pacing feet.

There's a coffee maker and that burned-coffee smell. Magazines so worked over their paper has become as limp as silk. Two prints on the green wall: a waterfall, a field of daisies; real soothing. The ubiquitous TV high in the corner. Stressed-out fat people, and stressed-out skinny ones, the terrified and the smugly faith-full, the sweatshirted, the St. John suited, young and old and attractive and not so, we're all equally screwed in this room, waiting, waiting like a bunch of sitting ducks. We leave; we go to the cafeteria; we return with cracker crumbs dusting our bitten lips. A nurse appears. She calls the family name. Somebody's father or somebody's daughter stands and slowly follows her to a secret room for The News. Sometimes they don't come back. When they do, even the best of us wonder, so how bad was it? Believing that there is a pie of bad news and a pie of good, and which slice you get depends on what's left; if that guy got bad news, I'll get good; if he got the good slice, I'll get stuck with the bad. Not everyone can win; someone's got to lose, right? The only sounds are the flipping of month-old *Newsweek* pages and the xylophone paging bells and the names of doctors floating down from the tiny speaker holes in the ceiling like confetti from heaven: *Dr. King, Dr. King. Dr. Yi, Dr. Yi*. Bobby's gone to have a hundred cigarettes. Maddie is having an abortion.

Last Thursday she came down with leukemia. Well, that's when she was told she has it; no one will ever know the day, the hour she actually contracted it, or whatever it's called. Is there a single moment when a single blood cell goes from healthy to deviant, a moment that could have been stopped if, if only —? Or is it a more gradual, global kind of thing? Well, before last Thursday, six days ago, her only medical condition was pregnancy. The chemo and radiation could kill or maim the baby, and carrying it to term would endanger her life, so. So this is what you do.

They said the abortion is a bit dangerous because of her low-platelet situation, there's an outside chance she'll bleed to death, but hey, it's necessary and will save her life. I bet this is the kind of goddamn statement you hear a lot around here. The kind that should tear your brain in half it's so internally contradictory: it's a life-threatening life-saving procedure. I thought medicine would be more rational than the movie business, but so far I don't see any evidence of that. And don't talk to me about paradoxes, okay? Paradoxes are just intellectual jingles for mysteries no one understands, for things that make no goddamn sense. People confuse illogic with profundity.

Maddie's taking it surprisingly well. She said, If I wasn't pregnant, I wouldn't have had that blood test, and if I didn't have that test, they would never have caught it in time. The baby saved my life.

They're also surgically implanting a phone jack into her chest. It's not really a phone jack, of course, it just looks like one. It's actually a Hickman catheter, sometimes cunningly referred to as a Life-Port. It's a white plastic square with two thin spaghetti-like tubes that will slide into an artery near her heart, and the "medicine," which I prefer to call it, will shoot right in there, no poking or burning of the spidery veins in the arms. They did a MUGS test to see how much of the "medicine" her heart could take before it'd start screaming bloody murder, and apparently she's got just a fabulous heart because the doctors were all very excited; they were licking their chops when they delivered the news. I know what you're thinking, Michael: good thing it's not Olivia; she would have failed that MUGS test, since her heart's about as stout as a soufflé.

I'm the one who smokes, eats animals and delicious fatty things such as french fries and foie gras, who drinks perhaps a little more red wine than a person without repressed anger does, who's six years older, who's maybe a little bit bitter, who's maybe a little existentially *irritable* — who just days ago would have welcomed a little poison in her veins. You're taught to believe in causality. If you act up, you'll get punished; if you're good, you'll get a star. If you eat broccoli, you'll live to eighty-two. But that only works in grade school. If it worked in life, I'd be the one having a little surgery right now.

It was only supposed to take an hour. She's been gone for three. I'd like to call you. Maybe you could send me your new number?

I'd have a cigarette if it was allowed. They don't let you smoke anywhere in this hospital, which is simply cruel. Don't they realize that this is precisely when people are fucking *desperate* for a smoke? And it'd be good business for them. They could put a turnstile in the smoking lounge and do future-profit projections. It's a win-win.

In pre-op, Maddie looked up at me from the gurney and said, I never thought I'd be the kind of person to have one. I always thought I'd go through with it, no matter what. Even if it was an accident, you know? Like even if I wasn't married, I'd still have it.

Yeah. Well. This is different.

I know. Still. I just never thought I would. You know.

I know.

I didn't think I could. You know. Do it. It's a living thing and I . . .

Out of solidarity I thought of saying, Hey, it's no big deal, it's just a bunch of cells. The size of a guppy, maybe two inches long. When you don't want to be a mother yet, you don't think about what it could *become* — a five-year-old boy, a fifteen-year-old girl unlike any other girl in the world. You don't think about how unique it is, or how it'll never come again. You think about your own life, weighed against that guppy-sized clump of cells. You think about how after the procedure — which is what they called it, and which only took ten minutes — how after those ten minutes you would resume living the life and future you planned — the career, the travel, the freedom; you'd have some control over the random and invisible forces of nature, you'd be as free as a man, you'd vanquish this thing that was threatening to vanquish you: a baby. I was a temp. You were a bartender. We'd only been going out for a few months. A baby felt impossible; there were so many other things to do first and we were barely providing for ourselves. I'm not saying I regret it or anything. But thinking about it today after so long — what, six years now? — I realize that we never talked about it, did we, Michael? The night I told you, you simply said, Are you sure? I said yeah. And we never talked about it again. Were you relieved? Or were you saddened? How could I not have asked you?

Through the chrome guardrail of her gurney, I rested my hand on Maddie's arm. You'll have another, I told her. Later. You're too young to be a parent now. You still act like a baby yourself.

She half smiled at me and said, Thanks for coming, Liv, which pissed me off. I told her not to thank me, and then a black orderly came and wheeled her away. She waved and I gave her a thumbs-up, *Go get 'em, tiger* smile and felt like a fool.

Bobby's back, so I'm going to mail this downstairs before I lose my nerve. I hope you don't mind me writing to you. Five months is a long enough silent treatment, isn't it? I mean, this letter shouldn't derail your resolve or anything. I thought you should know about Maddie. She always liked you more than I did, anyway. Men generally do look better from a distance. You might not even read this; you might return it unopened like the last one. If you do read it and you've gotten this far, I just wanted to say I'm sorry I didn't think of you back then, of what you might have wanted. I'm sorry I didn't even ask.

With love (even so),
Olivia

Date: September 2, 1998
From: OliviaHunt@usol.com
To: Dr_Jones@leukemiahelp.org

Dear Dr. Jones,

I read your article in *Blood* on untreated ALL and allogenic bone marrow transplant versus aggressive induction chemotherapy. My sister, who'll be twenty-seven next month, is Philadelphia chromosome negative: would you still recommend a BMT immediately or only after conventional therapy has failed? I'd love to talk to you if you have time. I can be reached at the e-mail address or phone number below. Thank you for your help.

Olivia Hunt

—·—·—

September 3, 1998

Mr. Mel Gibson
Icon Entertainment
5555 Melrose Ave.
Los Angeles, California 90038

Dear Mel,

Just wanted to say hi. It's been a while. You were great in *Conspiracy Theory*. I loved it.

I also wanted to mention that I've hung out my own shingle — yes, I finally left Universal to start my own production company — and I hope we can work together again soon. Working on *Lethal* with you was one of my most rewarding movie experiences.

I've got a few scripts in development, and one has a great role for you. It's about a priest who saves the Aborigines from a smallpox epidemic. Think *Dances with Wolves* meets *The Mission*. As soon as it's ready I hope you won't mind me sending it to you.

All the best,
Olivia Hunt

September 3, 1998

Mr. Jerry Bruckheimer
Jerry Bruckheimer Films
1631 10th Street
Santa Monica, California 90404

Dear Jerry,

It was great catching up with you on the phone today. My résumé is enclosed, as requested.

I've always admired you, your exquisite taste, your incredible box office. The opportunity of working with you is something I've always dreamed of. Your filmography, from *March or Die* to *Armageddon*, has inspired me since I was a temp at Warner Bros. in New York.

You mentioned that since your pictures have grossed a billion dollars (mazeltov!), you've now got your sights set on Oscars. I'd like to call your attention to my role in spotting *Silence of the Lambs* (and feel free to call Jonathan about this) and my New York publishing experience. Many Academy Award winners come out of books, so I'm well-positioned to provide you with a plethora of possibilities for those much-sought Oscars.

I look forward to hearing from you soon.

All the best,
Olivia Hunt

P.S. Still playing tennis? Let's have a game sometime.

September 3, 1998

Alan Ladd, Jr.
Paramount Pictures
5555 Melrose Ave.
Hollywood, California 90038

Dear Laddie,

It was great catching up with you on the phone today. My résumé is enclosed, as requested.

You know I've always admired you. Your exquisite taste and your incredible box office. Your filmography, from *Blade Runner* to *Braveheart,* has inspired me since I was a temp at Warner Bros. in New York. The opportunity to work with you is something I've always dreamed of.

You mentioned that since *Braveheart* you want to make only potential Oscar winners. I'd like to call your attention to my role in finding *Silence of the Lambs* (and feel free to call Jonathan about this) and my New York publishing experience. Many Academy Award winners come out of books, so I'm well-positioned to provide the Ladd Company with a plethora of possibilities.

I look forward to hearing from you soon.

All the best,
Olivia Hunt

P.S. How 'bout a game of tennis sometime? David says you're pretty good. . . .

Date: September 5, 1998
From: OliviaHunt@usol.com
To: Dr_Jones@leukemiahelp.org

Dear Dr. Jones,

I'm writing again because I haven't heard back and I imagine with something called acute, time is of the essence, right? Obviously my sister's life is not as urgent to you as it is to, say, her, or me even, but you are a doctor, you did encourage people to write to you with questions, so I don't think it's impertinent of me, having done that, having asked you a simple question, to expect a speedy reply.

Thanks,
Olivia Hunt

Date: September 5, 1998
From: OliviaHunt@usol.com
To: Bigdick@worldlink.com

Johnny,

I'm not the one who's "dumb as a dirt hole." It's been your childhood dream to make this movie and you're digging in your Houston heels at the wrong moment. We've worked on this script together for months — I sank my last ten grand into it — and you won't even *discuss* changes that might spring the financing?

I admire your determination to make the movie you want. You're the director, you have to be committed to your vision (like

Quixote himself), but no one else likes it, so it doesn't do you much good. When you need $60 million you've got to at least *act* like you're listening to the people who have it. It's not like *Lick Creek*, which you know I loved, but which only cost $4 million. I thought after your experience on *Stay the Night* you wanted to "fuck Hollywood and get back to movies you'd actually go see yourself." Back to your roots as "the John Huston of the eighties." Well, you can't have it both ways, JD. You can't demand Hollywood dough and then go make art house stuff with it. This is why you haven't made a film in five years.

I know it's not in your nature, but if you decide there's a middle ground — where the cynics in the audience see one thing and the sentimentalists another — there might be life left in old Q. But without some accommodation to the saps out there, I don't see the studios financing what some have called "too Beckettian." If we try to get a star first, like Robin Williams or Danny DeVito, you know as well as I do the first question from their agents will be, is it financed? So — another waste of time.

I guess this is good-bye. I'm sorry I couldn't come up with the money. You know how much I loved this project. And you're the only director for it. It would have been a great, great film. I hope we can work together on something else someday.

All the best,
Olivia

September 20, 1998
Somewhere over Nebraska

Dear Klein,

I wonder if you read my last letter. Maybe you're out of town.
Maybe that's why you haven't called.

Maddie began her third week of "medicine," and they say she's
sailing through it. So far it's been totally smooth. No infections, no
nausea, nothing nasty whatsoever. Her hair hasn't fallen out. I
knew she'd be okay. It was a little disconcerting that when the
nurses administered the "medicine" they were wearing astronaut
suits, and the "medicine" was in a steel box labeled with Zeus-like
thunderbolts, and this "medicine" that went into her veins could
strip the varnish off a gymnasium floor — it was a little disconcerting, but they say it works, and from what I read, it does 67 percent of the time, which is a nice high number in this game of odds.
There was no alternative: Maddie felt that when you're told ALL is
so ferocious it could kill a twenty-seven-year-old woman in four
months, a diet of soybeans and ginseng, dairy abstention, and
other new age remedies don't pack quite enough punch to inspire
confidence.

I managed to get her a private room by promising the floor
nurse I'd cast her in my next film. Luckily, the dear woman believed there might be one. Ah, the power of Hollywood. Imagine if
I was Julia Roberts, what I could do for my sister. It's a mauvey
room, a color that's not color enough to offend anyone, a color
Swedish psychologists probably found to be subliminally soothing, womblike, perhaps. The shelf under the window is crowded

with flower arrangements, get-well cards, and cheery crayoned rainbows and balloons from Sophie and Nell. There's a TV, of course, bolted to the wall opposite the bed, its remote attached to one bed rail, a Slimline phone to the other. There are chrome ports and nozzles and outlets in the wall above her bed, for procedures we hopefully won't find out about. Through the window you see the heliport and beyond, a fringe of leafy treetops whose green is just succumbing to yellow. I love this time of year. I love how the moment the leaves reach their brightest color, they fall. Maybe this fragility is what makes a golden maple so beautiful; you know the next time you look the gold will be gone, the branches black and bare.

We watched a lot of daytime TV, which inflamed my misanthropia but which inexplicably had the opposite effect on Maddie. She's been watching *All My Children* for fifteen years, so these psychos have become her family and friends; I believe she knows more about the Chandlers and the Cortlandts than she does about us, so she was happy to have this chance to catch up with them all. She even cries for those embarrassing slobs on Jerry Springer and she laughed — even now! — when Jerry Seinfeld had a tough time finding a parking space. You'd think she'd be too preoccupied with her own problems. Then there was the floor show. Day and night a parade of people in PJs (those blue and green scrubs) appeared, asked a question, made a notation, drew a little blood, changed an IV, and then exited offstage, sometimes never to be seen again. It was a cast of hundreds. There were janitors, dieticians, RNs, PNs, residents, interns, and every morning for about thirty seconds, surrounded by seven sycophantic sleepy-eyed students, the familiar face of her very own oncologist, who asked brightly, How are we today, Madeline? *(We? We?!?)* And the most amazing thing of all, Michael: Maddie was nice to each and every one of them. She smiled, she laughed, she asked how their day was going, she thanked them for dumping the garbage or injecting her with Cytoxan, and she always said she was doing just fine.

To us, her real family, she was somewhat less deferential. Maddie wouldn't touch the hospital food, of course; she wouldn't if she was well and now, now more than ever she's entitled to have what she wants, and what she wanted was Belgian waffles from the Breakfast Club, turkey wraps from the Pita Pocket, gnocchi from D'Angelo's, roast chicken with rosemary from Terry's. Food runs were done every few hours. How could anyone say no? We never have before. She's always had the whole family scrambling. She was the baby. An accident, no doubt: "Martini." She came out screaming, clamoring for a place that had not been prepared for her in a symmetrical family of four; my parents felt guilty, so they indulged her, and Jim and I were much older, so naturally we lost interest in her. "Don't 'nore me" was the first sentence Maddie spoke.

At Mercy I slept in her room four times a week and Bobby took the other three, because we couldn't leave her alone at night. When she was a kid, she wouldn't go upstairs without me. I'd read to her until finally, finally her eyes would fall closed and I'd gently slide out from under her, my side suddenly cool where her small warm body had been holding mine; I'd position her rag-doll arms under the covers and have my hand on the door when she'd sit up and shout, Where you going? Don't go. Tell me another story. I'd sigh, furious, resentful, wishing she would just go to sleep, just grow up, just shut up. I had homework to do; I had to call Tina; I wanted to practice piano; I had about a hundred better things to do than read *Madeline* for the twenty-seventh time. Maddie would fight to stay awake. I tried to outfox her. She grew bored with store-bought books; she wanted only the stories I custom made for her: *The True and Outstanding Adventures of the Hunt Sisters*. One night I decided to make the story so boring that she would fall asleep fast. I repeated the same lines again and again, hypnotically: *And then the sisters walked into the woods. The woods were vast. And then the sisters walked into the woods. The woods were vast.* Over and over, until I could see the curved lines of her eyelashes resting like two furry black caterpillars on her pink cheeks. Just when I thought she'd conked out, she sat up and spat, That story is boring! Make it better! When she was older, when she was nine and I was fifteen, she'd want to talk all night. From her twin bed across the dresser she'd ask questions and chatter on endlessly: Are you going to marry Tony? Margaret is not my best friend anymore; do I still have to invite her to my birthday party? Do all parents fight as much as ours do? Are French poodles from France? So at Mercy for the last couple weeks it was like old times, only I was in the sleeper chair next to her bed, a brown vinyl recliner, and the night sounds were the beeps and clicks of the IV, not the TV downstairs or the cicadas outside.

Last night we were watching the six o'clock news. After the reports on a stabbing in Cincinnati and some kid's incredible science project, there was a piece on Robin Williams being in town for a charity bowling event. In fact, Robin Williams was the advertised story, because Robin Williams being in Shawnee Falls was certainly Big News. Maddie said, Isn't he who you want for your movie?

What movie?

Don Quixote? Didn't you want him to play Sancho?

Or Danny DeVito. The studios all passed on the script.

But won't they make it if he wants to? He's huge.

(I explained you have to make stars financial offers or they don't even read the script.)

What if you just left it at his hotel? He must be staying at the Royal Oak, right? How do you know he wouldn't read it?

Because fifty other dopes are leaving their scripts, thinking the same thing. He'll have his assistant write a nice letter referring me to his agent.

You're so negative.

Please.

Maybe *Don Quixote* is like his favorite book or something. You don't know.

Maddie, it's not the way it's done, okay? You need —

It's not the way you do it.

That's right, and I'm the one doing it, not you —

And the way you do it is working so well.

She was annoying the hell out of me, but since she's sick, I couldn't ask her to lay off.

She has about a week to go, then, assuming she's in remission, which they expect, she goes home and just has "maintenance chemo" for a couple years, which means periodic injections and oral medicine to sustain the remission. Her boss at the county executive's office is being great about the whole thing. He's going to keep her on full pay, and she can come back to work when she's ready. Maddie hasn't really stopped working — from the hospital she was making calls for this chef apprenticeship program she had just started, and she talked to the constituents whose cases she was personally handling. The thing she's really mad about missing is Bobby's final softball game tomorrow against The Alibi team.

We're landing soon. I'll be back in L.A. tonight in case you need to reach me for some reason, like out of fondness or nostalgia or if no one else is still up in your time zone. I'm not sure why I'm writing to you. I guess I must miss you. Even though the way things ended was pretty unsatisfactory. I mean, I understand the *fantasy* of calling up and saying, Hey, I've had it, I'm not coming home — but to actually do it, and stick with it all these months, well, I'm surprised, that's all. I know things weren't great last spring, but there were some good years before that and, well, a lousy phone call wouldn't kill you. After all those years together I'd have thought my friendship would mean more to you. Yours does to me.

Love (but autumnal!),
Olivia

9/22/98

Hey Maddie —

This postcard is from my new employer. I start next week. You know how I love coffee, so it seemed like a natural. And did you know Starbucks offers health insurance after only two years of service! This one is located on the edge of the Mojave Desert, so it shouldn't be too busy and there's little chance I'll bump into anyone I know.

Write soon. I miss you,
Liv

Mr. Robin Williams
4575 Cherokee
Beverly Hills, California 90210

Dear Mr. Williams,

If you're reading this it means I haven't been arrested for trespassing on your, may I say, exquisite lawn. Please forgive me. It's really not like me to do something so rude, something so insane, but my sister reminded me that Steven Spielberg got his start by hopping the fence at Universal, and she just about challenged me into doing this, so I hope in the spirit of giving a fledgling producer a chance, you'll read the enclosed script, a truly fantastic adaptation of Cervantes' masterpiece, *The History of That Ingenious Gentleman, Don Quixote de la Mancha.* Johnny Ray Dickerman (*Lick Creek* and *Stay the Night*) is attached to direct, and I think you'd make a brilliant Sancho.

I've enclosed a brief synopsis of the script. Sancho is a heartbreaking comic character. He starts out a practical peasant who just wants to get himself and his old neighbor Quixote safely back home and ends up, after many hysterical adventures, becoming as idealistic as Quixote. He can't save Quixote from reality, but Quixote saves Sancho from a life without dreams. The role is full of physical comedy and heartwarming pathos, and there's no actor alive who can do both as well as you. (I forgot to mention, I've been a huge fan of yours since Tuesday nights in 1975, when you played Mork, all the way up to your recent totally underrated performance in *What Dreams May Come,* which I absolutely loved.)

I hope you'll see what a magnificent, funny, and important film this could be. Although the story takes place in Spain in the 1600s, what could be more relevant today in this age of cynicism than a movie that celebrates "the impossible dream"?

I haven't submitted the script to any studios yet, because I prefer to present a complete package in order to maintain as much creative control as possible. If you're interested in the role, I'd like to talk to you about who you think would make the best Quixote.

I look forward to hearing your thoughts. Please call anytime.

Sincerely,

Olivia Hunt

September 24, 1998

Mr. Danny DeVito
1122 Beverly Avenue
Beverly Hills, California 90210

Dear Mr. DeVito,

If you're reading this letter, I'm already ahead of the game. I know your agent reads everything first, but I can't wait that long, and I promise if you read the enclosed script, you'll be glad you did.

I recently ankled my job at Universal to start my own production company. *Don Quixote* will be my first picture, and you'd be perfect for Sancho. I've enclosed a brief synopsis in case you're not familiar with this literary classic.

I hope you'll see what a magnificent, funny, and important film this could be. Although the story takes place four hundred years ago, what could be more relevant today in this age of cynicism than a movie that celebrates "the impossible dream"?

Johnny Ray Dickerman (*Lick Creek* and *Stay the Night*) is attached to direct.

I haven't submitted the script to any studios yet, because I prefer presenting a complete package in order to maintain as much creative control as possible. And you are the only actor I've given the script to, because *only you* can play Sancho. If you agree, I'd like to talk to you about who you think would make the best Quixote.

I look forward to hearing your thoughts. By the way — you were fantastic in *The Rainmaker* and I've heard great things about *Living Out Loud*. I can't wait to see it.

Sincerely,
Olivia Hunt

- - -

September 24, 1998

Mr. John Cleese
Burlington Hill Mansion
London, England NW11 89J

Dear Mr. Cleese,

Please forgive me for taking the liberty of sending you this script directly. Your agent is a lovely man but so busy, and I'm confident you will not want to miss out on the chance to play one of the greatest literary creations of all time: *Don Quixote*.

Johnny Ray Dickerman (*Lick Creek* and *Stay the Night*) is attached to direct.

Robin Williams has expressed strong interest in playing Sancho, as has Danny DeVito, but I think Quixote must be cast first, so I'm eager to hear who you think would be best.

If you've read this far, I'll be honest: I haven't set this up at a studio. As a great artist, you know how meddlesome Hollywood studios can be. I've decided to put the entire creative package together first and then raise the money in order to retain as much artistic freedom as possible.

I look forward to hearing your thoughts.

Sincerely,
Olivia Hunt

September 24, 1998
Los Angeles

Dear Tina,

This is a Mayan fertility goddess. It's ugly as hell but why not try it? Hang it over your bed and you know the rest. I bought it at the Rose Bowl Flea Market yesterday, where I was scouting for the best stall location in case I need to start selling my earthly possessions. Get the guest towels out. I may be moving in soon.

Broke but cheerful,
Olivia

P.S. When you find yourself weeping to Muzak versions of "How Deep Is Your Love?" and "If You Leave Me Now," does that mean you want to get back together with your ex? Or you're just tired?

✦ ✦ ✦

September 24, 1998
Los Angeles

Hey Warrior-chick,

Congratulations on getting out of prison — and earlier than expected. I knew you'd sail through it.

Here's a little welcome-home present. Sorry I couldn't be there to give it to you myself. I'm busy building an empire out here. I know how much you love fresh pasta; now you can make it yourself. By Thanksgiving I expect you to have it mastered. (I prefer penne to spaghetti, in case you've forgotten.)

I'm glad Klein called you. He always had a soft spot for you. If he calls again, tell him I did *not* say hello, but I am eager to know if he has started going bald yet.

Love to you & Bobby,
O.

P.S. Hey, how 'bout a letter sometime?
P.P.S. You could also just casually mention to Klein that I have a date with a major celebrity next week, but you're sworn to secrecy.

September 25, 1998
The Bean & the Leaf, Sunset Blvd.

Edward Hunt
Hunt & Stanfield
101 Edison Avenue
Shawnee Falls, Ohio 45200

Re: Your investment proposal

Dear Dad,

Just wanted to say thanks again for the offer, but I'm okay. I didn't mean I was broke-broke, just very nearly broke. That's your stash; you should do something fun with it. Anything except buy that condo in Florida. Jim said you asked him if he wanted to go in on it with you. Could you have overlooked the well-established fact that Mom hates Florida? Who would wash your socks, make you ham sandwiches? And come on, admit it: you'd miss her. Because you know she's not retiring to Florida. Maddie wouldn't like it, either. If she had her way, we'd all live on Elmhurst together. She told me she called those people on Monroe Boulevard. She sure wants that house. Do you think she'd like it if she bought a house a block from yours and then you guys moved to Florida?

Life in L.A. is disturbingly languorous. I haven't heard from any of the companies I sent my résumé to. If only I was still *inex*-perienced, I'd have great potential; but when you're experienced and *un*successful, what do you have to offer but excuses? Nor have I heard from the actors for *Don Quixote,* but I didn't think I would. I half did it just to prove Maddie wrong: stars don't look at scripts unless they come from their agents. And their agents don't even return my phone calls. When you asked me the other day if I love this business and I said no, that wasn't the whole truth. I don't love it *yet*. I remember when you taught me how to ski, how much I hated it at first, but you wouldn't let me quit till I was off the bunny hill, because only then would I know if I liked skiing or not. Well, I guess I'm saying I'm still akimbo on Hollywood's bunny hill.

I know you've never loved your job. After thirty years of it, no wonder you're so desperate to retire. And to win the lottery. But with odds of a billion to one, the Ohio Lottery is a colossal waste of hope, Dad, let alone the $100 a week. That's five grand a year!! I'm getting worried about you. Mad says every day you bring her those scratch-offs and ask her for her lucky numbers and you drove to Pennsylvania last week to buy tickets for their $120 million drawing. It seems the more you lose, the more determined you are to win. But I don't think determination helps much when it comes to the lottery. Do you really believe you're going to win? Has a small-town lawyer ever won?

Time for me to sign off here. Thanks again for your offer to "invest in my company." I'm having dinner tonight with a screenwriter who has a pitch that I think I can sell to a studio. If I do, my development fee will pay off some debts and cover me for another few months. If I don't, I might have to take you up on it after all.

Your daughter,
Olivia

P.S. And since you asked, *my* lucky numbers are 34, 52, 46, 5, 18, and 1.

September 29, 1998

Los Angeles

Dear Maddie,

Just a quick note before I get back to cleaning the toilets here at the Daily Grille. It's the hottest lunch spot in town. Waitressing would be too public. This way, I might bump into someone in the restroom and I'll pretend I'm having lunch, not replacing the toilet paper, and strike up a friendly, do-you-have-a-job-for-me or would-you-like-to-finance-my-masterpiece conversation.

I have something to get off my chest, Maddo. When I told you I had a little inappropriate sex the other night, it wasn't an invitation for you to lecture me. You keep forgetting I'm the older sister here. I don't regret it. Well, not totally. I am not, as you kept saying, on some sex-drugs-and-alcohol binge. Pot makes me paranoid (*not* what I need these days), I can't afford cocaine, and I never drink between meals. I heard what you said — "sex without love is bad for your self-esteem" — but did you hear what *I* said? That sometimes, sex without love is *precisely* what the old self-esteem is screaming for. It's not like I do this all the time, Maddie; think about all the times I've wanted to have sex with a stranger and didn't. In fact, I think that's what happened — and that's the part I forgot to tell you about. The context.

I was walking past Ladder #10. A few of the firemen were standing around, and one of them, Lt. Harrigan, asked me if I wanted a tour. Having nothing else in the world to do, I said, Why not? After months of no sex (with or without love), I was highly horny, and as I followed the lieutenant's broad shoulders, I found myself fantasizing about them and other, what I hoped would be equally *heroic,* attributes inside that snug navy blue uniform and, okay, yes, about doing it with a fireman. Don't pretend you, too, haven't had this fantasy, Madster; who hasn't? Inside the truck, Lt. Harrigan called my attention to certain hoses and other vital equipment, and then this *completely chaste* tour ended. I went home and got ready for dinner with Sean Rutledge, a writer I've been working with and whom, a few hours later, after that encounter at Ladder #10 *and* two post-pasta grappas, I found myself wrapped around in the backseat of his black BMW. One minute I'm having an all-American fireman fantasy and the next I'm screwing a second-rate screenwriter. The only thing depressing here, the only thing I regret, is that I didn't even have the courage of my clichés.

But okay, I know Sean. I think this disqualifies me as a slut, doesn't it? I've always liked him, and as much as I might want to be — and you think I am — in fact I'm *not* the kind of girl who can sleep with a total stranger, even a strapping neighborhood hero like Lt. Harrigan. Sean and I are both young(ish) and single and, last night, a little drunk, alone in a big car on a lonely street in Los Angeles. He kissed me . . . and. Well. I needed it. I just needed it.

Your (damn-near) virtuous sister,
Olivia

◆━━◆

October 5, 1998
Los Angeles

Dear Tina,

Just a quick note to tell you that I've moved.

I never thought when they evict you they literally put your stuff out on the street and lock you out, but that's what my super did. There had been some correspondence, some red-lettered notices and such, but I fully expected the handjob I gave the guy in August would carry me longer than three unpaid months; guess I've lost my touch, ha ha ha. Fortunately, I've never been materialistic, so I gathered up the things that matter most to me and they all fit into my Karmen Ghia — the bag of curling snapshots, my journals, my one pair of Manolo Blahniks, a few suits in case I ever work again, my $23 shampoo, and key pharmaceuticals — and instinctively I drove west, to the sea, to Venice, to the Bay View Motel. For $65 a night you can hear the Pacific Ocean, and if no SUVs park in the front lot you can see it, too. All this and the Coke machine is right outside my door.

Just as I was wondering if the Bay View management would notice I was four days shy of my Visa credit limit and what I would do if they did notice, good fortune in the 6'3" form of Lee Hassler walked my way down an aisle at the Chalet Gourmet. I was there for the canned-baked-bean close-out, and Lee was there buying some white truffles just in from Tuscany. I acted delighted to see him. He asked if I was still in that house on the hill, where he had enjoyed some great parties. Funny you should ask, I said, stalling. In Hollywood you don't want anyone to know you're in trouble, because they'll recoil as if you're a scabrous leper, as if failure might be contagious. But if no one knows, how can anyone extend that much-needed helping hand? Here's that old tone problem popping up again. I don't know Lee Hassler well, but he's the only son of the Hassler Aviation empire and currently launching some video game business; I had the feeling he's the kind of guy who might have a few extra apartments lying around. I told him I was having my place renovated.

You want to stay in my old office while it's being done? he asked. My friend's moving out in a couple days.

Really?

Sure. There's no kitchen, but it's got a shower and a little fridge, if you need a place to crash. I'll tell the doorman you're coming.

So here I am, splayed on the beige fold-out in Lee Hassler's subterranean, fluorescent-lit office, floor B for Basement of the Dorset Condominiums in Century City. It stinks. Of carpet rubber and piss, but hey, it's free, right? And Burt Reynolds keeps an apartment twenty-three stories above me on floor P (for Penthouse), so you see it's a tony address. Maybe I'll bump into him in the laundry room, which is conveniently located right next door. I've discovered the rhythm of the dryers is an excellent soporific.

Last time we talked you expressed some low body image, Tina; there was some mention of cellulite and your darling husband's obsession with said "pock-marked under-butt thighs." Unless Stephen has lost about twenty-seven pounds, I daresay this is a case of the pot calling the kettle black. He's lucky to have you. Besides being beautiful and a great mom *and* Director of Sales and Marketing, you're the sturdiest, most optimistic and fun-loving person I know. Cellulite is trivial in the face of these facts and, contrary to popular-magazine propaganda, it is not the mark of a gluttonous sloth — they're dimples, the natural dimples of a fully grown woman. Stephen should savor each and every feminine indentation.

And I've been thinking about your work problem, too. Don't assume because your rival for that promotion is single, your boss will choose her over you. I know business socializing is important, but it's not more important than the job itself, which you must do very well or you wouldn't keep moving up the ladder so quickly. You work hard, Tina. The fact that you also work hard as a mother only makes you *feel* like you're not working as hard as someone who isn't one, because you're exhausted, you're drained, you're guilty for not being wherever you're not. Your rival is just spending those off-hours differently. She may be less exhausted, less guilt-ridden, but that doesn't mean she's doing the job better or is better qualified for the job you're both going for. So don't panic. I'm sure you're going to get it. And don't tell me you can only hope for one thing at a time. Why can't you pray for a baby *and* the promotion? That's not being greedy, Tina; only a stingy (or sexist?) god could think that it is.

So much for a short note. Tomorrow Maddie finds out if she's in remission. She feels good, so I hope that means she is good, that this round worked. The doctors are confident, which is making even my mother, the Queen of Darkness, feel a wee bit hopeful.

Give Ryan a kiss for me, and Stephen, too, but only after he apologizes for that cellulite crack.

Reporting live from
Burt Reynolds's basement,
Olivia

＊＊＊

October 6, 1998
Los Angeles

O Silent One,

Don't worry, Michael, this isn't another sob letter. It's just to tell you that I've moved. In case you were thinking of responding to my letters, please note the return address and my new-but-only-temporary number, should you feel the urge to hear my voice ever again.

The good news is that Maddie "achieved" remission. The bad news is that we didn't understand she must now have seven spinal taps. Plus two bone marrow biopsies and a partridge in a pear tree. It's the CNS prophylaxis act of the show: they need to get the medicine into her central nervous system or else the cancer could "jump" to her brain. Lumbar puncture is what the professionals call a spinal tap, which is onomatopoeic, don't you think? Puncture: a straight pin pricks a red balloon, a nail pops an inner tube, a needle pierces your spinal cord. She had one when I was still there. The men in white came in and asked me to leave. Knowing what they were about to do, I felt like I was selling her out to the enemy. In the small waiting room next to hers, I flipped through a dog-eared *National Geographic* from August last year — the month she married Bobby. She was beaming that night. In the stall of the ladies' room, as I held up her huge tulle dress, she whispered, Livvie, I can't believe how happy I am. I kissed her forehead and said, Why are you whispering?

If I say it too loudly it'll seem like I'm bragging and then something bad will happen.

Nothing bad's going to happen.

In the mirror I fixed her hair and makeup. Her eyes were shining from champagne, her round cheeks red. I can't believe he loves me, she giggled, mystified, delighted. Then she shrugged and said, But he does! as if she were pulling one over on him.

We were pretty happy that night, too, weren't we? You even deigned to fast dance a few times — once to "Celebration" with my mother. We walked onto the golf course and saw Bobby kissing Mad; her white dress glowed in the dark. I was remembering all this, how your tuxedo shirt glowed, too, as I slipped my hand inside it — and then I heard Maddie's sighs, her muffled soft cries, and the doctor's reassuring manly voice. My palms got sweaty.

After the doctors were through, I went back in and noticed her temples were wet and her pupils black holes staring up at me like the gaping mouths of baby birds.

Was it terrible? I asked.

Not really, she said softly. Bone marrow's worse.

How could you be going along just fine one day, getting married, getting pregnant, cooking a little spaghetti, watching *Wheel of Fortune* on the couch with your husband, etc., etc., and the very next you're someone who has spinal taps and bone marrow biopsies every Wednesday and Friday? Where's the transition? It's irrational, but I keep feeling there must be a higher level of management we haven't talked to where we could get some satisfaction. There must be one, somewhere. It's obsessive; I've become a little obsessive. I'm obsessing. Over and over I think, *What* happened? And when? What should we do now? Are we doing everything right? Are we doing everything we can? Is there something we're not doing? What can we do? What can we do now?

Sometimes this obsessing leads to you, as humiliating as this is to admit. I go to the videotape. The instant — well, not so instant — replay of various moves over the years. Lately I replay the first time I saw you. It appears involuntarily: I'm sitting in the car at a traffic light or I'm in line at Starbucks, and then I see you, in the Carnegie Deli. You have a bagel in one hand and a book in the other. I loved your face immediately. It's one thing I never got tired of. Looking at you. Who knows why one face moves you the way it does. You're a handsome man, of course, but that's not what it was. I recognized something, something sad, maybe, something that made me think I could trust you and that you'd see the same thing in me.

But why this first moment? Of all the others to replay — drinking in bars in New York and kissing in doorways, painting our first apartment, or driving the U-Haul cross country, watching the World Series with hot dogs in bed, our trips to Maine, the birthday parties — or of all the bad ones — the night in L.A. when you shattered the windshield with your fist, or when I stormed out of that gallery, or the post-premiere fights about the movies and what the movies were doing to us — of all the moments from our story, why do I keep replaying the very first one? I wonder if you even remember it. I was sitting with some friends from work. You talked to the waitress, and when you did you saw me watching you, and I didn't pretend I wasn't. Do you remember? You didn't look away. You looked as startled as I felt. Then you turned back to your book, but a smile crossed your lips, a sly smile. I had to meet you. Then. Somehow. I willed you to come to me. To say, Hi, mind if I join you? But that would have been so slick I'd have hated it. I couldn't do it, either; you might have found it too slick, too. My girlfriend caught me checking you out. He looks like trouble, she said. He looks like Sam Shepard, the other one said. I disagreed, and when I looked again you were gone.

That's the moment. When you caught me watching you. It's like David Hemmings in *Blow-Up,* who keeps looking at that photograph, looking for something in that bloody picture; he knows there's something there, a clue, he knows he missed something, he knows if he just keeps blowing it up and looking at it he'll find what he's looking for and be able to stop. I am looking for a clue, but to what?

It's time you wrote back. A postcard will do. Even better, a phone call. You're not proving anything by this.

Love (begrudgingly),
Olivia

October 9, 1998
The Basement in Los Angeles

Dear Mom,

We just hung up. I'm going to try again this way.

Of course you're so anxious you can't breathe. A dream about a coffin-shaped baby carriage would have anyone clutching the sheets. When you said, I'm just so scared, Olivia, and I said, For chrissakes, Mom, don't be, it doesn't mean anything, I wasn't saying your *feelings* don't mean anything, I meant the dream. I wasn't denying your feelings, Mom. I just meant it's not prescient. Dreams are just your subconscious giving shape to your conscious fears. Random electrical impulses. It's not the future; I know you don't really believe that. The fact that Maddie is starting to lose weight and weaken was expected: she's basically being poisoned to *near* death, but not death. Her counts are low, but they should be; she's on track, she's where the doctors thought she'd be at this point, which is a little sick. I know you are fundamentally, or should I say matri-instinctively, opposed to the protocol, which is understandable: a treatment that nearly kills your daughter, that wipes out her already embattled immune system, does seem counterintuitive, barbaric, even criminal, and I bet one day we'll look at chemotherapy and radiation the way we now look at bloodletting, but until something better comes along, something that offers as good a chance at full recovery as this does — 67 percent, Mom! — we've all got to get behind it and not let any nocturnal doubt seep into our waking life and make us all gloomy, okay? They caught it early. She's not Philadelphia chromosome positive. They're good doctors. It's not the Mayo Clinic, but from what I've read, at this stage any decent hospital gives the exact same treatment as the top places (it's later, if she should need a bone marrow transplant, for example, that she'd best go someplace else). But for this first round, for conventional treatment, she's in good hands, Mom. I don't like these hands any better than you do, but remember they're oncologists, not Methodists; scientists, not public relations executives, okay? And Maddie's got a great attitude and lots of support, which all the cancer books say is as important as the actual treatment, if not more. As long as she keeps in close contact with the doctors, something minor like that runny nose won't get major — that's what antibiotics are for.

So don't worry, Mom. Read that folder I put together, particularly the stuff I highlighted. And I beg you: get a prescription for Xanax. You needn't be anxious about taking antianxiety drugs; you won't become an addict, you'll just be able to do things like breathe and sleep, which will be good for you, and for Maddie. And you'll sleep so deeply you won't suffer from any more *meaningless* electrical impulses. I thought you were the rational one. Dad's already staked out irrational, so you have to hang in there, Mom.

With love & wisdom, your daughter,

Olivia

◆◆◆

October 12, 1998

Somewhere in Marin County, California

Dear Maddie,

As requested, I am writing this on the desk in Robin Williams's guest house. The view from this window is breathtaking. Cedar and cypress treetops in the near distance, and then, farther on, down a moss-green slope, a valley with horses lolling around chewing tall grass, and behind them on the horizon, a dark ridge of mountains. The stone guest house itself is bigger than your whole house, complete with two upstairs bedrooms, each with its own marble bath, a downstairs study, living room, and eat-in kitchen with a fireplace. Robin's house is the size of about ten of yours. Tastefully decorated in that Sundance style but with tons of money. Every French pine table is crammed with silver-framed photos of Robin smiling with everyone you've ever wanted to have your picture taken with — three American presidents, Princess Di, Mother Teresa, Bill Cosby, Mick Jagger, Cindy Crawford, Catherine Deneuve, Pee-wee Herman — basically the top 100 greatest people on earth. I've noticed these same pictures in every celebrity home I've been in: Mel Gibson's, Richard Gere's, Michael Caine's, and the top executives' and agents', too: instead of antlers and tiger heads on their walls, they have trophy photos on their $12,000 French walnut sideboards. Where do you think the family photos are displayed?

As you must know, being such an *Entertainment Tonight* devotee, Robin Williams is completely covered in hair. There are tufts flying out of his ears and collar and cuffs; he's like a beaver in a sweatshirt and jeans. A manic beaver: he literally cannot sit still for more than ten seconds. He'll start a sentence like a normal person, just talking, making his point, and then suddenly he's doing some rap, then he's a tight-lipped bureaucrat lecturing you on the dangers of eating red meat, and then he's back to being your normal hairy guy, but only for thirty seconds, because then he's off again, this time doing his impersonation of the president defining "sexual relations." He's hysterical, but phewww, it's exhausting being a captive audience for hours and hours, especially when one finds smiling such an imposition. I kept thinking: does he ever settle down? What's he like alone? Is he ever alone?

After his opening act, we sat down to a gourmet meal of line-caught roasted salmon with a sublime chive sauce (I've asked for the recipe for you), spinach pie (not as good as yours), heirloom tomato salad, and fingerling potatoes with butter and a hint of garlic, which you would have loved. I think you're right about garlic. A little goes a long way, and one clove too many and you've overdominated the dish. Robin has three chefs: a Japanese, an American / French, and an Italian. This was obviously a California menu. It was just me, Robin, and his wife, Marsha. Johnny wasn't there yet because Robin wanted to talk to me alone first. He's not sure about Johnny directing *Don Quixote*. He thinks he's good, but maybe not the best choice for the project. He said, His last two pictures tanked, didn't they? Yes, but the reviews were good, I said. He knows JD's attached, so he's open to hearing his thoughts, to meeting him, seeing how well they get along, but he wanted me to know he's not sure he's the best choice. Which was code for: If I don't like what he has to say tomorrow, it'll be me or him. You've asked me to explain just what a producer does? This is one thing: keep the movie together. Robin might get a studio to finance the movie, but if I replaced Johnny I'd have to find another director, and I might not be able to find one as good in the time available. Besides the loyalty question.

Robin went on to tell me what he liked about the story. (Which is, as you guessed, one of his favorite books.) It's about a regular guy, this peasant, who stands up to the establishment, the Inquisition in this case, and wins. A classic underdog story. (This isn't exactly what *DQ*'s about, but my feeling is, Robin can think it's about Rice Krispies as long as he makes the movie.) Especially with a few changes to the script, he added ominously.

I didn't pick that up, thinking, wait till he signs, wait till a studio has agreed to make it, before you start mucking around in the morass of the script. This is the critical moment when many movies are stillborn. The script gets so mangled by so many interpretations that your green light turns red before you can say the word *turnaround*. Another job of the producer is to make sure that doesn't happen. But with the eagerness of a game-show contestant, I said, Of course we'll make whatever changes you need, Robin! Because Rule #1 is Don't Lose the Star. Then I generally reassured him (Rule #2) and maintained my wholly false level of confidence and enthusiasm, which is actually also Rule #1.

I called Johnny after dinner to brief him. He's the most antagonistic person I've ever known. He grew up in a trailer park in Texas so he has that *Don't fuck with me because I'll kick your ass* chip on his shoulder. On his other shoulder there's the *I hate Hollywood but desperately want Hollywood's approval* chip, and both chips got even bigger last month, when he turned fifty. He thinks he's the arbiter of taste and that it's his job to educate and elevate the world; he's a real drag, is what I'm saying. But he's made some great movies (I know you liked *Stay the Night*, Mad, but rent *Lick Creek;* it's his best); he could make a great one out of this — and he's stuck with me this long; I have to try to make it work with him. He promised me he'd be on his best behavior tomorrow, then added: If that prick doesn't like me, fuck him. I'm not auditioning. I hung up and walked outside.

It was a crisp and clear mountain night. There's a bench on a bluff where I sat looking at the wall of stars. I wished you were there to help me make out the constellations. I still can't do it; I've even used books. Since you were a little kid you could pick them right out. At Aunt Louise's, floating on our backs after a moonlight swim, you'd call out the shapes: there's the ladle; there's a man with the body of a horse. I knew the names but could never see what you saw. You called them the "consolations."

The meeting the next morning started off well, and I was thinking maybe, maybe this one's actually going to happen, I'm going to make this movie, I'm going to make this and it's going to be good. Robin's wife (who, I'm sure you know, used to be his kids' nanny) is very nice and now his producer, too, so she was in attendance, although she didn't say much. Robin did some schtick. I laughed. Then Johnny said, Olivia's just sucking up to you; I don't do that. Now listen, he said, leaning forward, his finger pointing up Robin's nose, this could be a good fucking movie, but I'm not going to fuck it up just to please those cunts in Hollywood. It's not about the Inquisition. It's not man against the establishment or any of that other horseshit. It's about the death of idealism. That's the picture I'm making. And it'll be fucking great.

Things kind of deteriorated after that. Not openly — we're all professional bullshit artists after all — but it was pretty much over for old Johnny the minute he told Robin his ideas were sentimental slop. But we talked for a couple hours more, Robin giving JD some ideas for the rewrite, JD telling him they were stupid but he'd surely consider them. No wonder Johnny hasn't worked in five years. Then Marsha suggested we go for a walk.

Their compound is on a hilltop, so the walk was downhill at first, a narrow path winding through pine groves and grassy meadows. It's their 1,000-acre backyard. What would it feel like to know that every single thing you see, you own? To look at a hundred redwoods and that hill and that one over there — it's all yours. I tried to find some context: for Robin and Marsha, looking at these thousand acres is like me looking at my closet of clothes, my 25-inch Sony Trinitron, my red Karmen Ghia.

It's kind of hard to grasp, Marsha said as she tried to delineate what was theirs and what was their neighbors', the George Lucases. We just love it here, Marsha said. Robin needs it. You know, to get away from it all.

It's wonderful, I said.

Where do you live in L.A.?

If they knew the truth — a borrowed basement office in Century City — I'd lose too much altitude. A power address was crucial. In Bel-Air, I said.

Oh, that's lovely. Are you married?

This is always always the second question I'm asked. First one is, Where do you live? Then, Are you married, or, Do you have children? (Do men ask each other these questions in business meetings? Don't they talk about sports or the market?) It's just harmless socializing, I know, Maddie, but it always makes me feel like a dog being sniffed by another dog. I'm being sized up, defined, categorized; if the dog is a single man, he takes another reconsidering sniff; if it's a woman, she gives me a consoling or sometimes resentful sniff and we move on to the *other* topic in L.A., which is movies. It took me too long to realize that no one *really* wanted my opinion when they asked what I thought of last weekend's top grosser, they weren't actually asking for my mini-review; I was supposed to just root for the home team if it was a hit and share condescending condolences if it had bombed. Like when you're asked, How are you? No one really wants to hear, A bit gassy, thanks, and you?

We spent the rest of the day in the great room, talking about the script. I kept thinking, all must not be lost or Robin wouldn't still be going through the script, would he? He could end this meeting whenever he wanted to. He and JD seemed to be actually bonding in some way. Johnny can be very convincing, and Robin seemed to be buying it. After all, Sancho isn't the defeated one: Sancho carries on with the idealism Quixote awakened in him. I felt all must not be lost. I might be making a movie soon.

Whatever happens next, thanks for getting me this far, Maddie. I wouldn't be here if you hadn't made that absurd suggestion. And if we make it all the way to the Oscars, of course I'll say, If it wasn't for my little sister, I wouldn't be here tonight. . . .

Love,
Livvie

P.S. Here's an autographed picture of the beaver for you, as promised.

◆ ◆ ◆

October 14, 1998
Los Angeles

Dear Tina,

Would you relax? Look at the math:

Conservative estimate for the last good year for conceiving:	40 years old
Age you are presently:	35 years old
Conservative estimate for years left for you to have a baby:	5 years
Ovulation cycles per year:	12

$$5 \times 12 = 60$$

Number of chances to get pregnant: *at least 60!!!*

If necessary, some of those later years might be medically enhanced chances, in which case add:

$$y = \text{the turkey baster factor}$$

$$5 \times 2y \times 12 = 60 + y$$

You know I slept through Algebra, so that last equation is

probably off somehow, but you get my point. Dozens of chances ahead of you. Please try to stop worrying. Eggs might suffer from performance anxiety, too.

And another thing. Quit worrying about that bitch at the office. So what if she wears short skirts and has a drink with the boss now and then? Those girls usually lose, even though for a while it looks like they could even steal their boss's job. I bet she's gone soon. She'll sleep with him and then he'll have to either transfer her or marry her. Either way, she's history. So steady on. Just make sure he knows how good you are and how much you want the promotion — don't be your humble, nice Midwestern-girl self — grab that power, and next week we'll be celebrating. Call me as soon as you hear, okay?

Maddie's doing all right. She has a little cold but nothing serious. She's excited because she got some seed money from the county for this chef apprentice program she started. I can't imagine doing all that hard work, finding the chefs and the kids, coordinating with the schools, etc., without some personal financial incentive. Especially now, you'd think she'd want to enjoy herself a little more. I know I'd be spreeing. I'd go on food and wine sprees, Paris sprees, Caribbean, movie, music, and, if possible, sex sprees, too. But she's just gone back to normal, going to work, cooking dinner, and watching TV on the couch with Bobby. Jim has a similar routine: he goes to work, he comes home and plays with his kids, and they both seem happier than I've ever been. Maybe I *was* adopted, as my siblings both insist.

It's hot and smoggy out here. I'm missing the fall, and to me, missing the seasons is missing life itself. But Hollywood calls. How can anyone refuse her?

Sixty chances. Don't forget.

Olivia

Date: October 15, 1998
From: OliviaHunt@usol.com
To: Bigdick@worldlink.com

Dear Johnny,

I've asked you nicely about two hundred times: please refrain from calling me "cutie-pie" or "cunt-face" in meetings. Thanks.

We've also talked about Universal before, but I'm putting this in writing for the record: *There is no way in hell we are submitting* Don Quixote *to Universal.* Understand? I have few reasons to live and, as you might expect, I'm clinging to them, and one of them is for the opportunity to humiliate Josh Miller. The other is for the opportunity to say to Josh Miller, "I'm sorry, but *nooooo,* you can't have it." This may be my only chance to achieve both, so *back off* this Universal idea. I know they love you there, but now that we have Robin we'll get offers from other studios, don't worry.

Olivia

October 16, 1998

Josh Miller
President of Production
Universal Pictures
Universal City, California 91608

<u>Via fax</u>

Re: *Don Quixote*

Dear Josh,

It was great catching up with you on the phone today. And mazel-tov! on the numbers on *Total Annihilation*. I haven't had a chance to see it yet, but I hear it's fantastic. It sounds like a real winner.

I'm glad you (now) love *Don Quixote* as much as Johnny and Robin and I do. It's the same script you passed on a couple months ago, but hey, didn't Emerson say a foolish consistency is the hobgoblin of little minds? Can't say that about you.

Just to underline a few things:

1) Robin is only available till June; we need to start preproduction by *January 1*.
2) The budget is $56.3 million. I've attached the budget top sheet.
3) We are discussing the project with another studio at this time, so we must receive your final offer by close of business October 21, 1998.

I look forward to hearing from you, and I truly hope we'll be working together again very soon.

Sincerely yours,
Olivia Hunt

Date: October 20, 1998
From: OliviaHunt@usol.com
To: Bigdick@worldlink.com

JD,

You do realize this is the very same script Universal totally trashed three months ago? The only thing different is that Robin Williams wants to star in it, so they *will* want a rewrite. You've seduced your share of women, and actors, Johnny; can't you tell when you're being snowed? Miller's promise that all they require is a polish — *it's all lies.* We must hold firm on this point: the money *cannot* be triggered by a rewrite or we'll never make this picture. Don't buckle on me, goddammit. I know how they think. I used to be one of them, remember? I asked you not to give the script to Universal, and now we're in bed with them, so at least trust me on how to be sure *we come first.* (Pardon the double entendre.) And if Warners coughs up a matching offer, we have to go there; Miller cannot be trusted, I'm telling you.

— O.

October 20, 1998
The Basement

Maddie,

I thought you of all people would be excited about me dating a celebrity. That jab about forgetting who I am was out of line. (And what did you mean by that, anyway?) Robin Williams wanted to introduce us; I'm going to say no? I don't think it's going very well, anyway. I just got home from my third date. I wish you were up, because I'm *dying* to talk to you. What do you make of this?

After dinner (cooked by his private chef, of course) I asked Steve to show me his art collection, which is incredible. Most of it was on loan to a gallery in Aspen at the moment, so where all the Hoppers and Picassos usually hung were only rectangles lit by spotlights. A few lesser works still remained, but the best pieces, he said, were in his bedroom.

Aha, I said. Are you going to show me your "etchings"? I was making a joke, and since he's a comedian, I thought he'd get it, but he looked sickened, like either it was a really *lame* joke or he was horrified that I was serious and might jump him. Still, he led me down a long hallway, I mean *long* hallway, to his bedroom. A white bedspread covered a king-size mahogany four-poster, which dominated the room. I saw a painting and made a beeline for it. I stood in front of it, looking at it. It was an unamazing landscape by some very famous midcentury Californian artist I've never heard of. I said, This is amazing. I said it a few times: This is amazing. He told me about the artist and the painting, but if I found it interesting then, I sure don't now; I can't tell you a word about it. I remember thinking, Wouldn't it be ironic if this movie star falls in love with me because Michael taught me enough about art that I could spew some decent art-appreciation nonsense about the artist's brush stroke and color palette evoking the late-afternoon light of the dying frontier? It's the way life works. All those afternoons at the Met or MoMA with Michael end up paying off big.

I stepped over the sisal to the other lit landscape, this one by some other guy, don't ask me who, and that's when I heard the first tentative twangs of the banjo. Steve was sitting on his bed strumming his banjo. He was. And what was I supposed to do then? Continue to express my appreciation of the famous painting or direct my admiration toward his musical talent? I felt like a mother of hungry twins. I love this, I said, nodding at the painting, I just love it.

It's beautiful, isn't it?

Very. Then, smiling at him adoringly, I said, You're good.

Oh, thanks.

He kept playing. Now I'm standing there in his bedroom, and he's playing his banjo. Should I sit on the floor at his feet? Pull up a Biedermeier and settle in? I remained standing, arms folded across my chest, grinning at his banjo, nodding my head. What should I have done, Maddie?

He played for about twelve minutes. In fact, I know it was twelve minutes because I couldn't help seeing over his shoulder on the bedside table the red numbers of his LCD clock. It felt longer. Like an hour and a half. At 9:53 he stopped playing, and the minute he did I said, God, you are good (and he really is).

Thank you.

Then he walked me to my car.

What's that? You know this happened the last time, too, when I sat on the couch in the living room: out came the banjo. I listened and wondered, Could this be a pass? How do I get by the banjo? If I make a move will he think I'm just a star-fucker, some cheap groupie who's only attracted to him because he's a celebrity? If I *don't* make a move will he think I'm not interested? The first time he played I assumed I should sing along. I wasn't familiar with the song so I just hummed, demurely slapping my hand on my thigh to the rhythm, but he got that pained look on his face, which is why this time I just listened rapturously. I waited for him to throw the banjo aside and make wild love to me, but as painful as this is to admit, he somehow just didn't find me irresistible.

Even if tonight I did find a way to his heart (or whatever), I don't see why you're not more supportive. You hinted that I might have had ulterior motives — i.e., all that money! — but that's not true. I think he's cute. And obviously very funny. And smart. I'd never marry for money. I know too many girls out here who did and they paid with their lives, Mad. I may be desperate — well, yes, I am desperate — but I'm not easy, so I'd never get that kind of job offer. Men who buy their wives prefer models with fewer neuroses, slimmer egos, and hobbies, not career ambitions — usually just plain models. I don't think I'll be finding my way out of this hole I'm in with the help of a rich husband. Besides, I'm too romantic. There is only one way I'd live with a man again, and that is for true love. The kind you have with Bobby. The kind the movies portray so well. The kind I had, briefly, with Michael.

It's late. I better sign off. I have an early meeting with Warners tomorrow; they seem pretty serious about the movie. You're not lying to me about your counts, are you? Mom says you don't look so good. I hope you're being straight with me, Madeline Anne. Don't sugarcoat things for me, okay?

I love you,
Liv

October 22, 1998
Los Angeles

Edward Hunt
Hunt & Stanfield
101 Edison Avenue
Shawnee Falls, Ohio 45200

Re: Schmuck vs. Killer

Dear Dad,

Thanks for the advice yesterday. It's good to have a lawyer in the family. When we hung up I felt much better and convinced that I should go with Warners even though Universal's offer is better financially. You're right: the people in a business deal are as important as the deal itself, and I just don't trust Josh. Unfortunately, there's a new development that changes everything: Warner's offer is highly conditional.

I should have guessed there was a catch when I was invited to have lunch today with Eric Moriarty and Irving Lowenstein (the president and CEO of Warners). Shall I call Johnny or will your office? I asked Moriarty, whom I met when he was just a veep at MGM. Uh, actually, we'd like to have lunch with just you, he said. Okay, that gave me the creeps, but it happens; sometimes the money guys want to talk freely without the *artiste* around.

It was good to be back on that lot, and the day was sunny and bright and not too warm, this being November, when the temperature does dip below 80 degrees. Some studio lots feel more like elite college campuses than others: Warner's has a few ivy-covered brick buildings and well-manicured lawns, and not a lot of golf cart traffic; there's a quiet studiousness, whereas Columbia and Universal are more like outdoor malls or amusement parks, with low buildings covered in adorable fake Main Street Americana facades, which suggest that human beings are working behind them, just like Back Home, that earnest hard work is going on, not the treacherous, vicious, backstabbing, cynical trash recycling that's really happening. You feel like you're at Williamsburg, where girls in long dresses and bonnets reenact candle making at 1, 3, and 5 P.M. Gullible writers and producers, with optimism and hope in their hearts, are lured into these office buildings expecting to be treated with the same honesty and decency suggested by the movie towns created by the people inside, people who are in fact conniving, weak, fearful cowards. But I digress.

I wanted to be sure I wasn't late, so I arrived with enough time to pick up a few souvenirs for Mad and Bobby and Tina's son. I got Maddie a WB baseball cap and Bugs Bunny pajamas (with feet), and Bobby a WB travel mug. As I walked into the inner gray chambers of the executive dining room, I bumped into Mel Gibson. He was as charming and handsome as ever. Hey, Olivia, how are ya? he said. Mel didn't mention the letter I sent him a while ago, or the script I mentioned in the letter, so I mentioned it again, and while I was doing this mentioning, Irving (the CEO) and Moriarty walked in and saw me talking to Mel, which suggested I was actually a player, on the team, *inside,* not just another desperate nobody indieprod living in a basement in Century City. It's like that exploding paint used in bank vaults that covers the thief and the cash in an identifiable dye. Only with celebrities it's a good thing. They each have their own paint color, and if you get close enough to touch them, a little rubs off on you, so when you walk away, everyone knows by that brave blue color that you've been with, say, Mel Gibson, and the more powerful you are, the more colors you have sprayed all over you.

Lunch was gorgeous. Another thing I miss about being an executive is all that great expense-account food. Seared New Zealand lamb chops, roasted tomatoes, couscous, and a dozen oysters from Hood Canal. Yes, I ate a lot. Like you, I enjoy it, and it seems to impress men. They think because I'm not a salad eater I'm not the enemy, I'm like them, so I can be trusted; also, a meat eater suggests other possibly *carnal* appetites. It took me too long to learn that the opposite rules apply when dining with women: anything *but* a salad makes you an enemy, and don't even *look* at that dessert menu or your name is *bitch*. I don't know how many female colleagues I inadvertently alienated by naively ordering a little carbonara or crème brûlée.

I was knifing into my first lamb chop when Irving said, We want this picture, but we don't want Johnny. We want Fred Schepisi (*Roxanne, Six Degrees of Separation*). He loves the script and is ready to go. Robin will approve him. By my third lamb chop they said the script might need a "comedy punch-up," but other than that, they're ready to make the deal, which would be better for me than the one Universal was offering.

Fred Schepisi would make a great movie, and working with him and the WB executives could only be easier for me. But Johnny and I have been working on this together for months. He's wept over it, he loves it so much. So here's the question, Dad. Despite some of your heartless moves over the years — not showing up for my sixth-grade piano recital, falling asleep at Jim's Indian Guide meetings (even when you were the Chief!), singing along with "Start Me Up" at my first boy-girl party, to name just a few — still, I know you're a man of integrity. So what do I do? Look out for me or honor my commitment to Johnny? Given my recent history with Josh & Co. at Universal, working there will be sheer hell for me. I know what you'd do. But I think that's what's called a schmuck move out here. I want to be a killer, Dad, I do, I do, but something always holds me back. This feels like a critical fork in my road — success lies to the left, moral integrity to the right; are they ever on the same road?

Your little killer,

Olivia

October 23, 1998

Josh Miller

President of Production

Universal Pictures

Universal City, California 91608

<u>By hand</u>

Re: *Don Quixote* budget

Dear Josh,

As promised, here's the full budget *($56 million)* for the meeting next week. It's wonderful to be working together again, and Johnny and I both look forward to making a brilliant picture for Universal.

Sincerely,

Olivia Hunt

October 25, 1998
Shawnee Falls

Dear Michael,

I've decided I like writing to you precisely because you don't respond. You're like a dog that way. A great listener. Man's best friend.

Maddie's resting on the couch. She asked me to come home for the weekend, even though Thanksgiving is only a few weeks away. She said, Livvie, I'm scared. She's always been manipulative. Why she wants me around I don't know. We fought all the time as kids, and now she's judgmental about every move I make. You remember how she'd demand that we spend every holiday together "as a family" and then proceed to bitch at me the whole time, criticizing everything in my life (except you, for some reason) — my Cartier watch, my suede pants, my forgetfulness about recycling. You'd think sisters, who share more DNA than anyone else, would have more in common.

Another mystery to me is Bobby. I guess I underestimated him. I wrote him off as just a good-natured jock who loved my sporty sister; they'd be happy with a life of kids, barbecues, boating on Red Lake. I don't know why I assumed a guy like that couldn't handle what's going on now. Last night Bobby and I were walking to Elmhurst to pick up their casserole pot. We both needed a cigarette, too, which is obviously off limits around Mad; it always has been. After a block of crushing silence he said, This is just a test. And I'm going to pass it.

A test? Of what?

Of how much I love your sister. What kind of man I am.

See what I mean? He's devoted and solid and thank god Maddie married him. His confidence seems unshakable and has a calming effect on her. It must be that Jesuit education. Those Jesuits look at things like leukemia differently, like there's something enriching about it and you'll discover it if you just pray your balls off. I'd love to buy that. I'd love to come up with a way to believe there was something good in all this.

At Elmhurst my mother was delighted to see us. She was working on her latest children's book; I think it's called *Don't Kid Yourself — The Worst Will Happen: How to Be Prepared for the Seventh Grade*. She hasn't had good industry feedback on it. She asked me to read it on my last visit home, and I told her I thought it was a bit of a downer for kids. She burst into tears, so I capitulated and suggested maybe the illustrations were the problem. Is it the human condition, as natural as hunger, to believe you're good at the very thing you're the worst at? There's a nice familiar ontological cruelty that rings true to me, a good symmetry of the pairing up of your greatest desire with the abject deprivation of that very desire. A natural balance. My mother actually thinks she's an authority on parenting, can you believe that? Look at me! Look at Jim! (If you can ever reach him.) I obviously can't include Maddie at the moment, but as soon as she's better we'll take a closer look at her emotional retardation as well. Maybe we're all born with a protective mental coating like a pomegranate seed has, an invisible placenta that prevents reality from piercing our tender brains, that allows us to fool ourselves until our last breath, that lets us actually believe that one day we'll be discovered and one day we'll be rich, one day the world will see our hidden genius, that lets me believe that somewhere in the recesses of your sweet heart and hard head you still care for me.

When we lived in New York it was good; that's true, isn't it? This isn't revisionist. Happy, even, though I hate to sentimentalize here. We lit candles at dinner, in the bath, and whenever we made love. We found a drop-leaf table on Waverly after dinner one night; you fixed its broken leg and painted it white, and we loved it because it was our first piece of jointly acquired furniture. At MoMA and the Met you were my very own docent; you taught me how to see things: shadows, angles, color schemes. You had your first group show and sold both paintings; we celebrated the news on the tar roof, we felt too grand to be in our tiny airless apartment, we had to be outside where the lights of the stars and the city could at last shine down upon us and welcome us to the world. When the *Times* review singled you out, you bought me a Tiffany's silver bracelet engraved *forever yours.* I got promoted, my first expense account, my first subscription to *Variety,* and on my first first-class trip to L.A., at the pink Beverly Hills Hotel we made love, delighted by the high life in a way only visitors to it can be. Back in New York, on hot nights we ate Ray's pizza on the bench outside, watching the shirtless tall boys play basketball, and sometimes you played, too; I watched you through the fence for hours: your straight shoulders, your lean legs. You started a new series, full of long urban shadows, and Barbara gave you your first solo show — which didn't sell but should have; it was great work. I got promoted to L.A. You said a change of scene would be good for you, too, so we moved, and it all went to hell, and lately I've been trying to determine why. What happened, why you turned away from me, why I turned away from you. Why you were always leaving, first on fishing trips that turned into weeks away, and then to New Mexico, because the light was good there, because L.A. was turning you into a zombie, because you needed time alone. Why you never came with me when I had to travel for work: except for that first time in the Beverly Hills Hotel, you never joined me in the first-class life I led on location in London, in New York, in Vancouver. Why we stopped making love. I'm sure you have your theories. In fact, I think you shared them with me a few times before you left. But they're incomplete. Compulsively I seek the correct telling, the right version: the truth. I feel I've just climbed out of a car wreck and I'm staring at the mangled frame, wondering what the hell happened, because the last thing I remember we were driving along okay. I'm not asking for help here; you don't need to weigh in on the matter — *although it would be nice to hear from you* — I'm really just working it out myself, and you're my silent confessor, a breathing face on the other side of the screen: Forgive me, for I have sinned and all that. And may I say your silence is about as comforting as God's.

Maddie is stirring. It's dinnertime, but she can't eat anymore, because the nausea has begun. She has a little cold, too. Last night we watched *Phenomenon* on the fold-out, the three of us lined up like whole fish at the market. Travolta was pretty good but I know he has an outrageous perk package, so I couldn't enjoy the picture as much as Maddie did. She said, Thanks for coming home, Liv, which always makes me feel just lousy. I think I'm getting to know her in a different way, more like a girlfriend, not just my little sister; it's actually okay doing nothing together, just talking about things like our upper arms, our parents, our dream bathrooms. She's a strange mix of righteous and kind; she's unnecessarily nice to everyone, but she's also judgmental as hell: I think *intolerant* is the word. I agree with most of her politics, and some of her judgments, so it usually doesn't bother me, but I do wonder, how did she get to be so sure of herself?

When the movie was over, she sat up and her hair stayed on the white pillow, a brown wig of it, not a few wisps but a wide swatch, like she'd been scalped. She looked at the hair and touched her hand to the back of her head — *Oh, god, oh, no* — then her hands fluttered over her head like birds and handfuls of her long brown hair came out and she curled over and covered her face and her body heaved. I put my arm around her and was surprised to feel her shoulder blades through the flannel shirt and said, It's going to grow back; it will. Bobby held her as she cried hard, her whole body trembling for all the crying she hasn't done and is yet to do; she cried about the unfairness and uncertainty, the terror and the sickness, she cried because until then she hadn't lost anything, she wasn't one of those chemo-bald people you pity, that children are afraid of and adults politely turn away from, she was still Maddie.

Hey, thanks for everything.

Love (barely),
Olivia

October 25, 1998

Marguerite Dunning
Hollywood Wigs
3333 Melrose Place
Hollywood, California 91229

Dear Marguerite,

As discussed, enclosed please find your round-trip plane ticket for L.A.-Cincinnati for October 27, and returning October 28, as well as a check for $2,000 for the purchase of a human-hair wig, which you will fit and make for my sister immediately. I appreciate your speedy response to this. (I'll need a receipt for insurance; the term they use is "cranial prosthesis.")

By the way, I know I must have told you this, but thanks again for your help with Dom DeLuise on *Lloyd the Hamster*. The picture didn't work, but your wig did; I think he looked better than he has in years, and your marvelous wig was the reason why.

I'll meet you at the airport. See you then.

Gratefully,
Olivia Hunt

— ◆◆◆ —

Date: October 26, 1998
From: OliviaHunt@usol.com
To: Bigdick@worldlink.com

Choose your battles, Johnny. Universal is going to put on a line producer they trust, that's nonnegotiable and you know that. I liked Cully Davis the best; I think he's got good instincts and I talked to Kenneth Branagh and Martin Scorsese about him and they both raved: he's good with scheduling and the budget, and crews love him. So let's cancel tomorrow's meetings and hire Cully before he takes the Pollack picture. Just because Universal recommended him and they like him doesn't mean he's "in their pocket." You're so paranoid. Only insane people are paranoid.

Let me know if I should cancel the other interviews. I can call them from here tonight.

— O.

October 30, 1998
Outside at The Basement

Dear Tina,

There are days when the Santa Ana winds blow and the sky is so clear blue you want to dive in and disappear into that blueness and swim through space looking down on all the human struggle on earth like the bluebird of happiness herself. Or at least after a certain kind of day at the studio you might feel that way. It's five o'clock, and I'm sitting at a patio table by The Basement's pool eating my sushi take-out, wishing you were sitting across from me, a Corona in your hand. Two working girls having a beer in their panty hose.

I just read your letter. I can't believe you didn't get the promotion. I'm really sorry. I know how much you wanted it and, of course, I also hate being wrong: I thought it was yours. Is it possible your boss is threatened by you? How could he not choose you? Maybe it's time to change companies. (I can't believe it has to do with your wanting another baby. He probably assumed you want more kids — most people want more than one — and lots of working mothers have more than one. And wouldn't that be grounds for a lawsuit? Do you think you can prove it? Didn't you have more seniority than that other woman?)

I'm having some trouble at work myself. I'm not complaining, because I'm grateful to have work. Universal has agreed theoretically to make *Don Quixote,* but there are still many conditions we must meet before it's truly green-lit — and I don't get paid till it is, so I'm not buying any new underwear *just yet.* (But I do have my eye on a peachy lace ensemble at Victoria's Secret.) Today the head of the studio called me in for a private meeting. You're already familiar with my former boss Josh Miller, who was also in attendance. Well, this was Josh's boss, the CEO, Howard Trammel. He's shorter than I am, but so are feral pigs.

You think you can control Johnny? he asked before I sat down in his 1,800-square-foot office full of Francis Bacon paintings of men screaming.

No, I said honestly, knowing it would stun him quiet for a few seconds. (You should try this sometime, Tina: a good comeback not only impresses them, it buys you some time.) No one can control Johnny, I said. You know that, Howard.

Well, that's precisely what we're worried about, Josh said, as if he were making a new point. Duh.

I have his respect, I said to Josh, suggesting *he* didn't. And that's more important.

Howard was watching me. I crossed my legs, glad I'd decided on pants instead of a skirt. When I worked for Universal I saw Howard maybe four times and talked to him less. I wasn't on his radar, so his only opinion of me came from Josh, who preferred to pay me to go away rather than have me at another staff meeting. Howard twisted the soles of his tiny, shiny shoes on the edge of the glass coffee table, assaulting my ears with an irritating *squeak*.

So Johnny listens to you? Howard asked, *squeak! squeak!*

No. He ignores me. He disagrees with me. Then, eventually, usually, not always, he comes up with the idea — mine — that he rejected three weeks earlier. You know what it's like, I said to Howard, flattering him.

Josh looked at Howard for a cue, not sure if it was his turn to talk. Howard's feet squeaked. He continued to examine me.

I'll be fine with Cully, I said calmly, casually, confidently. Even Johnny has to respect him.

Why?

He's worked with other directors Johnny admires, on tough pictures. And, of course, he's a man; that helps. Doesn't it?

Howard's thin lips curled. He said, Well, we all heard about the bullshit on *Stay the Night*. I'm not going to put up with that, Olivia; this picture can't cost a nickel over fifty million.

Fifty? The budget's fifty-six —

Josh said it was fifty.

Now *that* was unmistakably a cue: That's what it should be, Josh said. We'll get it there.

Howard was back at his desk. The minute I see overages I'm pulling the plug, because I'm not going through that bullshit with Johnny, he said, picking up the phone.

You can't make this movie for fifty, I said. But only Josh heard me, because as far as Howard was concerned, the meeting was over.

I don't know what Howard made of my bravado. I know Josh can't stand it. He's afraid of women who aren't afraid of him. And he hates women who hate him, which I suppose is fair enough. Can you believe I'm back working with this guy? No wonder I'm not exactly thrilled about my first green light. And this is just the beginning. Robin Williams is only available till June, so the schedule is nearly impossible to make: we need twelve weeks to shoot — if Robin will agree to six-day weeks instead of five, which historically he hasn't — which gives us only fifteen weeks of prep, and normally you'd need about eighteen for a movie of this size. If Robin won't work six-day weeks, we have even less time to get everything ready: to find the locations, design and build the sets and costumes, plan the schedule, cast every part. There are two key meetings next week on the budget and the script, and then I go to Madrid on Monday with Johnny to scout locations. We'll come back to do some casting, then move to Spain sometime in December and stay there till July.

A great crew will help make the impossible possible, and we're off to a good start with Cully Davis, who will be our line producer — the guy who figures out the shooting schedule and manages the day-to-day physical production, the budget and crew. He looks like a sixty-year-old Clark Gable: he's tall, broad shouldered, with a strong jaw and silver Brylcreemed hair, and his blue eyes have seen enough to spot bullshit at five hundred yards. He's like a general, but not a chauvinistic one, which is a welcome contrast to ass-kicking Texas Johnny. He's made huge movies for relatively low budgets, so he'll find ways to cut ours — which is obviously my biggest challenge at the moment.

I keep saying to myself, aren't you excited, Olivia? You're making a movie! But whenever you have to ask yourself, the answer is no, otherwise you'd be too busy being excited to bother asking, right? The realization of something that's lived in my head for so long is exciting; maybe like seeing your baby's face after wondering what he'll look like for so many months. It'll be great to make some money again, and buy that new underwear ensemble, hell, maybe even an apartment. But I dread the actual work ahead, the months in Spain. The weather has to be perfect or we'll be screwed, because most of the movie takes place outside and we don't have the money or time to wait out a squall or downpour. I need a rewrite that will satisfy Johnny, the two stars, and the studio, and naturally none of them agree on what needs to be done — or even who should do the rewriting: everyone's got a favorite writer. Yet they've all committed to doing this picture believing they're each big enough to trump the other guy. I'm hoping Tom Zane, who's Robin's choice and the perfect writer, will be the only one available, or else Johnny will push his guy, who's not right. My job is to make — and keep — everybody happy, yet I'm the one with the least juice: why would Robin Williams or Josh or even Johnny listen to me? I'm the only one without a film credit. But if I don't get Johnny to do what Robin wants, and Robin to do what Johnny wants, and Universal to do what we want, then there will be no movie, and it will be considered my fault.

But it's only a movie. I think about what Maddie's going through. The chemo side effects have begun. Her hair started falling out when I was home last weekend. She asked me to cut off the rest. I set a kitchen chair in the middle of the living room and draped a blue striped dish towel around her shoulders. She said, I wonder if it'll grow back a different color? I've always wanted to be blond, like you.

Give your boys hugs from me,
Olivia

November 1, 1998
Universal commissary

Maddo —

Here's that article I told you about on Turks and Caicos — doesn't it look amazing? That hotel on page 147 is the one Robin Williams told me about, and the beaches are supposed to be incredible. So what do you say, Christmas in the Caribbean? Doesn't that sound blissfully free of all that corny Santa Claus crap? I bet Mom and Dad would pay for it, too. Don't annoy me and say, But I love Christmas at home. Okay, if you insist on the tree, the mall, the shitty presents, the sawdust turkey, we'll go the day after. Think about it. That hotel books up months in advance, so we have to decide right away.

Let's do something special to celebrate your graduation from the Misery Motel, okay? Sunshine, tropical breezes, pink drinks on a white beach . . . Think about it.

Hope you're feeling better,
Liv

- - -

November 10, 1998
Mercy waiting room

Dear Tina,

I've been resisting the urge to write you, hoping if I put it off I wouldn't have to, that things would get better before I had to burst here on the page.

Maddie's in intensive care. The story they tell me is she got an infection, that's why her nose was running and why she was coughing last week, and the antibiotics couldn't stop it, and of course her immune system has been destroyed by the "medicine," so without white blood cells the infection got worse and injured her lungs, which are now like sponges so thick with wet plaster she can't breathe. She was sedated and when she woke up there was a ventilator in her throat.

The pain was not bad because they had her on some good drugs, but she couldn't talk. Being understood, sharing words — you wouldn't think it's so important till you can't do it, and then you realize it's as necessary as water and air, just to talk to one another, to be heard. We wrote notes. I think the last time we wrote notes was on a trip out west in the Winnebago, when we were supposed to be asleep and my parents were watching TV up front. Under the covers with a flashlight we planned the next day and played hangman and tic-tac-toe till she fell asleep under my arm. This time, from the raised bed, she wrote, *How's movie going?*

Fine.

Pls scratch my forehead. Thnx. Luv you.

Luv you.

Then she started hallucinating. They had to increase the Ativan because she was fighting the ventilator. She wrote: *Jimmy Buffett wants toothpick.* And: *Get goat off the bed!* And then: *Where's the baby?*

Eventually she got too weak to hold a pen and she slipped, with another push of Ativan, into what I sincerely hope is a sugarplum fairy–filled dream. Her body is still instinctively fighting the invasive vent, so she isn't getting enough oxygen and is using up too much precious energy resisting it. Now they want to paralyze her so she can't resist anymore. She won't know the difference, they say, since she's already out of it, but Bobby is reluctant to authorize this because naturally there are risks when anesthesia is involved. The doctor rattled off numbers, odds of this happening if you use the paralytic drugs, odds if you don't, but he was acting like using them was the way to go. They're still waiting for Bobby's signature.

She'd hate this, he said. She'd hate to be paralyzed. And what if something goes wrong and —. I think we should wait another day.

I don't know, Bobby . . .

Fuck!

Her organs need oxygen. Her brain —

— I know, Olivia.

She won't know she's paralyzed. She's already in a kind of coma from the Ativan.

I don't know what to do. What should I do? He looked at me the way Ed did that night in the backyard. And then he went out for a smoke. My dad and mom are talking to a nurse, trying to understand what she's saying, to understand what the hell's going on.

I hope by the time you read this, Mad will be back home.

Freaked,

O.

November 11, 1998
Mercy

Dear Maddie,

It's three A.M. on the ICU ward. I finally convinced Mom and Dad to go home. Bobby's curled up in a chair in the waiting room. I can't sleep. I can't read. Novels demand some concentration and for what? People and problems that don't even exist. Magazines are trivial and garish. The grinning models and millionaires in *People* and *Vogue* are just asking for it; they make me want to stab their eyes out. All that superbeauty and happiness — how dare they? how can they? don't they know? There are not a lot of happy people around here. Everyone's either serious or scared shitless like us, which is fine since that way I don't feel like mutilating them. The nurses are great. They're like tanks. I'd like to bring them to Spain; they wouldn't take any lip from Josh Miller — that's how resolute they are. There's one doctor who is skating on thin ice, very thin ice, but until you're out we have to be nice to him. The first thing that pissed me off so deeply was his shoes. A man of medicine, a healer, should not do his ICU rounds in black Bruno Magli slip-ons, the kind O.J. wore when he allegedly sliced off his wife's head, the trendy tassled slippers every rich asshole with no taste prances around in, that arrogant alligator-skin shoe that stinks of entitlement; I hated him and his fucking shoes on sight. As he calmly explained that your lungs were filling up with fluid and that a lung biopsy might determine the nature of the infection, but it could cause permanent lung damage, and would Bobby just sign here to approve this procedure? I imagined ripping those shoes off his feet and ramming them down his patronizing pink throat. Money is okay — you want your doc to be successful enough to buy quality, and god knows you don't want those strung-out pasty interns in squashed Rockports keeping your sister alive — but the money should buy lastingness, because that's the feeling we want around here, goddammit, lastingness. He should be wearing wing tips. Church's sturdy brown oxfords. Shoes that say, This is the empire you're dealing with, and everything is and always will be under control, madam. And this guy should not have said to me, Oh, you're *the sister,* as if he'd already been warned I was going to be all over his high-and-mighty ass, which, as you know, I have been and will continue to be until you come home. Then he really blew it when he said, You're in the movie business, aren't you?

I swear it's the only time I've seen him smile. People always light up when they find out I'm in The Business; they're delighted, as if I'm not a marginal independent producer hanging by my last few grand but an elf from the North Pole, living proof that Santa really does exist, bestowing me with a power that priests and bishops must have enjoyed in the Dark Ages. Don't worry, I wasn't vicious. Actually, I considered offering him the role of the Knight of the Moon in *Quixote* if he got you out of here in one piece, but I've learned that when negotiating with men you never offer them what they want — you never say, I'll give you this if you give me that — because that would make you a whore and them a john, that would be so coarse. You have to make them think you just *want* to do what they want, without any incentive or reward, because that way they can feel adored *and* generous. If you were awake, you could tell me not to be so cynical.

Nurse Susan just came in and looked at the monitor, touched a few secret dials, and recorded her findings in your chart, which is now about three feet high. What kind of person signs up for the night shift on an ICU? Susan said, You really should go home and get some sleep. You need your strength, too.

I know.

Visiting hours are over.

I know.

Well?

I didn't say another word, but she left and I didn't. We never leave you alone. We take shifts talking to you; some study showed that people in a coma — even this medically controlled one — who hear familiar voices do better than those who don't. Like if you hear the party's still going on in the next room, you'll find your way back to it. Nurse Krystal told us this. As it happens, she's heavily into crystals. Funny how people's names can sometimes take over their lives. Krystal places crystals on your hands and chest and stomach, in between the Groshong and the Hickman catheters and the food tube in your nose and the tube that's draining your lungs and the oxygenation line taped to your forefinger; you're covered in purple rocks that emit good vibes from the Paleolithic era. Dr. Dickhead smirks and shakes his head at them, which makes me believe in them even more.

Dad's too freaked out to be dismissive. He's downright timid; you'd absolutely love it. He reads you the entire *Courier* on his shift, making some hysterical editorial comments along the way, e.g., The water board is drowning in their own bureaucracy, huh, huh; Look at this, honey, your fourth-grade teacher was arrested in the A&P for shoplifting artichoke hearts, etc. Mom's turned into a sheep; you could get anything you want from her these days. It's kind of pathetic but human, I suppose. Jim flew in and when he wasn't in here holding your hand, he was walking around the waiting room looking frantic and lost. His boss doesn't give a damn about you being sick, so Jim had to go back to New York yesterday, which made him even more frantic and lost looking. He wants to quit and move back to Shawnee Falls. I told you wouldn't want him to do that.

Your hand is cool. I've been holding it for nearly two hours. It doesn't warm up enough. I hold it and send you brain waves, fierce ones, like Uri Geller with his fork, willing you well, willing you to keep fighting, demanding that the infection be cleared, that your lungs start working again.

You know that first time we slept out in the tree fort? You must have been five, because I was going into sixth grade that fall, and it was a few weeks before school — I'd already participated in the Annual Fall Clothes Shopping Massacre with Mom. (Still she buys me plaid; why?) Jim dared me to spend the whole night in the fort; no one had ever done that before. You insisted on doing it with me. You always had to do whatever I was doing, which was really annoying; I'm sure I told you. I made you promise you wouldn't start mewling about going inside; this being a dare, I had to go through with it no matter what. We rolled out the smoky-smelling green flannel sleeping bags and filled the wicker picnic basket with Ding Dongs and cut carrots and PBJs and Fritos; we positioned the mesh citronella candles to maximize their mosquito killing. You filled the plastic bucket with the can of Off, the plaid thermos of milk, the big silver flashlight, and playing cards and whatever books we were reading — then you went up the ladder first because you wanted to pull the bucket up through the hole in the floor yourself.

And at first it was great. The night was humid and the sky was pale gold. The cicadas were buzzing like maniacs in their end-of-summer frenzy. We played Crazy 8s and Go Fish and I let you win (as always). We pretended we were sister squirrels, we pretended we were Jews hiding from the Nazis, we pretended the fort was our palace and we were Celtic warrior queens. We ate the Ding Dongs and curled the silver foil into engagement rings. You asked me, Why does Dad yell so much?

He doesn't yell. He just has a loud voice.

He yells at Mom.

Sometimes he's tired and he gets irritable.

What's irritable?

It's when you yell at every little thing.

Can I get it?

It's not like a cold; it's a feeling. And you do, trust me, you get irritable, too; everybody does sometime. Then you asked: Are they going to get divorced?

I said no, even though I was terrified they were. As much as I hated listening to them fight, I prayed they wouldn't get a divorce. I guess when you're a kid you only hope for the best: you don't hope your dad will get out, you hope he'll turn into the dad you want; you don't hope they'll get a divorce, which would end the fighting, you hope tomorrow morning there will be a sunny, loving couple living in your house.

A gust of warm air flipped the cards off the floor. The weather was changing fast; something big was happening out there. The trees swayed, rocking the tree house, the gray plywood planks groaning, the oak leaves fluttering so loudly they sounded like a roaring sea. I loved it; I was as excited as the wind. But you said, I'm scared.

Don't be, okay? It's great.

I wanna go in.

You can't, you promised.

But I'm scared.

Too bad.

Please, Livvie, I'm scared.

Don't be a baby.

The walls moaned again like they were dying themselves as the fort listed, and I thought of the lullaby: *When the wind blows, the cradle will rock; when the bough breaks, the cradle will fall . . .*

Don't worry, we won't fall, nothing bad will happen, I promise, just go to sleep, okay?

Tell me a story.

So I did, beginning as I began every story: *Another True and Outstanding Adventure of the Hunt Sisters. Once upon a time, there were two beautiful princesses named Madeline and Olivia Hunt. That day, the sisters set out on a sea voyage in their glorious red sailing vessel, the high winds tossing them forward toward the magical land of* . . . Your eyes were glassy and heavy, you were just floating off to sleep when the first crack of thunder smashed and you screamed and started bawling again. It was loud, it was right above us, so you weren't being pitiful. You climbed into my bag and I held you, and I promised we wouldn't crash down or get hit by lightning, and eventually you fell asleep that way, clutching my shoulder and my side, your breathing in sync with mine like we were one body, and though the storm rocked our tree ship, the rain pounding the roof, the branches scratching its wood sides, inside we were safe and warm and okay, and in the morning we woke with the sun and the birds and felt like heroes.

Date: November 11, 1998
From: OliviaHunt@usol.com
To: Dr_Jones@leukemiahelp.org

Dear Dr. Jones,

I've written you fifteen e-mails and you don't have the decency to reply to one. Why give out your e-mail address? I've put a curse on you. You're going to get this miserable disease yourself and then you'll know just how desperate life can be, you fuck.

Date: November 12, 1998
From: OliviaHunt@usol.com
To: Dr_Jones@leukemiahelp.org

Dear Dr. Jones,

I'm sorry my last e-mail was so hostile. I'm sure you understand how tense I am. I appreciate you writing back. You seem to be saying maybe my sister should have had the bone marrow transplant right off the bat, yet the chemo induction protocol would have been even tougher than what she just had, which has landed her in intensive care with some lung infection called ARDS, and now sepsis, so why are you suggesting we should have done that? Especially when, as I mentioned in my *sixteen* previous e-mails, my sister is not Philadelphia chromosome positive? No one ever said anything about the goddamned T-factor before. How were we supposed to know that was another indicator for early BMT? I assumed her doctors might know something like that. And so I have to ask you, with all due respect, what do we do now?

Date: November 13, 1998
From: OliviaHunt@usol.com
To: Dr_Jones@leukemiahelp.org

Dr. Jones,

Thanks for the totally useless advice. You don't even know these doctors; how can you possibly advise me to trust they're doing all they can? Trust? I trusted you, I trusted them, I trusted a whole bunch of people and now everyone's standing around scratching their fat asses while Maddie drowns in mucus. All doctors are not good doctors; it's like anything else — there's the top 10 percent and then there's the rest of the inferior cowardly quacks like you. You're an idiot and the curse is back on you. May you get acute lymphocytic leukemia one day and wind up drowning to death really, really slowly, like a minute at a time. Don't worry, this is my last e-mail.

⋅—◆—⋅

Date: November 13, 1998
From: OliviaHunt@usol.com
To: Bigdick@worldlink.com

JD,

It looks like I won't make the script meeting tomorrow. Things are still a little hairy here. But I did speak briefly (and confidentially, so don't mention this) with the reader who's preparing Universal's notes, and Josh's absolute deal breakers are the following:

1) *Quixote cannot renounce* his dream in the end. He can't say his whole quest was for nothing and that he knew it was just a dream; if he knew, why'd he bother?

2) *Q must be kissed* by Dulcinea at the tournament and she can't be a poor wretch, because "no guy in the audience will believe that Q went through all that trouble for a total dog." (Avoid discussing casting tomorrow; save that for Tuesday's meeting. I'll be there. But FYI — they want Penelope Cruz or Jennifer Lopez.)

3) *Q doesn't die.* He returns home, defeated at the tournament (like we want!), but he goes off into the sunset with Sancho, in search of further adventure.

I know some of these repulse you, but do me a favor: at the meeting, just go along with them; in fact, you might even suggest one or two yourself so the suits actually believe you. I know, I know, you don't "play these games," but you also haven't made a movie in five years, so now might be the time to reevaluate that strategy, Johnny. I'm not saying we have to actually *do* all their ideas, but in the meeting be open-minded and act like you think they're good and do-able, and then once we're alone with Zane, we'll get him to just gesture to them. I can hear you saying, Listen, dumbshit, you can't *gesture* about Death: Quixote either dies or he doesn't! But a good writer like Zane (and director like yourself) can *gesture* to the idea of immortality. Quixote lives on in Sancho, doesn't he? Even hardheaded secularists are in love with the idea that no one really dies, that we all live on forever, if only in each other's hearts and minds, blah, blah, blah. You accuse them of being literal minded; don't do that yourself — don't take their story notes so *literally,* Johnny.

I'm looking for more budget cuts; I see we're now at $54 million, inching south to $53 million. Josh said we have to get closer to $50 million before he'll approve the trip to Madrid. Yes, of course I reminded him that scouting Spain will give us more ideas on how to cut the budget. The first question — can we avoid three different production bases? — can only be answered there, on the ground. But in the story meeting, any cost-saving creative ideas — like cutting the Sancho island sequence, hint, hint — will go a long way to getting the scout approved.

This is the fantasy stage, Johnny, where we have to show we believe their fantasy (which is probably $53 million, not the $50 million they keep saying) before we get to live ours (making a great movie). Keep playing along, okay? And hopefully I'll see you in Spain next week.

— O.

November 15, 1998
ICU

Dear Maddie,

A new entry under the category *Huh?* is *Riverdance*. The way they jump up and down, they look like a bunch of little kids who have to go to the bathroom. We get only PBS in here from midnight till six, which is when I sit with you. I'd give them money to *stop* broadcasting it. I had to turn the sound off. I'm playing Bruce Springsteen for you (another personal sacrifice — boy, you will owe me big time when you wake up). So the Celts in leotards are now hopping in formation to "Tenth Avenue Freeze-Out."

Later, 4:30 A.M.

Having listened to *Born to Run* three times in a row, I must confess: you may be onto something with this Bruce infatuation of yours. I'm sorry I hid your album back in 1981 (but you had played it continually for three weeks). Earlier tonight, I couldn't get enough of "Thunder Road." The harmonica's opening, plaintive notes made me nostalgic, as if it's a song I used to know from some "glory days" I didn't actually have; and then when the melody cranked up, answering that sad harmonica, and the horns and other singers lifted up Bruce's bellowing voice like a baseball star on the shoulders of a cheering crowd, suddenly I found myself singing along, doing a little air guitar, sliding around the linoleum floor in my stocking feet, wanting to scream at the top of my lungs —

> *. . . what else can we do now?*
> *Except roll down the window and let the wind blow back your hair*
> *Well, the night's busting open, these two lanes will take us anywhere . . .*

— until I heard this nasal, indignant whine: What is going *on* in here?

An intern I'd never seen before was standing in the doorway. I looked at him (male, approximately twenty-eight years old, sleep-deprived, pale, skinny — in *squashed Rockports!*) and wondered: Why can't we just have two or three doctors, why a new series every day? Where are they all coming from — and going? How can each one possibly know what's going on with you?

I cleared out and went down to the cafeteria. Dolores, the cashier, told me her daughter passed the bar exam, so that was nice to hear. She said I looked tired. I sat in the empty dining room and ate some iceberg lettuce. The cafeteria offers that orange dressing you don't see much anymore and which is actually pretty wonderful. Three chocolate chip cookies topped off the meal. And now I'm back here with a Styrofoam cup of old 'n' gnarly coffee. Playing some Garth Brooks for you. But only for a few more minutes. He's too damn sad for the ICU.

Oh, Maddie.

The reason I'm writing tonight is Dad. There's no one else I can really talk to about this. Jim had to go back to New York; there's some crisis at work, and Sophie and Nell have strep. Even when he is around, Jim's so sweet and harried, I don't feel like adding to his plate of woes. I miss talking to him, though. We don't much anymore. I don't know why exactly. Maybe it's the time-zone problem. Then too much life passed and now it's hard to pick things up again.

But it's the other man in the family I need to talk to you about. Dad didn't show up for dinner tonight. We called the usual places, Shawnee Tavern, Roddy's, The Alibi, and they all said he'd moved on. Since you got sick, the bartenders don't lie to us anymore, so we knew it was true. Rich at The Alibi called back later and said Dad's car was still in the lot, so he must be on foot. It was snowing like hell, an early freak storm, so Bobby and I decided we better go look for him, he could die of hypothermia, that's all we need. We fanned out from The Alibi, trying to guess which route he'd choose, which destination. Bobby thought home; I thought Just One More Drink, probably at the Hi-Life or the Club, so I drove up Wabash and down Monroe, then over to Main. Wabash always reminds me of that summer I had the paper route and we'd get up so early the sky was still indigo blue; remember the smell of the inky papers and the dogs barking and you whimpering about it being cold, or being afraid of the dogs, or being hungry? You were always whimpering about something. I didn't want you to come with me, but you always did, and once we got out of the house, I was glad you were there. It was only one month of our lives, but every time I drive down Wabash I think of those dewy-grass mornings with you, and now that we're not doing it they seem really great, like it was the only time Shawnee Falls belonged just to us, and we were sneaking around in it free as the birds above us, these two girls tossing rolled-up papers at the sleeping houses, planning the rest of our summer day because it was all ours and we could do anything we wanted.

I found him on Adams, by that little triangle of vacant land. The snow had been falling since noon, so by this time there were six or seven inches and the roads were thick with it, slowing the rush hour traffic to a golden crawl. The Hahns already have their Christmas lights up, and that crazy Greek on the corner has started hauling out his mega display. (On the Action-7 News he said it takes him two weeks to get all the reindeer and Santas up. We'll drive by when you come home; I know what a sucker you are for that stuff.) I called Bobby and told him I'd found Ed.

I rolled down the window and cruised slowly alongside our father, who glared at me, furious and indignant, like your typical homeless raging nutcase.

Dad, come on, get in.

He kept walking, saying nothing, his camel hair coat and tweed cap white with snow.

Dad —

Go away! Go! Go away! Go!

Dad —

Go! Go away, goddammit! Leave me alone!

Stop! Dad, please! I screamed, and he stopped. He leaned into the window and whispered: I'm finito. Kaput. Good-bye, daughter.

I rolled along beside him. Dad, let's go have a drink. I've had some success with this strategy, and in fact for a moment there I had him. He stopped suddenly, his head cocked like a dog who's heard his master's whistle. He opened the door. Then slammed it.

I smell the rat, he said, and then he ran off like we were playing a game of tag, only it was disturbing, since there's something unnatural about seeing your father run away from you.

I parked the Camry and ran after him, hopping into his deep footprints, which wound along the road beside the cyclone fence, until we were walking side by side, no one saying a word, both of us breathing hard and shoving our feet forward into the snow, bending over the way you do in a blizzard or rainstorm, as if you're actually dodging a few raindrops or snowflakes. We were in the playground at Horace Mann when he leaned against the fence and slid down and said, I'm not getting up till I'm dead.

I've had that impulse myself from time to time. I didn't say anything. You never deny a drunk his fantasy — it's a waste of breath, just like reason, bribery, threats, love, hope, begging. This much I've learned. It was quiet for a while. We let the snow fall on us. I watched it cover the monkey bars and the slide, the crystals hissing as they kissed the white ground.

He said, I went up to the chapel in Mercy. I got down on my knees. That hurt. My knees are all shot. Like my hands. Look. Goddamned arthritis. He looked at them as if he didn't recognize them, and then dropped them with disgust. He continued. I said, Take me, goddammit, I'm a sonofabitch. I'm a sonofabitch! he yelled at the swing set.

Whatever I said would provoke him, so I remained silent.

You're not listening, he said.

Yes, I am. You're a sonofabitch.

Don't be a smart-ass, missy.

I'm not; you said it —

— You're no better than us, you know. You think you are, but you're not.

Thanks for the reminder.

Hey, kiddo, you're my daughter. I love you, do you understand that? And Jimmy and my Madeline — he broke down at the thought of you, moaning and groaning, the tears dripping down his swollen red face. It was terrible, Maddie; he was thoroughly broken apart. Just when I thought I couldn't watch another minute, he roared, Enough! Enough, goddammit! as if he were calling to someone far away, but the snow soaked up his voice so it was only a muffled cry.

She's going to be okay, Dad.

I'm going to kill those fucking doctors, strangle every one of them. I'm a helluva fighter, you know that? I was just a little shrimp on the South Side of Chicago; you had to be tough, so I had to fight dirty, kicking and biting. . . .

You can imagine my panic at this mention of his tragic past. He'd be asleep soon. I'd never be able to get him home.

. . . my mother died and I was only seven —

— Your mother died fifty years ago; get over it. (I know, I know, bold move, but I knew his bobbing head would snap up at such an insult.)

What do you know about it, huh? Miss Movie Business?

More than I'd like to, I muttered.

You don't know everything. Your sister worships you, did you know that? No. You're too busy to know anything. So just go. Go back to Hollywood. We'll be just fine without you.

Then he struggled to get up but fell headfirst into a mound of plowed snow. He didn't move and neither did I. It was one of those *Do I enable or don't I?* moments that I always fail. I don't know any other way. I grabbed a fistful of his coat and yanked him out. His cap stayed in the hole. I pulled it out and pushed it onto his head. He sat there stunned like a trout on a dock. His eyelashes were frozen and his eyebrows and mustache were dusted white with snow; he looked like he'd put his face in a bowl of flour. It was as quiet as quiet can be, the snow falling so silently all around us it was peaceful as hell and beautiful, beautiful.

He wiped the snow from his face and reached into his pants pocket. Here. Take this, he said, handing me his wallet.

What for?

Open it up. There were hundreds, twenties, the usual wad he likes to walk around with. In there. He pointed. Take it out.

There was a picture tucked in a credit card slot. It was of you, Mad. But as a kid. Maybe five years old. Your hair was short and messy, and you had on that hot pink T-shirt you wore every day one summer. You were smiling like you had a secret.

That's who I see. In that bed up there. You didn't know *that*, did you?

I slipped the picture back into his wallet and handed it to him.

I'd do anything, goddammit, he muttered soberly. Anything.

I helped him up. Would you quit?

He brushed off his coat and looked at me curiously. Quit? Quit what?

November 16, 1998
Shawnee Falls, Ohio

Johnny Ray Dickerman
DON QUIXOTE
Producers' Building 4
Universal Pictures

<u>Via fax</u>

<u>CONFIDENTIAL</u>

Dear Johnny,

I talked to Zane last night. I like his idea of killing Quixote at the tournament with the Knight of the Moon, then letting Sancho pick up his joust. It's a little obvious, but I'm sure the studio will like it better than killing Q off in bed later. And this way, you get to kill Quixote and they get the "up" ending.

I've gone over Cully's new budget. I see you're still insisting on a seventy-seven-day shooting schedule. Cully said we could cut four days if we dropped Sancho's island sequence — in time and construction and extras that would be a $1 million savings right there. We're still at $53.8 million; we have to start thinking of big cuts, Johnny, not a few thousand here and there. Creatively I STILL think this sequence, where Sancho is rewarded with his own island to govern, slows the movie down and takes away from Quixote's influence. Q should be able to inspire Sancho *without* Sancho actually getting a taste of his fantasy. That's the whole idea, isn't it? To believe even when there is no reason to believe? I know it's funny, and "never cut funny," but we can lace other physical comedy opportunities for Robin elsewhere.

The other place for big savings is above-the-line perks: they're huge and they don't show up on the screen. I'm not going to pussyfoot here, Johnny: your demand for two round-trip L.A.-Madrid first-class tickets for each of your five children — a total cost of $90,000 — is outrageous. You don't even have custody of three of them, and the other two are toddlers; why do they have to fly first class — and twice? And your third wife and that nanny? Your current wife and nanny I understand (but another $48,000), but why should the picture pay for her OB/GYN to fly over to deliver the baby in March? And a six-bedroom house for the run of the picture, plus first-class suites on location? I know this is the same perk package you enjoyed on *Stay the Night,* but that was a Tom Cruise vehicle, and the budget was (or at least it started out to be) $90 million. Be reasonable. Give up some of those first-class tickets. Accept $10,000 a month for your apartment rental in Madrid. Show the studio you're trying to help.

I'm going to talk to Jay Kerney about Robin's entourage, which will have to be reduced from twenty-five to ten, among other onerous sacrifices he may have to endure on this $15 million job. I wish I could talk to Robin directly about this. He's such a great guy, I can't believe these demands are coming from him; I bet they're his agent's way of being a hero.

I have a conference call set with Cully and Josh tomorrow, where I'll try to get Josh to sign off on the trip to Spain. I know how critical this is, so you don't need to scream about it again, okay? I think after our last chat I lost some hearing in my left ear, but don't worry, I'm too busy to sue your ass. Hopefully I'll see you in Spain on Monday.

Olivia

P.S. What about this rumor that Josh is out? What do you hear? Please, god . . .

◦—◦—◦

Date: November 17, 1998
From: OliviaHunt@usol.com
To: Jay_Kerney@Artistsmgtgroup.com

Subj: Robin Williams/*Don Quixote*

Dear Jay,

I'm sorry we're off to what could be called a bad start. The nurses are cooperative, but as much as I'd like them to be, they're not my personal secretaries, they're tending to twelve critically ill people, so please forgive them if they failed to be appropriately obeisant. Frankly, I don't think they knew who they were talking to. Between your stress and mine, words were spoken, words like "you're fucking out of your mind," and "do you have *any* idea what you're doing?" that only shed heat, not light, so I'm hoping you'll accept my apology and I'll graciously accept yours in advance, and perhaps in writing we can start afresh.

I talked to Robin directly about his perks package because he called me here at the hospital to talk about the script, and since it's so hard to connect, I decided to seize the moment and try to solve a problem that was only getting bigger the longer it went unresolved. Of course this was unorthodox; normally I would go through you, but desperate times, desperate measures and all that. You were yelling so much on the phone I don't think you heard what Robin told me, so I've put it in writing. Please call me back as soon as you've had a chance to go over it.

1. His two chefs, each at $2,000 per week, plus first-class hotel and travel accommodations, plus $200 a day per diem. Robin told me — which is contrary to what you said — that he's okay with leaving these guys at home.
2. His personal assistant's assistant — also not necessary, he said, since we'll pay for his assistant and have a PA available for him, too.
3. He'll even agree to a most-favored-nations trailer, which in this case will be a twenty-five-footer.

We didn't get a chance to talk about Dr. Woo. Couldn't we just fly him over a couple times? Does Robin's acupuncturist have to be on set, which requires buying out his Beverly Hills practice to the tune of $45,000, plus his $30,000 fee for the film, and flight and accommodations, a total of about a hundred grand? Johnny and Robin both use Dr. Woo, so I'm happy to have him make a set visit or two. Based on how well things went with Robin and his other perks, I'm sure this totally outrageous demand is coming from somewhere else, not him.

I appreciate all your help.

Sincerely,
Olivia Hunt

November 17, 1998
Shawnee Falls

Dear Michael,

I'm waiting for my bacon and eggs at The Alibi. It's seven A.M. I've been up for a few days. I shouldn't write to you in the state I'm in: I could say something tender and pathetic like please call me; I could confess things; I could apologize; I could say such things and I could say I guess I must still love you. It's Maddie's tenth day in intensive care. Even after a lung biopsy they don't know what caused the infection, so they can't treat it effectively. There's a tower of monitors beside her bed connected with enough wires and tubes to various natural and man-made holes in her body that it looks like she's ready for takeoff to a very, very distant star. Colorful graphs and grids and flashing numbers illustrate the devastation and the battle that's being fought inside her dwindling frame; they've become our only means of communication with her. I've learned what most of the numbers mean and I follow them as anxiously as most men track box scores or the stock market, and my mood, like theirs, can be improved or destroyed by a few digits one way or the other. I look at Maddie lying there in that techno-bed, motionless but not peaceful, a clear plastic mask taped to her face; I rest my hand on her hairless baby head and I wonder, Where are you, Madeline? Are you dreaming? Can you hear me?

Ed just returned from a two-day bender. Eleanor was her usual impervious self. Some might call it denial, but I think it's a kind of coping, a way of being blind to what you know you can't change, and maybe even a stubbornness that the future *will* be the way you want it to be. Yesterday morning I decided to walk home from the hospital and as I came up the driveway I saw them in the living room. It was still dark blue out; the bay window was lit warmly, like a stage. They were sitting together on the couch. His head was bowed. And then he made her laugh: she threw her head back and laughed — something I haven't seen her do in a long time. He looked up, delighted to have done that, and then she kissed him for it. I couldn't believe it was them. It was like watching actors in a play. In this simple affection, I saw that my mother actually loved the man she married, my father; she knew him and she forgave him — or maybe because she knew him she could forgive him.

Why am I writing to you again? I'm just gutted from days of waiting and nights of fear, maybe a little out of my mind. Lonesome and scared, I reach for you, even now. I want to be back in New York on any night when we were eating dinner together and just talking; I'd give anything for one of those ordinary nights. I would rewrite the next scene in L.A. differently: in this version I wouldn't have an affair, you wouldn't pretend you didn't care. When the credits rolled we'd be sitting on a park bench in Paris, continuing the conversation we started years ago, two people who had loved each other long and well. I could say such things in the state I'm in.

Could it all lead back to one bad move? With Mad's cancer, there was a single moment when a single cell mutated and then the others did, too, because there wasn't enough of a foundation of strength and health to stop them; is that what happened with us? My mistake led to your mistake, and without enough love we couldn't stop the blight from spreading. But is love so fragile as that? Why did I do it? I've been trying to pinpoint when the end began, to see if it was inevitable or just a mistake; to see if, had I done a single thing differently, you'd be here, sitting beside me. I was hoping to come to a different conclusion, because a mistake is harder to bear, a mistake begets those chilling words *if only*. At the time, I refused to talk about it — but that affair was a mistake, and I regret it. We were never the same, were we? Even though it happened while you were away and ended when you came home; even though I said it was "just sex," so it didn't matter; even though you said okay, that if it was just sex, it didn't mean anything. But it did, didn't it, Michael? It meant that I didn't care if I hurt you, and I didn't believe that hurting you would hurt us.

I must have eaten my eggs, because Rich just took away an empty plate and said, Guess you didn't like it, huh? Look, I'm not going to write to you anymore. You obviously want to keep more than just miles between us. It's over; why get all tangled up again? Even though I don't think our breakup was inevitable, by now you're probably doing just fine. But I had to tell you something that I should have told you before you left. I had to tell you I'm sorry. For not caring about you and for you, and for not protecting what we had as if it meant more to me than anything in the world, because of course now that it's gone, I realize it did.

Love (anyway),
Olivia

November 18, 1998
ICU

Dear Maddo,

For tonight's listening pleasure we have some of your all-time favorites, dating back to the very first album you bought, Michael Jackson's *Thriller*, which I interpreted as another grave mistake — your first expressions of taste in music and clothes worried me deeply — but perhaps I was the one who needed instruction, because *Thriller* is in fact a brilliant album that has withstood the tests of both time and danceability. I even caught that cretin Dr. Hayes tapping his alligator shoe to "Beat It" as he reviewed your chart. I sure hope you can hear it. I hope it's the soundtrack to some great dream you're in.

I'm a little buzzed. I spent the afternoon at the mall with Mom. I took Mom to the mall because I love her. Why else would I be there, at the mall, with her? She looks like hell these days. I thought it was the least I could do, take her shopping, buy her something nice. Mom's okay; it's the mall and the combination of Mom and the mall that is so challenging. Besides my androphobia — fear of other people, all other people, but particularly Midwestern, Southern, and Western people, which I suffer most acutely in airports, malls, and stadiums — I also detest shopping. (Another sign that I am a mustache away from becoming a man: I do not possess the female gathering instinct.)

We were in one of those tiny fitting rooms at Nordstrom's. I was sitting on that corner shelf, a pile of rejected slacks and blouses on my lap, getting a little moody looking at Mom's half-nude body, particularly that loose flesh that oozes like pizza dough out of her bra-strap and underpants elastic, because I know that no matter what I do this body is my future. She's in good shape, but she's sixty, isn't she? And that's what happens. Your flesh loosens up a bit; it's an early molting that's inescapable. No matter how many cans of salmon and jars of vitamins you eat, how many speed walks you take and Pilates you push, your flesh is sloughing away from your bones a little every day. My pulse quickened as I remembered that I am still husbandless and soon my upper arms will be floppy bingo wings and then it'll be too late.

Your hips look fine, I said.

You think so?

Sure.

You don't think they make my hips look wider?

Wider? No. No wider than they are.

What's that mean?

Mom, you're not wide — you're fine. Do you like the pants?

They're black pants. That's all they are. They're just simple black pants.

That's right, they're just black pants. They look very nice on you.

You think so?

Yes! Buy them, for chrissake.

Shhh! Maddie's a much better shopper. She actually cares.

I care. I'm here, aren't I? Those look better. Get those.

These?

Yeah. They look better.

But they're not really black.

Why are we whispering?

Because I don't want the whole world to hear this conversation. Maddie actually enjoys shopping with me.

No, she doesn't.

Yes, she does.

She only pretends. She hates shopping with you.

That's ridiculous. We go all the time together. I don't force her.

Are you going to get those or those?

I don't know.

Buy both, and we'll show them to Mad.

Those doctors don't know what they're doing.

Yes, they do. Her oxygenation is up to eighty-nine today, she's using less of the ventilator, that means her lungs are healing. It just takes a while. That is a hideous top — don't even put that on.

I like it.

It's South Side. You've been trying to deny that's where you're from all your life; you'll blow it with that top.

She really liked it, but I couldn't let her go through with it. Big and loud purple and orange flowers, very Polish. I put my head around the adjoining fitting-room curtain and asked the woman there, Felicia (we later learned), for her opinion on the hideous blouse.

Ees nice. Looks good on you. What do you think of this on me?

The woman, who was super-stacked and about four-foot-six, had on a black leather miniskirt and a sleeveless red blouse. She looked terrible. We told her she looked great. Then another woman, on the other side of us, required advice on her outfit, which was a stunning black Donna Karan suit. Mom wanted desperately to get out of that girl pit, but the zipper on those not-black pants had become jammed and she was growing increasingly but demurely frustrated. While Felicia and Donna Karan complained about how everything, everything they show now is black, I tried to unjam the zipper, which was stuck about three inches above

Mom's you-know-what. I realized this was the closest I'd been to "it" in thirty-some years. I yanked the zipper up toward heaven and then down toward hell until Mom, whose hot breath I could feel on the back of my neck, said crisply, Well, don't *break* it; I don't want to have to buy these. I then got down on my knees and prayed while simultaneously attempting a more surgical attack. The thing was really jammed. Before I could stop her, Felicia asked to have a go. Oh, I hate when this happens, Felicia said, crouching before Mom's crotch. Eleanor shot me a nasty look, which was caught by the Donna Karan woman, at whom she smiled and rolled her eyes apologetically.

I have some Vaseline in my purse, Donna Karan said.

This on top of everything, Mom said, chuckling through her clenched teeth.

Felicia said, We'll get you out of here, don't you worry, honey.

Donna Karan approached with the jar of Vaseline. Don't worry, she said, I won't get any on the pants, just the zipper. This usually works for me. The kneeling Felicia scooted over but didn't get up — I liked that about her; she wasn't a quitter — and Donna Karan kneeled down beside her with the Vaseline, so it looked like they were worshiping at the altar of Mom. It's too bad she couldn't see it that way. Desperate to do something, Mom could only oversee the work taking place near her privates. Her head was bent down and when it came up to look at me her eyes were brimming with tears and for that split second the whole world stopped moving and breathing and in our silence I looked at her and she looked at me and we both knew we were terrified about you but we hadn't said it out loud and all we could do was hold on to each other with love; with a love that survives all the mother-daughter fighting and disappointment, that endures and even grows, and is why I was at the mall — and then

Donna Karan said, *Motherfucking zippers,* and Mom's face relaxed into a huge smile and she laughed. I laughed, too, then all four of us were laughing harder and harder; it was that kind of infectious, jittery laughing you do when you're pre-something, pre-pubescent, pre-menstrual, pre-menopausal, that joyous hysteria only girls enjoy and is in fact one of the few benefits of being female, the giddiness that is as involuntary as sneezing and that can so easily turn into crying, which is what happened. Mom wasn't laughing, she was bawling. It was something, Mad. You've probably never seen it, since at home when Mom cries she always makes a good Protestant dash for the nearest bathroom or closet. Felicia noticed she was sobbing and stood up and threw her arms around Mom — being a quick embracer must come with big boobs, like you know that's what everyone, even other women, want to do with you, we want to dive into your bosom and be smooshed with unconditional maternal love — and Donna Karan said, Oh, don't cry, we'll get you out of those fucking pants. (You think I swear; Christ, she was foul.)

It's not that. . . . Mom said, gasping the way you do when you are trying so hard to stop crying. She'd found the corner ledge and was sitting there, her hand over her mouth like she was holding herself hostage, shaking, tears pouring out of her squeezed-shut eyes. The well-equipped Donna Karan handed Mom a fresh folded Kleenex from her purse.

What is it, honey? Felicia asked, stroking her shoulder.

Oh, it's nothing, I'm so sorry, I'm so embarrassed. My god, I'm sorry.

Don't be. It's okay. We all get the blues.

Fucking right, Donna Karan said. When you find out your husband's been banging the baby-sitter for two years you get the blues, let me tell you.

That cracked Mom up, it cracked us all up, and we seemed to be swinging back toward laughter until there was that post-hysteria calm that settles, and Mom sighed deeply and to my astonishment said, It's my daughter.

You know how private Mom is. Never gossiping, never sharing with her friends. I was stunned she would confide in these two strange women — in half-unzipped pants, no less.

What is it? She sick? Felicia asked.

Mom gasped, nodding her head, her eyes brimming with fear.

What's wrong with her?

I swallowed and gave them the broad strokes, feeling increasingly like I'd stumbled onto the stage of the *Sally Jesse Raphael* show.

That is so, so sad, Felicia said, crying herself now, tears flowing freely down her brown face. She lose the baby?

Mom nodded her head.

Oh, no . . .

I'm so, so, sorry, Donna Karan said, to me and then to the floor, where tears now fell from her own sympathetic eyes. You must love her very much, she said, and Mom and I said together, We do.

Felicia took Mom's hand and declared, She's going to be okay. What's her name? I'll put her on our prayer list. It's a powerful one. There's about eight hundred people on it. It saved Herbie Palmer last year, I believe that, and he was in bad shape with emphysema.

I told them your name, Madeline Hunt Connor. Then a salesperson came in and asked if something was wrong.

Don't ask, Donna Karan said. Just get some scissors and get this poor woman out of these fucking pants.

The saleswoman, Ginny, had to cut Mom out of them, and after all that trauma I said, Let's go have facials and champagne at the Club, and Mom said, No, we should get back to the hospital, but I insisted and she was too worn out to put up much of a fight, so we did.

→→→

November 18, 1996
Shawnee Tavern

Dear Tina,

I was on my way to the A&P for some bananas. The king of fruit. Sweet, unmessy, easy to swallow, easy to digest, and so pleasingly shaped. I decided to stop here for a hamburger instead. You'll be glad to hear Stan is still behind the bar. It's nice to know some people don't choose to leave Shawnee Falls. His forehead is bigger, his chest thicker, otherwise, he's as bad tempered as ever. I took a booth so I could write to you. The tables are still gouged with initials and names, but I couldn't find ours. A few guys are playing pool. Stan's playing the Eagles — still. I can't believe this is the dump we were so desperate to get into we nearly got raped trying to acquire fake IDs from that dodgy bastard in Cincinnati. I can still see the glint in his slitty eyes when he asked you to take off your shirt first. (Men and breasts: it's a mystery, isn't it? Have you ever been walking down the street, or in a staff meeting or a restaurant, and wished you could just *glimpse* a strange man's penis? I'm not talking about wondering about a potential lover's physique; I'm talking about random and constant curiosity about total strangers' body parts. It's so *weird*.) You handled that creep beautifully, the way you handled all men, in fact; with a friendly good-sport smile you laughed, Yeah, right. You put them at ease with that smile, and without them realizing it, you reclaim control of the situation. Everything I know about men I learned from you, you know. Except maybe how to let them go.

I've been writing to Michael. I know you're thinking, Why is she starting that all back up? I had to tell him about Maddie, and that led to thinking about him, and us, and what went wrong. With some distance, and after being around Mad and Bobby, who are simply devoted to each other, who are so tender they hold each other's hearts in their hands, I now see I was guarded, keeping an arm's length between us, never thinking of him, or us, first. Withholding something. Feminism had left a profound mark on my adolescent head; I believed marriage was subjugation and I pointed to my heroines — de Beauvoir, Steinem, Hellman, Susan B., all unmarried — as proof that husbands suck the life out of you, that men kill women's spirits, so I believed men must be kept at bay, even the man you love. There's some truth to that. And I'm not saying our breakup was all my fault. You, who listened to me complain, know what a difficult man Michael was; how when he was painting he could do nothing else — not eat dinner together, wash a dish, go out with friends, for weeks we didn't talk — and when he wasn't painting, he was too miserable because he *wasn't* to do those nice and normal things either, things like have a conversation or fight about which movie to go to. I'm not saying it was all paradise and roses.

But I loved him, Tina; I loved the way he looked and the way he could make me laugh and see the world differently and the way we made love. When all else failed — which it clearly did — we had that; we could go there and wake up in the morning simply happy to be in each other's arms. I thought that was enough. But Mad has shown me what was missing — at least in me. It may be easier to express love when you're in a crisis, but it could also bring out the worst in you: imagine if she'd married her first boyfriend, that creep Ivan; he'd have disappeared faster than you can say Newt Gingrich and long before the word *cancer* had crossed the oncologist's lips. She could have turned into a bitchy, needy wife, but they always think of each other first and do things just to please each other. It seems so simple. How did she learn this and I didn't?

The first three notes of Neil Young's "Harvest Moon" have sent me sinking into a warm bath of longing for him. We used to dance to this in the kitchen. Michael hated to dance, but now and then he'd lean and sway with me. I miss him, Tina. I know you think we weren't good together, and I'm clearly confused; maybe this is just battle fatigue, emotional tailspinning, the confessions of a desperate mind; or perhaps *fantasy* is the right word here, since Michael hasn't called me in months. Still, there's no one I'd rather talk to, or hold on to, right now.

I just asked Stan if he could put on something peppier. He said, I'm not a damn DJ. Some things never change.

Sinking in Shawnee Falls,
Olivia

Date: November 18, 1998
From: OliviaHunt@usol.com
To: Bigdick@worldlink.com

JD:

I've decided I can't go to Spain tomorrow. Things are still just too touch-and-go here. You'll be fine with Cully. I've talked to Carlos (our location manager in Madrid) a couple times, so everything should be ready for you. Please call me when you can, let me know how it's going.

The Josh rumor is going strong, which just fills my heart with gladness — I think he's really going to be canned! Justice, sweet justice at last. But I heard another, more ominous rumor, Johnny. That Universal (as in Howard Trammel) is thinking of putting on another producer. You know this is the equivalent of demoting me, don't you? I'm fully committed to producing this movie. There may be those who think I'm not up to the job, even without the obvious complication of a sister with leukemia, but they be wrong, Johnny, and I hope you will persuade them on my behalf. I need this movie to be mine; I need the sole producing credit and the money, and after all my work to get to this point where we're actually making it, to then be elbowed out by some 800-pound gorilla would be — no pun intended — *crushing*. As soon as Madeline's out of intensive care, I'll be back on the job, full-time. Please, hang in there a little longer.

I hope the scout goes well. Talk to you soon.

Olivia

Josh Miller
Universal Pictures

<u>Via fax</u>

Dear Josh:

I wanted to be the very first to congratulate you on starting your own production company. How wonderful! Although I'll really miss you at Universal, I truly hope you find independent producing as rewarding as you have made it for me, and perhaps we can look forward to partnering on future projects together.

Best of luck!

Sincerely,
Olivia Hunt

November 22, 1998

Madeline,

Last night I was watching a little *Riverdance* with you and I was wondering if the jury would have mercy on me if I accidentally stabbed Dr. Hayes to death, he's so condescending he deserves to die, and then I was wondering how bad jail could be if I was convicted, I mean you get three squares and some time to read, and this perverse fantasy led to a lesbian nightmare of a smelly gray-faced fellow-murderer licking my cheek with her enormous yellow tongue, and worse, which somehow led me to wonder if I'll ever have children, since I'm going to be thirty-one soon, and if I really wanted children anyway, and just then who walked in the door but Michael. Michael. Michael. He stood in the doorway in his paint-spotted jeans, this dark-eyed man I loved and lost, and when I realized I wasn't hallucinating, I cried. Well, sobbed. I burst, happy, relieved, ashamed. He squatted down and put his arms around me. Hey, there, he said softly. Shhhh, it's okay, it's okay.

I just held on to him for a while, breathing in his piney scent, his arms on my back and his chest against mine and his chin resting on the top of my head. It's been over six months since I've seen him. I was kind of shocked by how good-looking he is; I mean, I know he's not your type, Mad, but he sure is mine. Not that I'd forgotten, but you don't think about someone's eyebrows, necessarily, or the fine shape of his lips and jaw, or his eyes; his brown eyes are what I've missed the most. We went down to the cafeteria for coffee.

I can't believe you're here. You came.

I left as soon as I read your last letter. How's she doing?

I filled him in as much as I could, which triggered a minor rant against the doctors, who I suspected didn't know what the hell they were doing.

Maybe they're keeping her alive, he said. Maybe without them she'd be . . .

He looked at me and I realized what he meant. I hadn't looked at it that way.

Bobby must be out of his mind, poor guy. He's so nuts about her.

He sits with her every night till midnight. The other day he told me he thinks this is why God put him on earth. To take care of

my sister. That before this, he didn't feel like he had a special purpose. Would you call that a gigantic rationalization?

He laughed. It's called faith, Olivia. And love.

Man, I'm jealous.

He ran his calloused thumb over my knuckles. He said, I
missed you.

Why didn't you write back . . . or call?

Let's talk later.

When Mom came in to relieve me at six, we went to IHOP and
ate plates of syrup-sogged pancakes. Since you've been in intensive care, all I eat are pancakes, mashed potatoes, spaghetti with
meat sauce, and Oreos. My nerves are getting such a workout that
I've only gained seven pounds. Michael wanted some privacy, so
we checked into the Paradise Motel on Lincoln instead of going
home. I asked if he wanted me to come in; I didn't want to assume
anything. In the front seat he kissed me and said, Hell yes.

He was very tired, having driven pretty much three days straight
through from New Mexico. While he showered, I pulled down the
brown flowered bedcover, remembering the lesson Mom taught us
when we stayed at Motel 6s on our trips to Florida: never sit on the
bedspread or that woven foam they call a blanket, because they don't
launder those every day and they could be covered in body emissions
from the previous potentially unclean customer. Strange the lessons I
remember. I took off my jeans and shoes and slid between the pre-
sumably laundered white sheets. There was a Bible on the laminated-
wood table. I decided whatever words first caught my eye would
be an omen, that I would follow them no matter what, because
Michael's arrival felt like a miracle that deserved some kind of decent
show of gratitude. I read: *"If I have told you of earthly things, and
ye believe not, how shall ye believe, if I tell you of heavenly things?"*

Precisely, I thought. How *shall* I believe? I flipped the white onion-skin pages again and my finger stopped here: *"Commit thy way unto the Lord; trust also in Him; and He shall bring it to pass."* Oh, Maddie, how can I believe that if I trust in the Lord he'll heal you if I don't believe in the Lord in the first place? Trust is generally something that you develop with experience. There's evidence. You trust in traffic lights because you've seen people obeying them; you trust the sun will rise tomorrow morning because you have a fourth-grade understanding of the solar system and you've seen it happen every day of your life. You trust the restaurant won't poison you, you trust the elevator won't drop, you trust your husband won't lie to you, but how do you learn to trust when there is no evidence, and in what are you trusting, exactly? When you hear the word *dog* you picture that animal in your mind, but what do you see when you say the word *God*? Most people I know deny they see Michelangelo's white-bearded, big-handed guy; now it's a concept, usually it's Love — God is Love, most neobelievers say — but if God is Love, then we don't need the word *God*, do we? We could just say, I hope to Love you get better. I pray to Love you are healed. Love, please heal my sister, Madeline. I really feel like I'm missing something here and I wish someone could tell me how to believe in God, the God who is omnipotent supernatural goodness, because I'd really like to; I'm willing. Just saying, Okay, I do, *I commit to you, Lord,* and I trust and believe, seems like pretending, because with something so monumental you should have to prove it, shouldn't you? It should change your life, right? You should feel *something*. Otherwise, isn't it just words?

Michael came out with a towel wrapped around his waist and lay down carefully beside me. He looked thinner than I remembered. I'm bushed, he said, stretching his arms over his head. I moved against him, into his open arms, and rested my head there, feeling his soft chest hair on my cheek, taking my place beside him, which still fits as perfectly as a pair of favorite jeans. The room was dark except for the gray morning light framing the curtained window. Trucks gunned down Lincoln. A car door thudded shut in the parking lot. I could hear the ticking of the antique Rolex I gave Michael for a birthday years ago and his heart beating steadily. Then I didn't hear anything, because I drifted off to sleep, and slept for hours, deeply and dreamlessly. Later, our mouths found each other's, and before fully waking we made love tenderly, so tenderly I never wanted it to end.

He said he can stay a couple weeks. Dad arranged for us to use the Stewarts' apartment over The Alibi. We move in tomorrow.

I hope you wake up in time for Thanksgiving. Maybe "He shall bring it to pass," which would be an excellent start in building a little trust.

November 24, 1998

Robin Williams
4575 Cherokee
Beverly Hills, California 90210

Dear Robin,

Just a note to say thanks for your help on the budget, and for that fantastic basket of food for my family — both are really appreciated. My sister's doing much better, so I hope to see you next week at the read-through.

Happy Thanksgiving,
Olivia

November 24, 1998

Marguerite Dunning
Hollywood Wigs
3333 Melrose Place
Hollywood, California 91229

Dear Marguerite,

The wig arrived today and it looks beautiful. The hair is as shiny and brown as hers was, a perfect match. Madeline will love it. I'll take her to the salon you recommended to have it trimmed and fitted once she's out of intensive care.

Thanks again for doing this so quickly.

Sincerely,
Olivia Hunt

November 27, 1998

Johnny Ray Dickerman
c/o Ritz Hotel, Madrid

Via fax

Johnny:

I hope the scout is going well. If you would call me back I wouldn't have to rely on something as flimsy as hope.

Since for some inexplicable reason you are not calling me back, I'll just have to put this in writing: We've finally got the budget under control and you're talking to Anthony Hopkins about doing a cameo? Are you crazy? We've got $200,000 for the Duke; Hopkins will never do it for that — and Universal will never approve what would be a gigantic overage for him. He just won't sell enough tickets to make a difference — not in this movie. It's not like Jennifer Lopez or Penelope Cruz — they actually could draw the younger audience, and Dulcinea's a bigger part . . . AND it's U's idea, so they'll have to pay for it if one of them agrees to do it. Please drop this Hopkins idea before he says yes and then I have to say no. And CALL ME BACK. You know how crazy I get when people don't CALL ME BACK.

— Olivia

November 29, 1998

Madeline,

Without you the family is just falling to pieces. Now Jim and I are at war. He let me have it as I drove him to the airport this afternoon. I guess I said something about how nice it must be to be able to leave.

You're just trying to make up for being so shitty to her, he said. Now you're the big hero.

What do you mean shitty to her? When?

He then rattled off what seemed like an *awfully* detailed list of transgressions that began in 1978 when I hit you and galloped right through the eighties and nineties, when I called you fatty

Maddie, when I predicted you'd end up a Shawnee Falls loser because you chose an AC/DC concert over studying for your algebra final, when I wouldn't buy a case of beer for you on prom night, when I reprimanded you for pronouncing picture "pitcher," and most recently to 1997, when I became "a Hollywood asshole," because it took me two days to call you back.

You've committed them to heart. I didn't realize you guys talked that much.

You think you're the only one, right?

How could I ever hope to make up for such crimes? I said, pulling up to the airport.

You're such a bitch, he said, and slammed the door.

Well, you're a fuckhead, I said, but he was already gone. The problem with Jim is he isn't a fuckhead in the least, which makes it so demoralizing to fight with him. He's affable, but you never know if he's really listening to you. I hardly see him when he's here, since he's either with Dad or Mom or here, with you.

I sulked the rest of the afternoon. I'm aware that I haven't been the greatest sister in the world, but, you know, neither have you. Maybe after all this we'll be better. I can't believe he remembered every act of bad sistering — or at least I hope that was everything. If you were awake you could tell me Jim's just jealous. He just wishes he could stay here with you, too.

My hand is resting on yours. The way it did when I taught you how to play the piano that day. Like a toddler standing on the feet of her parent, you thought you could memorize the songs by the movement of my hands. It was a totally lame idea, but it was a rainy Saturday; there wasn't anything better to do. The screens of the French windows were cloudy with water and a damp coolness whispered across the tip of my nose. With masking tape we wrapped your fingers under mine like a human splint and you were very pleased, because although you were only eight and I was fourteen, your hands weren't much smaller than mine. We needed help, so we got Dad out of his chair where he was watching an old movie and reading his weekly thriller. What are you girls doing?

I'm teaching Madkins how to play.

That's crazy.

It's her revolutionary new way to learn the piano. We're going to get rich off this.

Put that chair in front of the piano, you bossed him.

Please, Father, he said. He loved you bossing him around. I'd have gotten the evil eye for sassing him, but from you it was always charming.

This is pure and utter *ignis fatuus*, he said. He liked to dazzle us with his knowledge of Latin. You can't learn by copying, Maddie, you know that. You have to take lessons like Olivia.

I don't want to take lessons.

Knowing what a smelly creep my teacher was, I'm now glad you never did. "Father" removed the piano bench and placed that fiddleback chair in front of middle C.

Then we sat on the chair together, you in the front and me behind you, my arms around you like when we rode that pony at the Ohio State Fair.

You girls are silly, he said.

Go away, you told him. We have to practice.

We started with the simplest song, and one you would recognize, "Twinkle, Twinkle, Little Star." You were very serious, absolutely focused, for all of five minutes. Your fingers didn't move easily with mine, mistakes were made, which you found too discouraging and not enough fun for a rainy Saturday afternoon.

Your heart is racing today — flying between 89 and 91. What are you doing in there, goddammit? The oxygen rate isn't good, either; even with the ventilator your lungs aren't oxygenating the blood very well; your blood pressure keeps bouncing along the bottom, which triggers an alarm and the appearance of a nurse who comes in and adjusts the IV and resets the monitor. You look at this technology, the banks of machines and monitors, and you realize the human body is an astoundingly complicated organism that does all this — oxygenating, circulating, converting food into energy and waste, walking, talking, seeing, thinking, feeling — all this and more, pretty smoothly, without any help, for about seventy-five years. It's all done so well we never even notice, let alone appreciate the incredibleness of it. We don't see all the work that goes into every second of just being alive. It's like Heidegger said: we only understand the true nature of things when things break down.

Which leads me to Michael. It's been great having him here. We haven't talked about anything yet. He said he came as a friend and we'll talk about the rest when you're safe. He cooks dinner every night and runs me a bath every morning when I get back. He even gives me massages without me asking — and of my shoulders and back, not the softer places that don't get tense but which are probably more fun to massage. When we make love it's — different. It's the first time I've ever understood the phrase "making love." It does feel like we're making something, with all the discovery and release, the pain and pleasure that involves; we're making something as singular as any work of art, but it's love, and it feels more necessary than water these days.

Okay, that was probably more than you needed to know. He's also been hanging out with Bobby. He went over to your place the other day, and I guess Bobby's not much of a housekeeper, because *both* china sets and every fork, spoon, and All-Clad pan were dirty; there were pizza boxes and McDonald's bags everywhere. The place was absolutely trashed. By the time Bobby came home from work, Michael had cleaned the house, gone to the store, and made a pot of chili — he makes great chili. I'll get the recipe for you.

Yesterday they were here watching the Browns play Dallas, and things were looking dismal. Bobby said, Let's go eat; it's over. He looks pretty rough these days. His eyes are sunken and dull, his mouth defiantly downturned. He's lost a lot of weight. Michael said, Wait, things could turn around.

Bobby snapped, Yeah, when? When?

The next moment I thought he'd smash something. Or fling himself through the plate glass window. That's how angry he was. The last few days have been unbearable, with the doctors saying this is it, this is it, and we hurry around you, and then it's okay again, the danger passes. So Bobby wasn't talking about the stupid Browns game. Michael looked at him. Then he said, You never know, Bobby. Remember the eighty-two NFC championship. Bobby dismissed it with a flick of his wrist: Once in a fucking life-time, he said.

Michael added this: And Kirk Gibson. Bottom of the ninth. Only a home run would do it. He limped around those bases.

Bobby was still tense. You told me he's got a temper, so I thought we were about to see it in action. The last few weeks have to come out somewhere. Michael continued: It happens, he said. Why else would everybody watch, year after year? Because in any game it could happen. You could see one amazing pass or shot. He then named some more eleventh-hour sports miracles. He goaded Bobby into naming three more, bet him twenty bucks he couldn't, and eventually, begrudgingly, he did, and they both got into remembering and debating the details of each great feat. The Browns didn't enjoy such a miracle, but Bobby was calmer, and they laughed about some heavyweight upset and when they stood up to go to the cafeteria he hugged Michael and said, Hey, man, thanks.

- - -

Date: November 30, 1998
From: OliviaHunt@usol.com
To: Jay_Kerney@Artistsmgtgroup.com

Subj: Robin Williams/*Don Quixote*

Dear Jay,

I understand that it's been suggested we change the title of the movie from *Don Quixote* to *Sancho Panza*. Well, I thought about it. I thought about how the novel has been called *Don Quixote* for over four hundred years, but it's hardly a bestseller anymore, is it? Maybe it'd enjoy a resurgence if we renamed it. The word *quixotic*, which came from the title of this book, never really caught on — for example, when's the last time you used it? So maybe *sanchoesque* would be more popular. Maybe if we gave this four-hundred-year-old literary masterpiece a new name it wouldn't feel like "some old, stuffy period movie." I thought about how hard it is to spell Quixote, and how difficult to pronounce, whereas even a child could probably handle Sancho Panza.

So, sure, it's fine with me. Johnny asked me to deal with this, so that probably means he doesn't want to be the one to say Are you kidding? Ultimately, however, it's up to Universal, and I'll be sure to discuss it with them next week.

Thanks for the idea,
Olivia Hunt

November 30, 1998
Mercy ICU (still!)

Dear Tina,

Don't worry about your letters. Just a few words is great. You don't have hours in waiting rooms and on flights like I do. And writing for me is a way of making sense of what's happening. While I'm writing I feel some control over things, however illusory that is.

That's great news about your job offer. I knew your boss couldn't be blind to your talent. You said you're not sure about taking it because you'd have to relocate next year, but what would be so bad about that? You hate Portland. I know Stephen's family's there, but you are his family now; he should be willing to move if it's good for your career, right? You would for his, hint hint. I know you're worried about being pregnant and starting a new job at the same time, but you're not pregnant yet, so I think if you really like the sound of the job, you should take it. You'll be able to handle a new baby, too. You've done it before — to my amazement and admiration. You might be resentful if you don't go for it, right?

Thanks for the advice on Michael, but you're too late. He's here. I know, I know, but don't worry, Tina. We're taking it very slowly. Michael is now the guarded one, which could mean he's afraid to get involved again or that he knows he doesn't want to and is here, as he claimed, as a friend only. We have a quiet routine in the small slanted-ceiling apartment over The Alibi. Sometimes he sits with Maddie. Yesterday I found him reading to her, from Mark Twain. He said Twain's humor and indignation remind him of Mad. On the way home we stopped to take a walk around Red Lake. The crunching snow was the only sound until we reached the water's edge. I was looking at some footprints when Michael said, In your last letter. You were right. . . . It did matter.

I looked at him and knew he was talking about that affair. Why did you say it was okay?

He kicked loose a puck of ice. What else could I say, Olivia? He watched it skid across the frozen lake and said, I didn't want to lose you.

We were quiet for a while, both remembering things. A branch snapped behind us as a doe walked by. He broke up some more ice with the toe of his boot and said, I knew, anyway. Before you told me.

He saw me kiss Robert on the mouth. I'd been acting strange. He'd followed me to the airport because he had to know. Once he did, he decided it was up to me to tell him about it.

He went on: I told myself it didn't matter. We weren't married. We never promised we wouldn't. If you told me and you said it was over, then it wouldn't matter. But that was my mistake, he said, because it did.

He said when I wrote to him about it, he heard something in me he never had before. It was good just to talk, but there hasn't been time for more. There's too much to say for a stolen hour here and there. I also sense there's something he's not telling me — but maybe that's just his reserve. He thinks I should get back to L.A. and the movie soon. But I can't. I'm afraid if I leave, Maddie will — slip away. I think we all feel that way, which is why there's always someone sitting here, holding on to her.

Bye for now,
Olivia

— ◆ ◆ ◆ —

November 30, 1998

Maddie,

It's Day 21 on ICU and this isn't good. They say twenty days on a vent and your lungs are goners. Last night things were so hairy with you Dr. Hayes said there was nothing to do now but pray. Pray! Coming from your doctor, it was like hearing from the cockpit that it's time for the passengers to start flapping their arms. His Harvard Med School eyebrows jumped up like, Hey, don't look at me, I'm just the messenger, and Bobby nearly popped him. Your lungs were wiped out, Dr. Hayes said. There's an ECMO in Cincinnati, but it's not proven successful with adults yet. . . .

An ECMO?

Essentially, what we'd do is take all the blood out of her body, run it through a machine that would oxygenate it like lungs do, then run the blood back in. Like artificial lungs, he said, as if he were describing this really cool new stereo he wanted to try out. There's a trial going on with adults now, so it's worth a shot. You've got nothing to lose.

What's that mean? I snarled.

He put his hands up like I was arresting him. Then he said, Let me see what I can do, see if I can even get her in the program, okay?

But what is it? Bobby asked.

Rather than waste his time explaining something our puny lay-brains couldn't grasp, he simply said, Your only chance, like Dr. Clint goddamned Eastwood, and then he walked away.

It was snowing like hell. I worried about the transportation situation. You were too fragile to go by ambulance, a helicopter would be required, people were making phone calls, but a helicopter in this weather? All we could do was wait and hope you wouldn't pack it in before the helicopter arrived, before you got to Cincinnati and the ECMO. Bobby didn't like the sound of the ECMO and didn't know if he should approve it. The poor guy was wrung dry.

We have to keep talking, he said, so she hears us. Jim had made it in on the last flight before they closed the airport. He looked at me warily — we hadn't spoken since our little spat — and then we all walked into your room.

Your temperature was like 250 degrees. They had an ice blanket covering you right up to your chin, so it looked like you were just a bodyless head in a bed. The ventilator tube sprouted out of your mouth like a big plastic stem, and two white gauze patches were taped over your eyes. Hairless on top of it, you simply looked like shit. It was hard to believe you, Madeline Anne, were still in there, in that body, on that bed. We were supposed to be yattering away, but it was hard to strike up conversation, because even though no one was sure you could even hear us, we were never to discuss your condition in front of you, which would be rude and in your case probably totally disturbing. We couldn't say, for example, I'm scared. Jim reached for my hand. I squeezed his. It was sweaty.

I'm sorry, he whispered.

Me, too, I whispered back.

The vent *whooshed . . . whooshed . . . whooshed.*

So what'd you have for dinner, Olivia? Bobby shouted.

I stick with the salad bar. You?

The meat loaf.

Really? How come?

It looked better than the cod.

Jim chimed in, Delta Airlines peanuts.

And then it was quiet; we were conversationally tapped out. A few minutes passed before Jim came up with: The cafeteria cookies are good, aren't they?

Yeah.

Yeah.

Maybe we shouldn't talk about food, since she can't eat anything and she might be hungry, Bobby said.

I thought that was unlikely, but I didn't argue. How was bowling?

Michael sucks, Bobby said.

Then it was too quiet again, because we were busy praying our heads off that you'd stop dying, we were all just begging for that; Bobby begging God, Jim and I begging — I don't know who, but we were begging and praying, too. You couldn't hear it, but you could feel it like a vibration under your skin getting bigger and making it harder and harder to breathe; we were rushing, rushing, rushing, but where? I don't know how long it was quiet, but then I remembered we had to get the racket up again. We could sing, I said.

Oh, god, no.

Yeah, let's sing, she'd like that.

I'm not going to sing, Jim growled.

Do you know "You're the Top"?

No, Bobby said.

"Singin' in the Rain?"

Olivia, we're not singing!

It was quiet again, and we watched the monitor where the numbers were all flying up and down, your heart rate moving into the nineties; your body was under attack, and we were just standing there watching it happen. And then Jim started singing: *Come and listen to my story 'bout a man name Jed, a poor mountaineer, barely kept his family fed . . .*

Bobby and I joined in, and we sang the *Gilligan's Island, Cheers,* and *Brady Bunch* theme songs. We watched your heart rate slow to 91, then 89, 88 . . . When we ran out of TV shows we resorted to folk songs. *I've been working on the railroad, all the livelong day. . . . Can't you hear the whistle blowing?* We stood over your skin and bones, each with a hand resting on an arm or shin, because that's supposed to be good for you, too, to feel our touch, singing off-key and on, whatever songs we could think of, while out the window the snow was falling and silencing the helter-skelter world, everything soft and peaceful and magical, and for those hours we believed that as long as we never stopped singing it would all work out, that with our songs and the snow and the purple crystals and Dr. Dickhead's machines, maybe taken all together, we could save you.

December 4, 1998

Dr. Robert Smith
Director, Sisters of Mercy Hospital of Shawnee Falls
11367 Adams Road
Shawnee Falls, Ohio 45200

Re: Madeline Hunt Connor

Dear Dr. Smith,

What I'm about to tell you is the story of my sister, a patient in the "care" of your hospital. We aren't permitted to see her file for some reason. But you can. I expect you'll want to.

After twenty-one days in intensive care, Madeline had a "miraculous" turnaround. Although Dr. Hayes did recommend *prayer,* I believe his medical expertise, along with that of his staff, had more to do with this, and for that I am truly grateful. The nurses in particular were tireless, kind, and unflappable. However.

The ventilator was removed and Madeline was weaned off the paralytic drugs and sedation. My family was enormously relieved, as you might imagine. Only my sister failed to wake up. The nurses would yell, Maddie! Time to wake up! They'd tap her hands and we'd tap her hands, but she remained as "unresponsive" as Dr. Hayes, as deaf to our cries as the universe itself. The most implacable interns and nurses started to look a little freaked out, a little like President Clinton when he testified before the grand jury, like people who know something they wish they didn't: guilty, I guess is the word I'm looking for here. Finally one Dr. Y (you know the one, with the fifteen consonants in his name?) appeared on the scene and summoned me and my sister's husband, Bobby, into a small conference room, where he said — before he even sat down — Madeline has had a massive stroke.

He dropped the file on the table and looked at me with unveiled impatience; he had obviously pulled the short straw and resented having to deliver the bad news.

A stroke? But she has leukemia, how could —

It doesn't appear to have been an embolism, he said.

An embolism?

Two thirds of her brain has been damaged. Severely.

Two thirds . . . but how?

At this point my sister's husband, who married an athletic twenty-five-year-old woman not even two years ago, started wailing, but Dr. Y didn't bat an eye; he maintained his cool professionalism.

It's too early to know just what impact this will have, each patient is different, but it is possible that eventually she will be able to walk again, and her memory should be mostly intact —

— Walk again? Bobby cried.

But . . . how did this happen?

We can pretty much rule out an embolism, but to determine whether it was a clot would require further tests, which may not be advisable at this time.

Why not?

(There was a pause here, small but perceptible.) . . . She needs to recover first. Dr. Y then stood up to go.

Is that all? Is that all you're going to say?

Well, yes, he said, like, what more do you want from me?

Well . . . what now?

You'll have to discuss that with your doctor.

You're the doctor.

That seemed to confuse *Doctor Y*. Good day, he said, and walked out.

Can you believe that? You can imagine how confused we were. One minute she's got a lung problem, the next she's had a massive stroke that has left her a vegetable and no one knows how, or what to do next, everybody's scrambling back into their holes like a bunch of mad rats.

I thought maybe a meeting with everybody, Drs. Hayes and Callahan, the neurologists, and Maddie's oncology team, might fill in the gaps in the story, but I was told that a meeting just wasn't possible, the doctors' schedules being what they were, etc., etc.

We were standing in that immaculate, shiny ICU hall outside Maddie's glassed-in room. Her eyes had opened a slit by then. She might have been lying there wondering, Why can't I feel my legs? Why can't I scratch my nose with my fingers? Why can't I speak? Why is Olivia waving her arms at my doctors?

When can we all sit down and talk? I asked nicely.

Nurse Susan said, Why don't we answer your questions right now?

I explained how my sister's husband and parents had questions, too, we were all so confused and stunned, and I was told again and again that a meeting just wasn't something that could be done, until I lost it and yelled, I WANT A MEETING TODAY WITH EVERYONE. IT'S NOT ASKING TOO MUCH. HAVE YOU FORGOTTEN MY FATHER IS AN ATTORNEY? DO YOU HEAR ME?

I was relieved to see that this explicit suggestion of a lawsuit, delivered at an admittedly impolite decibel range, changed their attitude, and with what I'm sure was a *herculean* effort, a meeting was arranged for that very afternoon. It's inspiring to see what people can accomplish when they're threatened. At this meeting we were told that they didn't know how much functioning — walking, eating, talking, breathing — Madeline would regain, or when, but generallygenerallygenerally, right-side brain damage meant left-side paralysis.

Will she be able to talk?

They looked at one another and shrugged like the Little Rascals. Duh, we don't know.

My father started thumping the table, beating it methodically and rhythmically with his fist like he was tenderizing a piece of veal.

Where will she go now? Back to the seventh floor? I asked.

What do you mean?

I mean, will she continue the chemo protocol on seven or — what?

My father's fist was thumping faster now, like the piston of a speeding Mack truck. The medical team members looked at one another the way people who haven't had a chance to get their story straight look. Dr. Hayes took command and led off with an aria that was echoed by the chorus of his disciples in a cacophony that rang to me of utter bullshit:

She no longer requires intensive care.

And she's not strong enough to resume the protocol.

She'll need physical rehabilitation first.

There are some excellent private long-term-care facilities.

And outpatient therapy sites if. When.

The social worker will give you the list.

Whoa, whoa, whoa. Are you saying you're just going to discharge her? I asked.

The chorus resumed:

There's really nothing more for us to do. This is intensive care.

Her condition caused by the leukemia makes her too weak for rehab —

— or for us in oncology —

A long-term-care facility is what's appropriate —

She'll be discharged in the morning.

They all nodded and started making this-meeting-is-over movements, shuffling and collecting their files and almost standing up, and that's when my father's now-throbbing fist flew across the table and smacked into Dr. Hayes's mouth, smashing it open just beautifully, and, like at a school fair where a perfect throw dunks the most despised teacher, Dr. Hayes fell backward — kerplunk! — onto his superior bottom. Blood splashed from his split lip all over his white jacket and the papers on the bulletin board behind him, too, and he required urgent care. Fortunately for Dr. Hayes, he was in just the place for that.

Needless to say, the meeting was over. My father was hauled off by security (who I should tell you had more spring in their step than some of the doctors around here). The Shawnee Falls police were summoned. Officers Kowalski and O'Riley happen to know my father and were eager to resolve things without going down to the precinct.

I don't know if you were involved in this decision or not, but if you were I want to say thank you for not prosecuting, although I suspect there was some tacit quid pro quo in the gesture: we won't prosecute if you don't sue kind of thing. Don't count on it. My father and brother-in-law are still consumed with what could be called an avenging anger, and since God can't be sued, you medical experts might catch some of this. Consider yourself thanked if you deserve it, and forewarned if you deserve a lawsuit. I don't know which it is and I may never know, but that's not my point here. As I said earlier, I have to believe your doctors did the best they could, and who knows why things went so wrong? What they clearly failed to do, however, was display any courage, sensitivity, or acceptance of their part in a tragedy that has just begun for my sister. Dr. Hayes in particular acted like a kid who broke a vase and then hoped if he just tossed it out no one would notice and he wouldn't get in trouble. Something bad happened, and suddenly no one was around.

Despite all that, I am forced to make this humble request: that your hospital continue to care for Madeline while she is recovering from the stroke and through her initial rehabilitation. She can't speak, eat, or move her body. We've been directed by your crack staff to "long-term-care" facilities. As much as this place gives me the creeps, we've gotten used to it, and the idea of stashing my now-drooling sister in a nursing home is frankly unbearable to me. Please help me out here. She's a mess at the moment, but Maddie is full of fury and grace, which will speed her recovery; she won't be taking up space in Mercy for long.

Sincerely,
Olivia Hunt

December 10, 1998

Michael,

This is that new R. L. Burnside CD I told you about. Track #4 ("Don't Stop Honey") is how I feel about you. I also got you the Dusty Springfield CD just to prove I was right about that lyric, so you owe me twenty bucks.

I hope the sandwiches aren't too soggy by the time you're hungry — and that you still love pastrami with pickles. The plaid thermos is from my childhood, so don't lose it, okay? And Hostess cupcakes are actually delicious warmed up, so put them on the floor by the heater. I couldn't remember if you like Doritos or Ruffles, so you get both.

By the time you hold this letter you'll be driving away from here, on your way home, and I'll be flying over you. Maybe you're reading it with a cup of bad coffee in a bright truck stop somewhere on I-90, the curved crust of a hamburger bun on the plate in front of you. I wish I was sitting next to you. I miss you already.

You'll never know how much it meant to me that you came here. You were the only thing I wanted and there you were. No matter what happens now, thank you for that, for being such a true-blue friend.

It's been so good being together, despite what's been going on with Maddie, that I hope it's not stupid of me to hope that over Christmas we'll be able to work things out.

Love (more),
xxoooOlivia

December 10, 1998
Seat 24G, Delta Airlines Flight 32

Dear Tina,

We've reached a cruising altitude of 35,000 feet and I feel a sense of relief, of suspension; I'm hanging above the clouds and the earth and my life, and I will be for the next five hours as this Boeing 707 soars over the Great Plains and the Rockies and banks above the blue Pacific before landing at LAX. I love it up here. Despite how much flying I do, to me it is, like television and cellular phones, miraculous, and when we lift off, my spirits do, too: I feel optimistic, omnipotent, almost, reminded that if a plane can fly, miracles really do happen. And if later I don't find that to be true, at least while I'm up here my life is in a parentheses, and I don't have to deal with down there, which has now entered a new circle of hell.

Maddie is psychotic. Literally. They call it ICU psychosis, or sundowning, and it often happens when people are in intensive care for so long that they, well, lose their minds: the immobility, the drugs, the absence of day and night, and, in Mad's case, the stroke itself wreak havoc on the brain and leave the patient a raving, disoriented, hallucinating mess. Mercy finally agreed to transfer her back to oncology even though she's not undergoing any treatment. She is fed through a tube in her nose, she is catheterized, she is bathed by a candy striper named Sheryl who was on the Horace Mann tennis team with Maddie ten years ago. Maddie looks like a wild, frightened, hairless cat. At first she could only make sounds. Then, when she could talk, she begged for her baby and hallucinated that it was in a cage on the table. She clawed at the tubes in her body. The nurses tied her hands to the bed. She spat at me, I hate you. She hadn't slept in days. I pleaded with the doctors to do something, but there was disagreement over treatment: some said more drugs, antipsychotics; others said no drugs, that they would only delay this process. After three nights of her crying for her baby, I insisted that a psychiatrist talk to her. He recommended that we slowly start to tell her where she's been and where she is now.

Yesterday a group of high school students were caroling in the hall. I hurried to shut the door, but Mad stopped me and ten teenage do-gooders crowded into her stuffy room. Their faces paled with pity. One girl reminded me of Maddie when she was sixteen; she was buxom and big haired and her smile was both sweet and sour, and when she opened her mouth and raised her chin to sing, her whole face shone from the sound she was clearly proud to possess. Maddie sang a solo of "Amazing Grace" for the pops concert her senior year. (Were you there? I think you were, but why would you have been?) There was a backup band full of bongos and flutes, and she belted out an African-inspired version of the song that vibrated down the spines of everyone in that auditorium. Even Eleanor was swaying by the time the chorus was wailing, *and grace will lead me home.* With the same innocent spirit she was now joining these sixteen-year-olds, singing with her crooked mouth and in her screwed-up voice, *Have a holly jolly Christmas, it's the best time of the year.* I nearly lost it. I came dangerously close to really losing it, Tina. But Maddie was enjoying herself immensely.

After they left she said, That was great. I love carols. It's so early, though. It's not even Thanksgiving.

I told her Thanksgiving had passed. She was confused.

How long was I asleep?

About a month.

A month? So what's today?

December ninth.

As she realized how many days she'd lost, her face fell and then she looked at me and said, I missed your birthday.

That's okay, I didn't feel like . . . Don't cry, Maddie.

I didn't get you anything.

I don't care. Don't cry!

You've been so nice to me.

Hey, shut up, okay? Goddammit. Shut up. I sat next to her on the bed and put my arm around her. Stop crying, Mad.

I wanted to make you something, she said softly. Some cookies or something. I have to get out of here. I hate it in here. She slammed her good arm down on the bed.

I know.

I hate this. She slammed it again. I hate this.

You'll be home soon.

No, I won't.

Her gradual awakening to what's happened to her, to what she's lost and what may lie ahead, is harder to witness than all the spinal taps and puking, because I know this pain may not end. If she walks again it will be with a cane and she will never run or play tennis or dance again, and if she wraps both her arms around her husband's back or holds an orange in the palm of her left hand it will be a medical miracle. Watching someone you love being hurt is its own special hell. Because you are not hurt, because you are strong, you feel you ought to prevent the pain from being inflicted; her pain is blameless, while your psychic pain is laced with the guilt of knowing you didn't do anything to stop it, and the fact that you couldn't have comforts only your mind, never your heart.

From somewhere over Texas,
Olivia

••••

December 10, 1998
Santa Monica Jail

Josh Miller
12715 Miller Terrace
Beverly Hills, California

<u>Via fax</u>

Dear Josh,

I know you're inclined to press charges. But before you do, I ask you, please put yourself in my shoes. They're much smaller than yours, of course, so it'll take some imagination to achieve this, but you should be able to manage it, and I'll do my best to describe just what my Timberlands have walked through in the last few days. Don't worry: I'm not playing the cancer card here, so you're not in for some tragic movie-of-the-week pitch.

This morning my shoes and I walked into the production office, where I introduced myself to the first person I saw. This turned out to be Chloe, the stunning office runner. Her full lips quivered, How can I help you?

I'm the producer.

Of —?

This movie.

Ohhhh, I'm sorry. I'm sorry. Of course. You're the one with . . . the family problem.

Yeah. Is there a producer without one?

Her stunningness dimmed; Chloe was clearly confused. Then she laughed, Oh, I get it! Yeah, we're all a little dysfunctional in this business, aren't we? She thought I was making a joke.

At which point my shoes carried me spiritedly down the gray-carpeted hall. I say spiritedly because I was feeling some excitement as various staff hurried past and there was a general air of industriousness and I realized I was finally taking my place at the helm of a ship whose journey I'd been trying to finance for some time; I thought of Aubrey in the Patrick O'Brien series finally getting to set sail again after too many months on land. (In this case, I've been working on *Don Quixote* since you fired me last spring — did you know that, Josh?) On my way to Johnny's office I noticed on the closed door next to his a piece of paper marked with the word *Producer,* so I decided to check out my office and drop my bag. I opened the door and, lo and behold, who was sitting there behind the desk but you! I was momentarily confused. Then I figured out that you'd been given a deal as part of your severance settlement and this was your temporary office while you were waiting for your permanent office to be remodeled, and I quickly (and, may I point out, respectfully) stepped back through the door before I disturbed your phone call. I proceeded to Johnny's office, which had the word *Director* on the door.

Johnny was looking at drawings of Don Quixote's study with Matthew. He was surprised to see me, of course; he gave me a hug and introduced me to Matthew and as he did, another model — I mean PA — came in, Alisha, and Cully, and then Tom Zane, and while we were all shaking hands and I was telling Cully how my sister is doing (he very kindly asked about her), in you walked. You can imagine how bewildering that was to me. Johnny looked like a mouse had run up his ass, but there was no time for anything but the most perfunctory explanation.

Josh has joined us as a producer, Olivia. Don't have a cunt-fit about it. It's all decided and it'll be fine. Now, let's get into the script because I have my medical in an hour.

Having no time for a "cunt-fit," I dragged a chair over to join the circle and swallowed my pride, my fury, my frustration with doctors, Hollywood, and the universe, and opened the script. Chloe brought in a tray of coffee and Evian and bagels. Feeling freshly gutted, I didn't have an appetite.

Johnny began: Olivia, do you think Sancho's island sequence works now? You've always wanted to cut that.

It's got some pace, which helps —

You interrupted me, saying: It moves better. . . .

You may not have noticed, but every time I started to speak you did, too — did you notice that? Probably not, which is why I thought I should point it out to you. I'd hate to have a rude mannerism like that and no one tell me about it; it'd be like having a goober hanging from your nose all day. The first few times you did this I let you; you had probably just forgotten that you're not my boss anymore. But then I couldn't stand it and the only way to fight your conversational fire was with the same fire, which is when we started talking over each other until Johnny said, Hold on, hold on, one at a time. Then you resorted to the other rude conversational habit you have, which is a two-step thing, where you cluckcluckcluck and shake your head like a horse while the other person (me, in this case) is talking and then you rip apart whatever the other person just said. Even Johnny noticed it when you disagreed with something as irrelevant as the description of a sunset.

Later, when you said, Olivia, come on, have you even read the book? I couldn't say what I so badly wanted to, so my head at this point, after all that interrupting and contradicting and constant nippiness, was just exploding with stress. When I dropped that cup of coffee on you, however, it was an accident; I've become weak from little sleep and too much coffee, so my hand was shaking and the mug just slipped out of my clenched fist. Honest. It wasn't my fault that Johnny found it totally hysterical. I am sorry and I suppose now, given what else has happened, my insisting on paying the dry-cleaning bill for your Armani jacket seems laughable, but I meant it and the offer stands.

After the meeting Johnny told me how it came to be that you were on my picture, a story as old and common as prostitution. Putting you on solved two problems for Universal: they had a producer they knew and trusted on the movie (and, in all fairness, one who was around) and they had a sweetener for you to exit the executive office. It made perfect sense; if I hadn't been on ICU duty I would have seen it coming. Still, I didn't like it, and Johnny knew it, and you knew it: what's to like about being demoted, and, worse, by the very man who actually fired you last chance he had? Even you, who are not exactly the Dalai Lama, can understand how deranged my shoes were by this development, can't you, Josh? But, as Johnny pointed out, *Don Quixote* is my baby and I shouldn't abandon it even if it meant eating some humble pie. I had to be professional, not a quitter. He said, Remember, you're not a doctor, Olivia. You can't save your sister's life by ruining your own.

She was in critical condition, Johnny —

— Don't hide behind her illness. You're either producing this movie or you aren't, and if you are, you have to be here to do it.

Johnny then left for his physical. I went to find my office. But there was no office. No one had —. No one knew if —. Etc., etc. In fact, you were in my office, but that's okay, I thought, I'll be "professional" and just find another office. I did, and the size wasn't the problem; I'm small, you're substantial, it made sense we'd have offices that corresponded with our measurements. The problem I had with the office was its locale. I didn't mind being near the studio maintenance guys, they're a lot of fun, and the smell of the garbage wasn't that bad, it was being so far away from my ship — a twelve-minute walk or four-minute golf cart ride — that bothered me. As the ex-helmer of a much greater sailing vessel, I'm sure you can understand my feelings; you need to be in the center of the action. Still, the day was so young. I had to overcome the morning's setbacks. I got my lawyer on the phone.

You're being fucked, she said, dispensing with the usual salutations.

No kidding. Why didn't you tell me?

I just found out this morning. They want you to defer half your fee, since Josh came on —

— What? Josh was their decision, not mine, why should I be penalized?

— and take second position.

To who?

Josh.

Isn't he executive producer?

Honey, wake up, okay? You're a big girl. He was the president of the studio; he's not exec, he's producer, first position. So here's what I think. Defer another $50,000 —

— I'll be down to $75,000! What's Josh getting?

$750,000.

As she went through the rest of the deal my right foot started tap-tap-tapping. My shoes were pretty beat up by the morning's events, but there was still some life in that right one, and as I watched it tap I felt an uneasiness growing deep within me because it didn't feel like that shoe was on my foot any longer, it seemed to have a mind of its own, and that shoe's mind was out of control. Suddenly I was running.

It all happened so quickly. Like an accident. One minute I was in my Karmen Ghia pounding the steering wheel because it refused to start (again), and the next I was sitting in the cool leather comfort of your, may I say, *outstanding* automobile, the Rolls-Royce Silver Shadow. It was parked right next to mine, all butter yellow curves and shiny chrome, your pride and joy, just daring me. I knew the keys would be under the front seat where the valets toss them. The red-jacketed Mexicans had their backs to me. I could drive out the Universal gate easy-peasey. And obviously I did, or I wouldn't now be sitting in the Santa Monica jail facing a possible grand-theft-auto charge.

I was deranged, Josh. Once we were on the open road I couldn't stop, I was having such a gas, laughing my head off and crying and singing along with none other than Bruce Springsteen on the radio: *It's a town full of losers, and I'm pulling out of here to win.* . . . Don't you love when that happens? You wish for a song and your wish is granted. You could almost believe in something. You could believe there's someone out there actually listening to you. Not God, clearly, more of a Supreme DJ providing the perfect soundtrack for your life. In case you haven't discovered this, your car just hums at ninety. Like my shoes, she surged forward uncontrollably; we shot right through the Santa Monica beach parking gate and onto the sand, headed straight for the wide-open sea, and we'd still be screaming west if the tide hadn't been so high and strong in the bay — but alas, even a *custom-made* Rolls can't swim, so my joyride ended abruptly when the wheels sank into the sand and the surf splashed over her proud windshield. The smell of the sea was restorative: I suddenly realized what I'd just done and wondered how, *how* could I have been so *insane?* Officers Rodriguez and Johnson wondered the same thing. I don't know, I told them. I don't know.

You see I have no defense. I just snapped. Call it a post-traumatic "cunt-fit." I hope this time spent in my shoes will help you open your heart to be as merciful as Jesus himself. Charging me seems beside the point, doesn't it, Josh? It's not like I'm going to do it again. I'll pay for any damage to the car, although I didn't hit anything, it just got wet. I'm broke, of course, and with what I'm now getting on *Quixote* I'll require a long, *long*-term payment plan.

Remorsefully yours,
Olivia

◆ ◆ ◆

December 10, 1998
Jail

Dear Tina,

This has got to be the longest Thursday I've ever had. Twelve hours ago I wrote to you from the plane, chirping about the miracle of aviation applying to life, too, and now I'm in a holding cell in the Santa Monica jail. Who wouldn't draw some new conclusions? On the sunny side, I'm the only one in here, and Officer Brown has kindly provided me with this notepad and pan.

I was arrested for driving Josh's hideous fucking car onto the beach. I'd had a difficult morning. From where I now sit, I realize this *really* didn't help, but around noon I had to get away fast. I wanted to go far. And I badly wanted to steal something precious to Josh. One minute I was on the lot, the next I was tearing down the 405, and the next I was gazing at the green waves of the Pacific, watching the sea froth slide down the window, and hearing the echo from a long-ago memory: *Calico Jam, the little Fish swam, over the syllabub sea.* Maddie loved that patty-cake. She liked all the hand movements and she liked being the only one in her class who knew it. She used to think it was "Silly Bob's sea." One day she came into our room and insisted I play with her. I'm studying, I said.

Just do "Calico Pie," then. Just once. Pleeease.

Just once, I warned her. Once. We sat cross-legged, facing each other on her bed.

> *Calico Pie,*
> *The little Birds fly*
> *Down to the calico tree.*
> *Their wings were blue,*
> *And they sang "Tilly-loo!"*
> *Till away they flew,*
> *And they never came back to me! . . .*
>
> *Calico Jam,*
> *The little Fish swam . . .*

When we came to the syllabub sea I stopped, deciding it was high time to educate Maddie (and myself), so we hauled out the big dictionary my mother had given me and I read the definition out loud: a dessert made of cream or milk, flavored, sweetened, and whipped to thicken it.

Where is the syllabub sea? she asked.

Nowhere. It's just an idea.

How do you know?

Because I do. Now go. I have to study.

Why do they call it the syllabub sea if there isn't one?

To help you understand. The sea only looked like syllabub. It just looked like that. It wasn't really made of milk and sugar. It was just frothy like syllabub.

I think it does exist somewhere.

Fine.

You don't know everything, Olivia.

I know there isn't a sea made of milk and sugar.

I hate you.

Good. Then you'll go away.

You never want to play with me. You hate me.

I rolled my eyes and returned to my history paper. No, I don't, I muttered.

Yes, you do. She started crying.

No, I don't. Now go, get out of here.

You do, you hate me. You never want to do anything with me. If you don't get out of here right now I'll hit you.

She was on her bed crying, and when she didn't stop, when she kept wailing louder and louder, I crossed the room and smacked her arm, hard. I mean it. Now get out.

She stopped crying instantly and glared at me. See, she said. You do hate me. And then she left.

In the car I whispered, You were right, Maddie, I did, and as the water wept down the windows I cried, because I knew that I hated her now, too. For disrupting my life, for ruining everything, for her suffering and for loving me nonetheless.

Your jailbird,
Olivia

December 10, 1998
Los Angeles

Dear Michael,

I'm finally back on the fold-out couch in my basement pad and I can honestly say it's good to be "home." I'm desperate to call you, but the phone was disconnected while I was in Ohio.

After we hung up I spent another few hours in the holding cell. I was released to Josh's assistant, Josh (yes, his name is Josh, too), who drove me to Josh's place in Bel-Air. This Josh is a good-looking, obedient USC film grad who would have done well in the military. He opened the back door of his black BMW for me. Can't I sit in the front? I asked.

Oh, sure. I just assumed you'd want to sit in the back. That's where Josh sits.

On the drive I tried, even at my own expense (which wasn't hard, given the circumstances), to get a smile out of the young man, but I think Josh hired Josh because he's so efficient he doesn't have time for a sense of humor. We pulled through the gates and up the circular drive to Josh's Tudor mansion. Josh the assistant wished me luck. As I pressed the doorbell I imagined him and the other earnest assistants eagerly spreading the news — did you hear that other producer drove Josh's Rolls into the Pacific? They'd assume I was drunk or on drugs. I almost wished I had been; it might help explain it. Substance abuse buys a lot of goodwill out here. A liveried butler led me to Josh's mahogany-paneled study, which was as big as my current residence and lined with leather-bound gold-embossed scripts — *Against the Law, Below the Law, Under the Law, Lloyd the Hamster,* etc. — and the ubiquitous silver-framed photos of my tuxedoed host with the top coolest people on earth. Josh was on the phone, laughing hard, laughing like a hyena.

Robin, stop, stop, you're killing me, he said, laughing so hard I was hoping I might watch him choke to death. Robin, I'll see you and Marsha Thursday. Looking forward, he said, and hung up. Then he stared at me. His eyes are so wide set you can only look at one at a time; it's very disconcerting. He exploded: What the fuck were you thinking?!

I obviously wasn't, Josh.

He stood up and started pacing and flapping his arms. The British accent came in and out. Do you know what that car is *wuth?* Do you have any *idea* how valuable it is? And the kind of trouble you're now in? What *wuh* you thinking?

My car wouldn't start and —

— so you steal someone else's? That's so puhfect! That's so you!

What do you mean by that?

The first sign of trouble, you give up. Like you're too good to get your hands dirty. You know why I fired you, Olivia?

Because I wouldn't sleep with you?

That stopped him. What?

Okay, why did you?

You think that's why? You think that everyone wants to fuck you?

You did stick your tongue down my throat at the company Christmas party —

So?

So?

I didn't do anything else, did I? It was a party, for fucksake. I didn't do anything else, did I?

He seemed unsure; I let him sweat and said, Oh, I should be grateful.

You should get over yourself. I fired you because I couldn't stand your attitude. You have a superiority and an inferiority complex —

Don't they cancel each other out and make me kinda perfect?

See? Even now everything's a joke with you. I could press charges. You'd have a record.

His beady eyes were shining. I knew all I had to do was cry and we could cut through all this crap. He wanted to see me crumble; he wanted to *make* me crumble. But even then I couldn't give him the satisfaction.

Fortunately, his own mention of charges made him a bit defensive. He put his hands on his head and snapped it to the left — *crack!* — and then to the right — *crack!* — and then took a deep breath and said, You're a smart girl. You're good on story. You could be a good producer, Olivia. But you don't have what it takes. Things don't go your way, things get hard, you act like someone farted and walk away. Like you're too good for the rest of us.

Etc., etc. He carried on in this vein for what seemed like days. He then mercifully shifted his focus to the *cause* of my character deficiencies — my poor parents — and at last we agreed on something. By way of example, he told me about his father, and a speech he made at Josh's bar mitzvah and how it destroyed him at the time but ultimately made him what he is today. Josh recited the gist of it, happy to be able to share the wealth, to become the father figure I so clearly needed: "My son is becoming a man today," it began. "And I pray to God that his balls finally grow, at least a little bigger, because he's going to need them in this disgusting world we call our home. But there's only one way that can happen, isn't there? That's if he bests me. That's what the next generation has to do. So, son, good fucking luck. I was running Fox on my twenty-sixth birthday. You better get busy."

The point is, Josh said, it hurt, but it was good medicine. It gave me the stuff.

That dreams are made of? I wondered. I thanked him for sharing that with me, for passing on "the stuff." I have to admit, once I stopped treating him like an idiot, we did seem more at ease with each other. I was truly sorry for what I'd done to his car. He apologized for being so "hard" on me when I was a new executive. He said he wanted to work together on *Don Quixote,* he didn't want me to feel he'd taken it over, and that I should think of him as my proxy for when I couldn't be there. We wanted the same thing, after all, and that was to make a great movie. He opened his arms and said, Come here. He hugged me. It was disgusting, but it seemed necessary. He then called his butler in and said, What would you like to drink, Olivia?

A double Stoli on the rocks with a twist, I said.

We don't keep alcohol in the house, Josh said.

Oh, then — what are you having?

Carrot juice.

Even better.

A taxi arrived later and took me home. Tomorrow I'll have the Ghia towed — it needs a new battery. Car trouble always makes me feel so . . . desperate. I wish you were here. If you were, you could be the man and deal with the damn car. I could make love to you, gratefully, passionately, adoringly, for hours. I would, you know. God, I'd like to. You've made it so hard to sleep alone. I miss your warm body around mine. But it's only two more weeks. My flight arrives in Santa Fe on the 23rd at 11 A.M. and I leave for Europe on the 4th. Fifteen days together, alone. Maybe I'll make them so good you'll have to come to Madrid with me. . . .

Amorously,
Olivia

December 17, 1998
From my "office" on the lot

Dear Mom,

In case by the time you read this you've forgotten what I said last night, this is just a little reminder: There is <u>no way</u> I'm coming home for Christmas. <u>No way.</u> I'm going to see Michael. It's all planned. Pleasepleaseplease don't not-at-all-subtly hint about how totally *devastating* this will be to people like my father and my sister. (And I know you were only speaking on their behalf, not your own.) This is what out here they call non-negotiable. And no, Michael will not come there; it's my turn to go to his place. We hardly ever have time alone together in Ohio. And time alone is what we need.

And in case you are still clinging to the notion that this means I don't love you, I have three words for you: I love you.

Firmly,
Olivia

➻

December 18, 1998
From my "office" on the lot

Dear Maddie,

I just wanted to say again, I'm really sorry <u>I can't</u> come home. And please don't be mad at me. Michael and I need time alone together before I go to Spain. You can understand that, can't you? I tried to explain on the phone, but you sounded distracted, like you weren't really listening; I think at one point I actually heard you saying, Yeah, yeah, yeah. Which is why I'm putting it in writing here. It's one of the things I like about writing letters. I know I have the person's full and undivided attention.

I know how important Christmas is to you, Madster, but you've got Bobby and Mom and Dad and Jim and his family — it'll be plenty festive and crowded enough in that little hospital room without me. I have to do what's best for me and Michael, especially given how delicate things are at the moment. I'll be home again soon, but it just can't be at Christmas.

Resolutely,
Livvie

Dear Michael,

How can I *not* go home for Christmas? I agonized about this; this is not, as you said, "typical." It's true I've caved in before — okay, I admit, *every* other Christmas before — but that doesn't make this typical, anyone can see that. Maddie's in the hospital, all screwed up. I have a movie in preproduction in Spain — what's typical? Besides this fight you and I are having about Christmas. And your unwillingness to spend it with my family. It's a big deal to them, it's not to you. It's true you were just there. Oh, what's the point? I've said all this.

I've changed my flight. I go to Ohio for the 24th and 25th, then I'll be in New Mexico on the 26th. I'm not "squeezing you in." I really hate it when you say that; you always used to say that and it's just not true. *They're* the ones who're getting squeezed in. I'm adding *them* to my Christmas break, not you. You see the difference?

And please, think some more about coming to Madrid. If only for a few weeks. A couple Valium and you'll get over your problem with flying and wake up in my arms. And then the Prado, sangria, paella, and every night, a great hotel room. Think about it, okay?

Love,

Olivia

December 26, 1998
Cincinnati–London

Dear Tina,

Belated Christmas greetings. I'm really sorry I missed your call last night — I would have loved even a few minutes with you. I hope you got everything you wanted and a few good surprises, too. I know what you want more than anything and I hope that comes to you this year. I'm sure Stephen wants another baby as much as you do; he's probably just dreading the fertility struggle. Maybe in-vitro and artificial insemination are worse for a man, a kind of slap in the face of their manhood. I'm sure you'll be able to convince him. You're a persuasive, alluring woman, remember that. I know Stephen loves you, so don't despair, I'm sure he'll come around.

As you can see, I'm on my way to London. The flight is eight hours, so make a cup of tea and put your feet up; I have a lot to tell you.

Even though Maddie is feeling better, she hasn't begun rehab and Mercy said if she left the hospital for Christmas she couldn't come back for their inpatient stroke program — some insurance nonsense. She got on the Slimline and called her boss, the county executive, and the next morning a nurse came in and said, I don't know what you did, but you're out of here till the twenty-eighth. This was Christmas Eve. The second thing Maddie said to me after Can you pack my stuff? was Tell Mom not to put oysters in the stuffing, and I thought of you and your annual stuffing war with your mother-in-law. (I hope you won this year. Remember: it's your house!)

There wasn't going to be any celebration without Maddie, so nothing had been done at home; a mad dash to decorate the house began. Jim and his family went out for the tree. I found Ed on a ladder, struggling to string the Christmas lights along the gutter over the bay window. He climbed down and found the next set a tangled mess and we huddled over it, the steam from his mouth fogging his glasses. He was in a panic, his big crooked fingers shaking as they hurried in and out of the loops of twisted green vines. Rushing was only making the web more tangled. Take it easy, I said. Relax.

I have to get them up before she gets here.

No, you don't; she doesn't care —

Goddammit, Olivia, just be quiet and hold that end.

I held the socket while he quickly loosened the knot and wove the end in and out of various loops.

Every year I put them away carefully, he said, and every year I take them out they're all tangled up. How do you explain that? How do you explain it?

I looked at the box of lights at his feet. Where else are we putting them?

Where we always do, he said. On the tree and around all the windows. He was in a foul, agitated mood. I should have known; everything for this Christmas would have to be precisely replicated to be precisely like every one before, which is one of Maddie's greatest joys in life: recapturing peak moments of childhood. Even the order we came downstairs Christmas morning — Jim first, then me, then Maddie — had to be reenacted until she moved out a few years ago.

Ed jiggled the tangle and tugged it and said, I didn't want her coming home, you know.

You didn't?

I don't want to see my daughter coming home in a wheelchair. On Christmas Eve.

You'd rather she spend it in the hospital?

We should just skip the whole thing.

But Maddie loves Christmas.

Never mind. You don't know what I'm talking about. As usual.

He was talking about himself, of course. Is your dad like this? Maybe it's a generational thing. Maybe that's what men pre-self-help and pre-feminism are like; they can't get outside of their own heads because they simply don't know how to, they were never asked to. I decided to forgo Lecture #32 — the one where I point out that she's the one suffering, not him, that we should be happy to welcome her home in any condition and be glad we can — I decided to skip all that because, after all, it was Christmas Eve, the least I could do was ease up and be a little more kindhearted. I said, We don't have to put them all up, Dad —

— Why do you have to contradict me? Just do it.

We finished the Hanging of the Lights in silence. I went inside and threw the switch and then came back out to stand beside him and view our work. It's beautiful, I said. Icicle lights hung from the gutter and white lights framed every window and the big pine was dotted with red, green, and yellow teardrops.

It's okay, he said, still miserable at the thought of greeting the Caboose, as he sometimes called her, in a wheelchair. I guess for him as a father, her physical devastation registered as a failure of his own, a failure to protect her, a failure that he literally could not face. I left him in the garage tucked into his La-Z-Boy, watching the black-and-white TV and drinking a beer from his little fridge.

Inside, Eleanor was rushing around cooking and decorating at the same time. She was also frantic. Feeling bad about Ed, I stopped Eleanor midstride and gave her a hug, which was understandably confusing to her. It's going to be okay, Mom, I said. Everything doesn't have to be perfect.

I know, I know. But help me get the garlands up. We quickly wove the juniper rope through the white banister and I realized that like Ed, my mother was desperate to show how much she loved Maddie by decorating the house magnificently. They would give her what she wanted — a place where nothing had changed.

It smells great, I said, still trying to be nice to her. There was cinnamon and a roasting Butterball turkey in the air.

I hope she can eat something.

She'll be happy just to be here.

Can you make the salad and crescent rolls?

Sure.

Is your father done with the lights?

Not wanting to lie but not wanting to get him into trouble, either, I stalled. If she knew he was sitting in the garage drinking beer she wouldn't like it. She'd ask me to go get him to come inside and help — with something, there was bound to be something that needed to be done, and not just done but done by *him*. Her desire to get her husband in the house was a web of urges: one, to curtail his drinking; two, to flex her power to make him do things; three, to actually get some chore done that she couldn't do herself; and four, to enjoy his companionship, to feel him in the house, breathing, straining, moving, working beside her. Depending on what was going on between them, and what was coming up in the next few hours, one of these might color her desire more than the others. That night I'd bet it was equal parts of all four.

I don't know, I said.

Go get him.

I walked across the shoveled deck to the garage and imagined the next several minutes of my life. He'd moan and say, Jesus Christ, what now? and I'd mutter in a conspiratorial way, I don't know, which would in a single stroke make me a traitor to her and a pal to him, and then once inside he'd look at his wife of thirty-seven years and heave the monstrous sigh of the oppressed and exploited and say, *What?*

And that's exactly, verbatim, what happened, which for some stupid reason, I enjoyed. As I placed the baby Jesus in his cradle in the hand-carved crèche they bought on a trip to Mexico in 1972, I heard Bobby's Blazer crunch over the gravel driveway. In a moment my father was outside, offering help but relieved to find none was needed: Bobby carried a black wheelchair into the family room and then came back to lift his wife out of the front seat while Ed held the door open with a tense smile. As she crossed the threshold, we saw the joy on her face that told us it was all worth it, that what she'd endured was worth this moment of coming home for Christmas.

She wore a red zippered sweater and a red knit beret; she decided against the wig. It's fake, she said. And it itches. I'd helped her with some makeup, giving her some color with blush and lip gloss and a little eyeliner. At dinner Sophie and Nell couldn't really look at her. She was incomprehensible; she's their Aunt Maddie, but she's not the aunt they saw four months ago when we last sat around that table together: she doesn't have any hair, she can't walk, her voice is weirdly unmodulated, so who is she? They were very polite; they smiled but avoided looking at her. I remember being afraid of people in wheelchairs, don't you? On a primal level you intuit something your mind isn't ready to believe, namely that bad things just happen to people, that life is not fair or safe.

Eleanor wanted to make a toast. As she took a deep breath we lifted our glasses. She looked at Maddie and said, I'm so glad you're home, honey, and then burst into tears. Ed said, Jesus Christ, Eleanor, and swallowed his wine. Maddie said, I'm glad I am, too, Mom. Jim hugged Sarah, who was sniffling, and I wished Michael was there.

After dinner I was helping Maddie with her exercises when Johnny called from London and changed my Christmas plans. He hated the rewrite. He said he wouldn't shoot it. I thought Universal would like it. I suggested we see what they thought of it.

We're not giving it to them, he said. We have to rewrite it first. If we give them this draft, they'll want me to make it, and I won't do it. It's a piece of shit. You have to come to London tomorrow.

Tomorrow's Christmas —

— So what? You can take the night flight.

He wanted me to do the rewrite with him. Only I knew all the drafts and the book as well as he did; we'd do a cut-and-paste and write some new scenes before the studio started demanding the script.

What's Josh think?

Fuck Josh. We can't trust him, Johnny said. I haven't even given him the script. He'll just go right to Howard with it and then we're fucked. We gotta get the script right first, Olivia. Before Robin goes pay-or-play on the twentieth.

That's when the studio agrees to pay him even if they later decide not to make the movie; it's essentially when a flashing green light becomes a permanent one, because once the studio shells out $15 million they don't pull the plug.

I can admit to you, Tina, that I didn't hesitate. I didn't think, No, I've got to see Michael; I didn't say, I'm sorry, my life is more important than this movie. Yes was my reflex; yes, I'll be there, I'll do what's necessary, yes, I'm as serious about this movie, about this job, my career, as you are, just watch this. I felt afraid. And heavyhearted, but I didn't hesitate, and sitting here now, flying away from Michael, I wonder why. Was it to prove something to all the *other* men in my life — Johnny, Josh Miller, my father — and myself? Or simply because I knew that if I didn't go to London, the movie was essentially over? I know you're thinking it's because I don't love Michael enough. The right man would change that reflex in me. Like Stephen has changed you; if you weren't married you would have taken that promotion, right?

When I told Michael I couldn't come to Dixon, he didn't say anything for a while. He listened, and even to my own ears, I sounded defensive. Then he said, This is who you are, Olivia. This is what you do. He sounded resigned. I didn't want to hang up, but we weren't talking anymore; we were both just listening to nothing.

Oh, shit, what have I done?

Lost in space,
Olivia

December 26, 1998
Cincinnati–London

Dear Michael,

I want to be with you, not writing to you. I'm sick of writing letters. I can't think of anything to say. But this is the closest thing to being with you that's available: this blank page, my thoughts, your music. I'm playing that Billy Bragg & Wilco CD you bought in Ohio. "California Stars." It's so wistful I could kill myself.

Why do I feel defeated?

The first night in your apartment in New York. It was, what, a week after we met? I don't mean the Carnegie Deli, since we didn't actually meet then. Or in the elevator in the Brill Building later that day (what were the chances?), because still we didn't meet. I mean after I walked into Fanelli's a month later and there you were, this guy whose face I couldn't forget, standing behind the bar serving drinks. Who wouldn't think it was destiny? But it wasn't till I was in your apartment and I saw your paintings that I felt afraid it was true. They were melancholy but passionate, and somehow humorous, too; they expressed what I saw in your face that day. And then you put on Herb Alpert and the Tijuana Brass. This cool, serious guy was playing Herb Alpert. We drank tequila and danced around, laughing. I think I — or you? — started taking my clothes off before the second track.

And now it's six years later, and I'm not flying to you but away, reliving the past, longing for it, as I move further from it. The sun is rising over London; the frost crystals trapped in the window are tiny pink flowers. We'll be landing soon. On the phone you said, You sound like you have no choice. But you do, Olivia, and thinking you're not making one doesn't mean you aren't.

This isn't a choice, Michael, it's just a delay. Of a few more weeks. As soon as the script's approved and we're green-lit, I'm coming out there. Josh will handle things for a while without me. I told Johnny I'd come to London on that condition. See, it's only a delay, Michael. You said, You know where I am. Call me when you're back. I'm coming out in a few weeks, and after I visit, maybe you could come to Spain? You could even rent a studio here for a few months. Everything could be great.

Last night I was watching Bobby help Mad with her exercises. She was on the floor near the Christmas tree. Her beret had fallen off. Bobby sat at her feet. She slowly bent her right leg and Bobby bent the left and he held it gently so it wouldn't flop over. Her goal is to squeeze her thighs together. Her right leg was improving; in a week she'd gone from little movement to a few, slow inches. But her left leg was still as inert as a sock and every day that passes where it doesn't move means it's less likely she'll walk again. She concentrated, straining, biting her lip, jaw bearing down, her brown eyes willing that left thigh to move. I wondered what was going on inside her, how the intense concentration of what was left of her brain, a third of it, could translate — or not — into the tiny flex of a left hamstring.

You did it, Bobby yelled. It moved! It moved! She exhaled and smiled her now-crooked half smile. He held her face in his hands and when he kissed her mouth I saw his tears drop on her cheeks. Oh, baby, you did it. He was as relieved as she was exhausted; she was going to walk again. He lay down next to her by the brightly lit tree and she rested her bald head on his shoulder. Damn, he sighed. I never thought I'd be so happy to see you *close* your legs, Madlicious. They laughed hard and he hugged her close to him.

I had to walk away. I was jealous, Michael. I'm ashamed to admit it, but I was.

Love,
Olivia

Dear Madster,

I saw two kids with enormous backpacks tromping down the Strand tonight and I remembered my first trip here, with Tony, and how I wished we could afford to stay in a place with good sheets, any sheets, like this place, which not only has good sheets but beds with 836 springs — a feature for which the Savoy is famous. You were so mad at me for leaving you back then. My hand was on our bedroom doorknob when you hissed, Where are you going? and my heart sank, because I knew I might not make it if I had to say good-bye to you.

I'm going to Europe with Tony, I whispered.

You can't, you said, Dad'll kill you. Even half asleep, only eleven years old, you had strong opinions. You were wearing my faded Horace Mann Varsity Tennis T-shirt. You smelled sweet, like baking bread. Your cheeks were rosy from sleep.

He'll get over it. I have to go.

Why?

Because Tony's waiting.

No, why do you have to go to Europe?

Well, to see it, Madster. You looked like you still hadn't heard a decent answer. I just want to, okay? I want to see London and Paris —

Can I come with you?

You've got to go to school.

Just for a couple weeks?

Maybe you can visit.

How long are you going to be gone?

Till our money runs out. I hoped that would be about a year — which it was — but I lied to you and added, Not long.

Will you be back for Easter?

Easter's in two weeks.

You won't be home for Easter?!

No, Maddie —

What about Memorial Day? I'm going to be in the parade this year —

I have to go. Be good. Don't fight with Dad. And do your homework so you don't turn into an idiot while I'm gone. You have to study, okay? Promise me you'll study.

You started crying. I put down my knapsack and sat on your bed. Oh, come on, I said, I thought you'd like me being gone. You'll have the room all to yourself. You can play the stereo as loud as you want. It'll be great. Come on. Please don't cry. Mom will wake up and then I'll be mad at you.

Are you coming back?

Of course. It's just a vacation, for chrissake.

Then you hugged me really hard like I wasn't coming back, like last night when I left you and you held my shoulder in your surprisingly strong grip. You're lousy at saying good-bye. I'm good at it. Back then you said, Will you send me postcards?

Of course. From everywhere I go.

And buy me souvenirs.

Sure. You want anything special?

A carved duck.

What? Why?

I want to start a collection.

I kissed your forehead and slipped out the door. On the way to the airport in the taxi I remember watching the sunrise and being strangely happy that you were going to miss me, because I didn't think you would. You always seemed disappointed with me. I thought I just frustrated you. We fought so much. I never wanted to play with dolls, watch TV, or play Monopoly like you did; I wanted to study, to practice, to be left alone. I never wanted to just roll around with you the way Jim always would. Then I was gone, first to Europe, then college, then New York, California. I just realized now that you were right, Maddie: I never did come back.

Getting sentimental. Guess I'm overtired. I arrived around ten this morning and came directly here, to start going over the script with Johnny. Maddie, Johnny is crazy, have I told you that? He thinks we can rewrite the script in ten days if we work fourteen to sixteen hours a day. I don't know why Johnny thinks we can do this, but it is my only shot: he won't make the draft we have, and we've got to get Universal to approve a script so we can start hiring crew. We did ten pages today. The challenge in rewriting is to fix the problems without causing new ones or upsetting the intricate ecosystem that exists in a script. In his suite I sit at the computer; he paces. I say, That won't work because —, he says, You're such a cunt, Hunt. It's a compliment. I call him a prick. Because he is one. Well, sometimes.

Madinks, I miss you. You should be in this hotel room with me. It's gigantic. Pale pink walls with white-frosting molding. High-ass ceiling. A view of the Thames where the lights of the barges float by like fireflies. A brass button next to the bed that says "Service." I hate it all. I wouldn't if you were here, or if you weren't in the damn hospital. I keep wanting to say something about what's happened to you. We've never really talked about it; we're always talking about other people, politics, recipes, movies, Mom and Dad. I've tried to bring it up, but it seems pointless, too: what's to say? What are the words? We don't have religion to turn to for answers, and I sure don't have any. These words may not be necessary and they feel inadequate, but I just want you to know I am so sorry you're in this hell. It's a terrible time, but it won't be forever, Maddie. I never knew how fierce you were. I knew you had guts, but I didn't know how much. You're *formidable* (the French pronunciation — for-mee-dabl), which means tremendous. You'll be running down the beach again soon, you'll have babies and barbecues and all the other ordinary good things. You'll remember these days and think they must have been from someone else's life.

Love,
Olivia

— · · · —

January 4, 1999
Savoy Hotel, London

Katrina Kyler-Ross
President of Production
Universal Pictures
Universal City, California 91608

<u>Via FED EX</u>

Dear KK,

Congratulations!! I always knew you were next in line. Instead of the usual bottle of champagne, I thought you'd like this whip, which belonged to one of the most beloved matadors in Spanish history. Bring it to the staff meetings, see what happens.

Casting is going great here in London. Richard Harris wants to play the Duke, and his agent insists that he's been sober for months, so insurance won't be a problem. I'm still working on Johnny re: Jennifer Lopez. Dulcinea really should be older, KK; are you sure Sophia Loren couldn't work?

The script will be delivered to you Friday. I look forward to working together (again).

Sincerely,
Olivia Hunt

—◆—

January 5, 1999
Savoy Hotel, London

Dear Dad,

Maddie said those people on Monroe Boulevard are thinking about selling their house. You know the red brick with the big elm in front? She called them last fall and they said they'd let her know if they ever want to sell, and they just called her and said probably this spring. But they're asking $250K (!!!). Maddie doesn't have the down payment, of course. I didn't say anything to her about that secret stash of yours, but I was wondering if you'd consider loaning her some of it, and as soon as I'm paid, I could loan her some, and maybe that way she could do it? I could probably throw in $10K. And maybe Bobby's parents could chip in, too.

Don't tell her I said anything to you. Bobby's too proud to let her ask you, so that's why I did. He might not even want to buy it, so this could all be for nothing. But I thought you'd want to know it's something she's thinking about. You know, as kids whenever we rode our bikes past it she'd say, That's my house, I'm going to live there one day. Weird but true.

I'll call you in a couple weeks, when we're done with the script. I think it's pretty good. Let's hope. If it isn't, the movie could go up in smoke.

Love,
Olivia

— ◆ —

January 7, 1999
Savoy Hotel, London

Tina,

I did not say Stephen is as dull as a door. If you hadn't hung up on me I could have explained what you think you heard, and what I in fact said, and what I meant, because those things got all twisted up when we were talking. I apologize for even *suggesting* that your husband is in any way dull. I was in fact defending my man, who I felt you were attacking when you called him a self-centered jerk. You know only *I* can call him that, Tina, even now, when we're quasi–broken up or quasi–back together, whichever it is. My patience was just worn out after hearing about what a dysfunctional relationship we had — if I hear the word *dysfunctional* one more time, or that litany about what a "healthy" relationship is, full of mutual sacrifice and compromise (sounds great), or about what a classic ACOA I am and how I should join Al-Anon for a few hundred years and then maybe, if I'm really *lucky,* I could hook up with some "healthy" guy and not have a "codependent" relationship and finally be as "happy" (read alternately bored and irritated) as the rest of the long-suffering, sanctimonious married world; and that since Michael and I didn't get married, we must not love each other enough, because marriage is different than living together, it's transformative (yeah, right into misery), marriage requires putting the relationship first (is that what Stephen did when he made you move to Portland? and when you passed up that promotion because Stephen wouldn't *leave* Portland?); if I hear about how it's time for me to "settle down and get on with my life" (you mean without a husband I don't have one?), or that I have a "commitment problem," if I hear another drop of this thin-as-broth conformist Old Testament–laced pop psychobabble I'll just scream! — so I counterattacked by suggesting that you, after a period some would call *promiscuous,* when you screwed nearly every white boy at State (and one African American), married, some might say *hastily,* a guy so unlike all the guys you'd gone out with since middle school (and remember, I know them all), a guy so decent, so sensible, so solid (some — not me! but some — might say as *solid as a door*) that some might suspect you were so *spent* by all that freedom that you handed it over like a panting thief on the lam offering his wrists to the cuffs, so eager were you to get on with your "life" and have children that you chose someone you knew would never leave you, who would never challenge you or torment you — but who *would assume* you'd put your career second to his — which is why you must now defend your choice by urging me to make the same one, because the presence of someone who doesn't makes you doubt yours, and because, as everyone knows, misery loves company.

That's all I was saying. I love Stephen. I know you do, too. I think he's good for you. But just because he's good for you doesn't mean he'd be good for me. I mean — oh, you see how addled I am? I've been working long days on the script and I hope this letter isn't an indication of how it's going. I'm really sorry if I hurt your feelings about Stephen. You hurt mine about Michael, so I hope by the time this letter reaches you you'll have forgiven me, and now that I've spit all this onto the Savoy stationery, I feel better. I realize we were both too strung out to mean the things we said.

I'm sorry,
Olivia

January 9, 1999
Savoy Hotel, London

My Madster,

I know the food at the hospital sucks. It must be healthy, though; they have a nutritionist on staff. Just because it tastes bad doesn't mean it's bad for you or that you should throw the tray against the wall. You'll be out of there soon. And until then, here's a little care package to help prevent future outbursts. The cheese and biscuits are delicious, but I know your tastes have changed since the stroke, so you might find them revolting, but I hope not. The breadsticks are amazing, made with lots of lard and salt; definitely give them a try. I love the shortcake and Bendick's mints and the marzipan roosters; they fueled the rewrite Johnny and I finally finished last night.

The videos are Academy viewing tapes of last year's best movies, and, as usual, most were released in the fall, when you were in ICU, and some haven't even been released yet, so I'm sure you haven't seen any of them. They belong to Cully Davis, our line producer, who said you can just keep them. I'll send the rest (the movies from Warners, Fox, and Miramax) when he's finished watching them. You are probably the only person in Shawnee Falls — and maybe all of Ohio — who's got these movies on video. Mom and Dad will be jealous.

I'm on my way to Spain in the morning. Johnny and Josh are going to stay here in London and do some casting while I set up the offices and hire some office runners and make sure the coffee is hot when they arrive next week. Josh and I are so civil to each other you'd think we were a couple of Swiss figure skaters. I should have stolen his car ages ago.

Talk to you soon. Love,
Livvie

January 10, 1999
Ritz Hotel, Madrid

Dear Michael,

It's midnight here, four P.M. in New Mexico, but you're not home. You weren't home yesterday, when it was midnight in New Mexico and seven A.M. in London. This little world travel clock you gave me for my birthday is sure coming in handy. Maybe you decided to go fishing for a few days. I'm sorry I couldn't talk when you called Friday night. We were having a script meeting — yes, in my hotel room, because Johnny's wife was sleeping in his. It probably seemed late for a meeting, but we're really under the gun here. And the day before, when I had to go, I was late for a casting session. Here's another advantage in letters: nothing can interrupt me, or you. And if I FedEx this you'll actually read it before we talk next. Especially at the rate we're going . . .

My news isn't great. I don't think the script Johnny and I did is going to please the studio, and last night around three A.M. the phone rang; I was hoping it was you, but it wasn't, it was Howard Trammel screaming his head off. *Fifty!* Didn't I say *fifty?*

We're nearly there —

You're still at $52.5 million! The next time I see this budget there better be a zero after that five, Olivia, or you're all coming home on the next plane. Do we understand each other?

I spent the day with Cully trying to lose another $3 million. We have an idea, but I doubt Johnny will go for it. He loves the Sheep scene, where Quixote sees a dust cloud in the valley and, thinking it's a band of soldiers, charges into it . . . only to find it's a flock of sheep. Comic mayhem ensues, but to the tune of $400,000 and three days of shooting, plus some effects. Something's got to go or the whole movie could.

Meanwhile, back in Ohio, my sister has staged a hunger strike at Mercy. She can't get out of bed without help, she can't stand up or walk, but she organized a hunger strike to protest the culinary crafts of the cafeteria, and because she has connections in the local press, she made the six o'clock news. Jeff Johansen, the Browns receiver who's in the next room suffering from some brain injury, helped, too. They got a couple other patients to refuse to eat for two days, and then the press "heard" about it, and now I bet Mercy's wishing they hadn't let Her Royal Madness stay. They defended the nutritiousness of the food, which only got them in more trouble, because then Action-7 News did an investigation and found that the food is in fact about as nutritious as Styrofoam. She's tireless. Tiresome, too, but sometimes, as in this case, for a worthy cause.

I should be able to fly out there on the first. I miss you. I can't wait to see you. Call me when you can. Soon. Any time.

Did I already say I miss you?

Love,
Olivia

+ + +

January 11, 1999
Ritz Hotel, Madrid

Dear Tina,

Please just throw this away if you've called me back and accepted my sincere apology. If you haven't, read on.

I didn't mean it, okay? Just call me back. We have to talk it through or you're just going to stay angry or, worse, get angrier, so please call me back and give me a chance to apologize and explain. The longer you're angry the longer it could take to make you not angry. So come on. Call me back.

Even more apologetically,
Olivia

Dear Mom,

I told Dad about that house because I think we should help Maddie buy it. I know she can't even walk yet, but she will. And she's still very weak — all the more reason to get *something* you want. It's true it's easy for me to say, since I won't have to help her move in and fix it up, but you like redecorating; I thought you'd like a whole new house to do. Anyway, I'm sorry if, once again, I've "stirred the pot." I didn't realize you guys have a huge tax bill that you can't pay; I thought you might have some savings you wouldn't miss, that's all. As long as Dad doesn't say anything to Maddie about all this, we can put the lid back on the pot and forget I ever said anything, okay?

Once we're shooting, maybe you and Dad should come for a visit. When we move the whole company to La Mancha in April it'll be warm. I'm getting very excited, Mom, guardedly, but I think, despite all the budget bluster, we're going to make this movie. Yesterday on the scout, when our convoy of four green Range Rovers stopped in the middle of a wide golden valley and the location manager, Carlos, said this would be Scene 35, where Quixote sees in the distance a row of windmills and believes they are giants sent to destroy him, I realized that the next time we were there we'd be accompanied by a caravan of trucks full of props and lights and camera equipment, a catering truck and a makeup truck, and John Cleese and Robin Williams would be in costume and makeup, saying their lines: we'd be shooting film, film that would be developed and one day projected and watched in movie theaters in Omaha and Milan and Tokyo. This was the good part, the brief period when everything is possible, the period that follows the longer one when everything wasn't and that precedes the one when you face the mistakes you made getting the job done.

I wished Maddie were there; she would have loved that vista, the El Greco blue sky above the tawny land. I hope she makes it over for some of the shoot. Sometimes when I realize a few hours have passed and I haven't thought about her I feel guilty. Other times I have to will myself *not* to think about rehab exercises, blood draws, chemotherapy, leukemia. I wonder what Maddie does. Does she refuse to look at Damocles' sword or does she never let it out of her sight?

I've got to run, but here are the names and numbers of the studio marketing departments. You should probably ask for Special Event Marketing — the Oscar campaigns would fall under that. This is such a classic Mad move, isn't it? She couldn't just watch those videos I sent her, she has to launch a screening program for Mercy and try to get the studios to institute one for other hospitals. It's a great idea, but I doubt they'll go for it. I'm glad you can help her. Where does she get so much goodwill? I guess she got my share, too. Wouldn't you take advantage of the greatest reason in the world to be bitchy or lazy (cancer, a stroke!) and just watch those videos in bed yourself? She makes me feel guilty for working so hard to get one dumb movie made and not hiring, say, homeless migrant olive pickers to be my crew.

Love to you & Dad,
Olivia

January 13, 1999
Ritz Hotel, Madrid

Hey Tina,

You know, there's only so much groveling I'm going to do. Stephen sounded downright arctic on the phone just now, and the fact that you "weren't home" (at ten P.M. on a Wednesday?) leads me to believe you're still mad at me. I said I'm sorry and I am; I didn't mean to insult you or your husband. I was defensive. You weren't very nice about Michael, remember? And I'm not holding it against you. I value our friendship more than anything, and I certainly value it more than a few poorly phrased sentences about our respective relationships. I can only surmise that you don't feel the same way about our friendship. Otherwise you'd at least talk to me before you just dump it.

Still sorry but getting pissed now,
Olivia

← → →

January 14, 1999
Ritz Hotel, Madrid

Madwoman of La Mercy:

If I didn't know you better, I'd think all the trouble you're causing was some kind of sweet revenge. You've been back there three weeks and you've conducted a hunger strike and launched an Oscar screening program. If I say I'm proud of you it'll sound patronizing or worse — once again words fail me. Anyway, I am amazed at you, Mad. (But I hope all this civic do-gooding isn't slowing down your rehab. Remember what's important.)

I wish you were here with me in this big mirrored bistro. Writing to you is not nearly as good. If you were here I could complain about Josh, and you could complain about how busy I am or how noisy Madrid is; we could discuss the Basque problem, which is heating up again and which could force us to change locations. It'd be my luck that I finally get this movie going and then the Basques blow up our set or, worse, kidnap one of the actors. If you were here we could also check out the waiters together. There's one leaning against the bar who looks intriguing. He looks over here, then away, with brooding indifference.

More later, my meat is served.

Next morning:
As much as that young man's firm round buttocks and smoky wet eyes made me want to, you'll be happy to hear I did not have inappropriate sex last night. I looked at Raoul over the rim of my rioja and wondered, chest hair or no chest hair? I imagined closing my hotel room door behind him, unbuttoning his uniform, and slipping my hand inside to find out — and then he turned into Michael. He's with me now even when he's not. I know this feeling. I remember this feeling. These location nights. When I am alone because I love someone — a situation so familiar to me I usually overlook the paradox: you're alone because you're not alone. What good is that? Our time in Ohio together was so tender but so unreal, like a diorama that we stepped into and — now out of again. We keep missing each other on the phone. He was angry about Christmas, and I don't blame him, but then I think, hey, he could have come to

Madrid, right? At least for a little vacation? It was New Year's. I'm working long days, but we would have had the nights together. . . . This is a producer's life. Some men would love it. Well, I'm going to Dixon in a few weeks, as soon as Universal approves the script. Then I'll be back here till August (with some trips to Ohio, of course). I'm hoping once I visit him, I'll be able to convince him to visit here and then he'll like it enough to stay for a while.

. . . Like you. I found a great apartment today. I can't wait for you to see it. It's got a fireplace and terrace and a great kitchen with windows overlooking a lush garden. I hope the minute you're strong enough you'll come.

I miss you, Maddie,
Olivia

January 16, 1999
The Ritz, Madrid

Klein,

You never mentioned Willow. You never mentioned there was a girl named Willow who lived in Taos who was a friend of yours. An attractive friend. Half Navajo. Who you slept with. A few times last summer. But who was away taking photographs of Vietnamese orphans for her upcoming book of poetry and photography. Who won the Prix d'Or for her last book called *The Face of Hunger*. This attractive poet-photographer babe named Willow who is a friend but might become something more. You never mentioned her.

Not that I'm entitled to know anything, but I do wonder what kind of Christmas you were imagining we were going to have. I know she wasn't going to be there with us, she was still hunting photogenic orphans in the Mekong Delta, but when we talked about our future, was she going to be a part of the conversation? If so, you might have just mentioned old Willow to me before I made the trip to Dixon, which I realize I didn't make on account of the movie requiring my producing services immediately. Be that as it may. You were so disappointed and even angry when I told you I couldn't come, one might have believed there was no Willow in your life, only me.

Of course it's complicated, I so understand. Last summer we'd broken up, you were alone out there in the wilderness, who could resist a half-Navajo poet-photographer? And why should you? She was probably a centerfold before she took up poetry, right? And then she left town for a few months (women today!), the very months I started writing to you, and then there was our time together in Ohio, which confused you because it was so good but so unreal you couldn't trust it to mean anything; my tenderness might have just been a passing condition caused by sheer terror. It's easy to be yielding and vulnerable and grateful when you're scared shitless; once Maddie was better what would stop me from turning back into the selfish bitch I used to be? And then, sure enough, I did! You said something tonight about being tired of being the last on my to-do list, which isn't true. You're second, after work, which I thought you preferred, since it's where I am on your list and the mutuality of this made me your partner, not your slave. Should I quit and move to New Mexico? Maybe Willow and I could team up on a documentary about Romanian orphans rescued by Hollywood wives.

Should it be this hard? Is it always? Isn't it possible that my man could be here with me? Cully's wife is here, and Johnny's wife — and she's six months pregnant. As you've pointed out, I probably wouldn't like a man who would follow me around, whose own work wasn't important enough to keep him from doing that. Funny thing about you is, your work is mobile; you *could* come with me if your pride wasn't so cumbersome. But hell, you might like a woman who could stay with you in your adobe hut, dabbing your brow, stirring the rice and beans now and then, snapping the odd Worthy photograph while knocking off a few lines of a sonnet. Quietly, of course. Pregnant, perhaps. You might like that. What's not to like? I guess that's not me. I guess that means I should face it and move on. To something easier than this. Isn't that what love should be? Easier than this?

Rather pissed,
Olivia

Maddie,

Oh, my god, I just sent Michael the most humiliating letter. The minute I dropped it in the mailbox I screamed, realizing I was in the grips of one of those highly regrettable hormone-enhanced moments of rage. I ran back inside the hotel and called Michael and asked him to throw the letter out, but who doesn't read a letter you've been begged *not* to read?

We talked some more about this new girl in his life. Or not so new, since he met her last summer. Who am I to be upset, right? At least he waited till we broke up. He said it's not really serious.

They're just seeing each other again. But the simple fact is, Maddie, *we're* not. I'm in Spain. She's got a huge home-field advantage.

He said, You know, Olivia, love should be easier than this. I had come to the same conclusion in my letter. Maybe timing really *is* everything. The only timing we've gotten right is this moment when we're both thinking it's over.

Your sister,
Livvie

—•—•—

January 20, 1999
Madrid

Katrina Kyler-Ross
President of Production
Universal Pictures

URGENT FAX PLEASE HAND DELIVER IMMEDIATELY

Dear KK,

Please call me (back). I have some ideas that could solve what I've heard are your problems with the script and the budget. I've called you fourteen times, KK. I've put a lot into this movie. A phone call back isn't asking too much, is it?

Olivia

Date: January 21, 1999
From: OliviaHunt@usol.com
To: Katrina_KylerRoss@Universalpictures.com

Subj: A warning

Dear KK,

I guess you weren't in film school the day they taught that lesson about being nice to everyone just in case one day you fall from your totally undeserved place of power and need the plebes to help you out, because if you had learned that, how could you have pulled the plug on this movie without having the guts or decency to call and tell me yourself? As a former colleague, I just wanted to tell you that it's too bad you missed that class, because you'll be falling real soon. You're such a spineless fraud you'll be out before the summer movies are.

Oh, don't be so shocked. You think I really care if you like me?
See you down here on the bottom,
Olivia Hunt

January 22, 1999
Madrid–Cincinnati

Dear Tina,

I'm flying home. I still can't believe *Don Quixote* is really dead. After all that! All those sixteen-hour days, all that money, all those people dashing around to find locations, actors, camera crews, to build sets in time for the start date. The studio's $100 million remake of *Rudolph the Red-Nosed Reindeer* was trounced by Paramount's *Christmas with the Numwits,* and after a lousy summer and fall they weren't in the mood for a $50 million throw of the dice — especially when they hated the new draft, the one Johnny and I rushed to write. Johnny wouldn't shoot the one they liked ("It's *Man of La Mancha* without the music!"). Josh was the picture's only true fan, and KK-the-Dim reportedly said, You call this a movie? There are no cars, no sex, no effects — why would anyone go? Howard Trammel said, I'm sorry, Olivia, there are just too many reasons *not* to make this movie. They also heard that Terry Gilliam's *Don Quixote* might be coming alive. So you see what I was up against. It's hard to get so close and not make it. It makes me wonder both if there was something more I could have done and if I was a fool to try in the first place.

At least you and I are talking again. Those two weeks when we weren't were terrible. Even though we don't actually see each other very much — something I hope we can correct this year — you're one of the most important people in my life, Tina, and the idea of losing your friendship made me miserable. I hope you meant what you said — that the fertility drugs were making you hysterical — and that you understand I was just lashing out, trying to defend my weird romance by attacking your enviably healthy one. I know you were trying to help. You've watched Michael and me dance around for a while now. I think I was trying to explain that maybe not everyone *has* to get somewhere, or to the same place, that love can have different shapes, take different journeys.

But even I am not happy about this new shape. You asked if this means we've really, finally broken up. It's hard to break up when you're not together. In some ways, things won't change that much:

we'll still have words, which are what we've lived on for a while now. Don't worry, I know that's not a relationship. And I know I'm ready for a real one. I'm tired of eating alone. Among other things.

We've hit some turbulence over Newfoundland; I have to put the tray table up. I'm glad you're there again. I missed you. And I hope hope hope the in-vitro is successful this month.

Lots of love,
Olivia

❧

January 24, 1999
Seat 4A, Cincinnati–L.A.

Dear Michael,

As you can see by that single-digit seat number, I am enjoying first class for what could well be my last time. Unless of course I become a stewardess. I know the takeoff speech by heart, I know the safety procedures. And I need a job. Universal pulled the plug on *Quixote*. I didn't call you about twenty-six times. Even though you said I can still call you, that nothing's decided, that Pocahontas is just someone you're "dating," still, I thought I should try to break this habit of reaching for you when the news is good or bad. This desire to share the story of my life with you. When I hung up with Universal at three A.M. last week (they refuse to call at the *beginning* of their day, when it's only six P.M. in Madrid), I looked around my grand hotel room and felt déjà vu. It was like that time in London when my first movie collapsed on me. Except then I did call you, and you said, I wish I was there.

Oh, what could you do? I asked, bitterly blowing my nose.

Talk to you.

It was exactly what I longed for, both times, a rainy afternoon in bed with you talking, a dinner at Scalini's, talking, walking through Green Park, talking. Men think women want diamonds, but what they really want is someone to talk to.

Even Ed is learning that. When I flew in from Madrid on Friday he said, Let's have dinner together. I don't think I've eaten dinner alone with my father since — well, I can't remember when. A sandwich here and there. I was nervous; I thought he might have some more goddamned bad news. He assured me that he didn't. He just wanted to have dinner with me. I then wondered if this was something my mother had put him up to. (She later insisted it was his idea.) He said, Anywhere you want. I chose Lucky's because of their good jukebox and rib-eye. We shared a half carafe of red — that's all. He said he's been "experimenting" with drinking only "a little" red wine, nothing else. He was getting heavy, he said. It's hard, sometimes. But I'm sticking to it.

Good. I guess.

Your sister appreciates it. Eleanor, too.

I bet.

What's that mean?

Just that I'm sure they do. Jeez.

We ate in silence for a few minutes and then he said, Too bad about your movie.

Yeah.

Can you get someone else to make it?

Nah. It's period. Foreign. The lead's over twenty-one years old. It's pointless.

I'm proud of you, anyway.

Tears flashed up fast. I had to look down at my steak so he wouldn't see. What for? I asked. I didn't get it made.

You tried. That's a lot. More than I could do.

Trying's what losers do. It's another failure —

— No, it isn't, honey. It's a step. Toward another movie. You learned things. You'll use what you learned on the next one.

Next one? There's not going to be a next one. I'm going to be a stewardess. I always wanted to be a stewardess. I love those uniforms.

He tried to cheer me up, but I was like steel. He slid a stack of lottery cards in front of me. Here. Fill these out.

Now I really feel desperate.

It's fun. Go on.

You lose every week. How fun is that?

I like planning what I'd do if I won. Just thinking about having all that money makes me happy. I could buy all you kids big houses. And your mother a cottage right on Lake Michigan. I'd buy myself a sixty-foot sailboat and a Jaguar. I'd buy Maddie — he opened his hand, at a loss, because even a SuperBall jackpot couldn't buy that, and said instead — Anything. I love picturing your mother's face when I tell her I won. He smiled, imagining what it'd feel like to be a hero to his wife, to be the man he dreamed of being. He tapped his fingers on the table. Nina Simone was singing "My Baby Don't Care" on the jukebox. Listen, he said.

We talked about jazz — he knows so much; he was a real devotee when he was young — and the beat was so peppy it was just about breaking through my gloom. Then he insisted I dance with him. How many chances do you get to dance with your old man? He was already shuffling around on the smooth linoleum without me, snapping his fingers like Dean Martin. Okay, okay, I said.

We danced to the next song, too, because it was another one of his favorites, and the next, and that's when it dawned on me. These were Ed's jukebox selections. Our old plumber Red and his wife, Shirley, were celebrating their forty-fifth anniversary, so they joined us, and it was a good night and I forgot about things for a while.

Maddie's doing really well. Released early from rehab. (I think Mercy was afraid of what she might do next.) When we got to her place, she said she had a surprise for me. We were in her kitchen. She was sitting in her black wheelchair. She said, Okay, here it is. And she stood up. And took three steps toward me. Without any help, without a walker or a cane, just on her own, three careful, deliberate steps. She cracked her crooked smile and said, Pretty good, huh? It was incredible; the therapists said her improvement has been remarkably fast. Later that night I gave her a bath. After nearly three months in the hospital, where there's only a handheld shower, she was dying for a deep hot bath; she wanted to feel her whole body immersed in warm water. The tub was too shallow and difficult for Maddie to manage, so Ed got a plastic horse trough deep enough for her to sit in. In the laundry room, I placed candles on the table and covered the washer and dryer in pink sheets to make it as spa-like as possible. Bobby undressed her and set her on a kid's chair in the deep water and then went upstairs to watch the Red Wings game with Ed. I squeezed the sponge. Gardenia-scented water dripped down her back.

This feels amazing. I never thought I could feel this way about a bath, she said. I caressed her shoulder with the sponge. This is so nice of you, Livvie.

It's nice to do.

So what are you going to do about *Don Quixote*?

Nothing. There's nothing more to do.

Aren't there other studios or investors you can go to?

Maddie, leave it alone, okay? I'm done.

There must be other places. You just have to —

You don't know what you're talking about.

Don't I?

No.

I gently lifted her bad arm, the one that just hangs there, and washed the armpit. We were quiet. A sullenness hung between us. Later Bobby came down and lifted her out of the trough and wrapped her in a warm towel from the dryer. As he carried her away she looked at me and said, It's weird you're such a bad loser and I'm not, and you're the one with everything. It's always been like that. You make me sick, actually.

That hurt. Because it was true. You go so long without anyone pointing out your failings, when they do, it knocks the hell out of you. Especially when it comes from your little sister, who you want to look up to you.

Over breakfast the next morning I explained how hard a movie like *Don Quixote* is to get made. Even Orson Welles failed. She said as long as I knew I'd done everything I could, then I wouldn't be sorry later. I wouldn't wonder.

You have to know you gave it your best shot. It's all anyone can do. If you'd just listened to some Bruce Springsteen you'd know that, Livvie. She sang for me: *We made a promise we swore we'd always remember, no retreat, baby, no surrender . . .* She laughed. God, I'm tone-deaf now, too, aren't I?

I couldn't believe this was Maddie talking. The spoiled brat who always had to have her way. But as I write this I realize it's not so surprising. Her way has always been to fight for what she wanted or believed in; it just used to be for simpler things, like which sitcom to watch.

So *naturally,* Maddie thinks I should get my ass out there and kick your little girl out, but I think you should do that yourself — or not, it's your call. She says I'm too proud. I said it's honorable and decent of me to let you have your time with this wonderful girl-poet. Then, when you realize how much you miss me and that you want me more than her, you'll give her the heave-ho and give me a call. It's not like you don't know me, is it? It's not like you're lacking any vital information. Wouldn't you find begging incredibly unattractive? I've never liked it myself, even when it's being done by someone else. All I know is I'd like to see you and have that big talk we never had over Christmas. I could come out for a weekend. I could stay at a motel if your place is too crowded. I'll be back in the Century City basement if you want to call me sometime when your squaw is out picking berries.

Your old sweetheart,
Olivia

January 27, 1999
Los Angeles

Dear Dad,

Re: My progress as a killer

The first call I made when I got back to my Tinseltown bunker was to Eric Moriarty, the president of Warner Brothers. Remember

WB was the other studio that wanted to make *Don Quixote*? Moriarty, like the entire town, had heard about our demise. Good news is, they're still interested in making it; bad news is they still don't want Johnny. The director WB wanted last fall, Fred Schepisi, is no longer available; Bob Zemeckis and Ron Howard were looking for movies, and Moriarty had heard there might be cast trouble on Ben Wilcox's movie at Fox. If I could get any of these guys — and keep my cast, and the budget to $53 million — he could almost guarantee they'd make it. I didn't want to lose Johnny before I had another director, but the others are all represented by the same agency as Johnny, so it'd be hard to find out if they were interested without Johnny finding out that I was sniffing around to replace him.

That day I was having lunch with Casey Levine, a CAA agent who's been a friend — a real friend — for years. I walked into the Daily Grille and guess who was standing there, waiting for his lunch date? None other than Johnny himself — with Josh. Once again, Johnny looked like he'd just been goosed.

I thought you were in Ohio! He laughed.

If you called me back you'd know I was here.

They were meeting with Andy Malacara, an ICM agent, to discuss financing opportunities. Without me. Without even telling me about it, Dad. Johnny graciously invited me to join them for coffee after my lunch. Which I did. And after talking the situation through with Casey, I was emboldened to do what I probably should have done last fall: I fired Johnny. He seemed confused. I had to remind him that I controlled the rights to the script; he never paid me for his half of the option so legally he didn't have any claim to it. The script we rewrote together I didn't want anyway. There would have been some added delight in firing him in front of Josh, but I'm not that advanced as a killer (yet), so I asked Josh to give Johnny and me a moment alone, and that was pleasurable in itself. I'm not sure if this gamble will pay off. Now I need $50 million *and* a director by March or it'll be too late to make the movie this year. At least it was fun firing him. Johnny said the words *lawyer, buncha bullshit,* that kind of thing, which is understandable, but they don't worry me. It just comes with the job, doesn't it?

Your little killer,
Olivia

.

January 27, 1999

Casey Levine
CAA
9830 Wilshire Blvd.
Beverly Hills, California 90212

Re: *Don Quixote*

Dear Casey,

Thanks again for lunch today and for your generous offer for me to take care of your place for a while. I spoke with Christy, who's going to meet me there tonight with the keys.

I'm also really grateful for your advice, which I followed. So now I need a director — and fast. I lose Robin June 21 to *Mrs. Doubtfire Returns,* so we need to start shooting by March 30.

Enclosed is what I think is the best draft of the script, which, fortunately, I control.

What about Rob Reiner?

Talk to you soon,
Olivia Hunt

Encl: *Don Quixote*, Sept. 17, 1998, draft

—•—•—

January 27, 1999

Ursula Jackson
Universal Pictures Marketing
Universal City, California 91608

Re: Oscar Videos / Hospital screenings

Dear Ursula,

I hope you're well. You heard about *Don Quixote*. I don't have the greatest luck at Universal, do I? Hopefully you'll be the exception and help me with this program my sister would like to launch.

As you may have heard, my sister, Madeline, was diagnosed with leukemia recently and has spent months in the hospital. Cully Davis (our line producer on *Quixote*) was generous enough to send her his Oscar tapes. Madeline shared them with the other patients and came up with this great idea: each studio could send a set of Academy tapes to hospitals across the country for their long-term-care patients.

If you've ever had a long hospital stay, you know how grim it can be. You can imagine how great it'd be to watch a first-run movie now and then. Even start an Oscar pool with the other "inmates."

My mother, Eleanor Hunt, is helping Madeline with this. She wrote to you a few weeks ago. I'd really appreciate it if you could give her a call and share your thoughts with her. It's a wonderful idea that could really use your support.

Thanking you in advance,
Olivia Hunt

January 27, 1999

David Vekich

WMA

151 El Camino Drive

Beverly Hills, California 90212

<u>Via fax</u>

Re: *Don Quixote*

Dear David,

Thanks for offering to help me find financing for *Don Quixote*. I look forward to meeting the Colombians next week.

I'm a big fan of Michael Bay's work — *Bad Boys, Armageddon* — who can argue with that box office, huh? — and his idea of updating the story, setting it in the American Southwest, making Quixote and Sancho men in their early twenties riding Harleys to an Eminem concert that turns into a terrorist hostage situation, is really hard to resist. But it would require an entirely new script and cast, and I was trying to get *this* movie made, not secure another development deal. Thanks anyway.

I'll let you know how it goes with the Colombians. You're sure they made their fortune in *cable,* right?

Sincerely,
Olivia Hunt

January 27, 1999

Rachel Wolff
CAA
9830 Wilshire Blvd.
Beverly Hills, California 90212

Via fax

Re: *Don Quixote* / Spike Lee

Dear Rachel,

It was great catching up with you today. And congratulations again on having twins!

You know I'm a huge fan of Spike's, and I love the idea of making an African American *Don Quixote,* set perhaps in the South, or the urban North, Detroit, maybe. It's a great idea, but it would require an entirely new script and cast, and I was trying to get *this* movie made, not secure another development deal. Thanks anyway, and I hope I'll find something else for Spike soon.

Sincerely,
Olivia Hunt

January 30, 1999
Los Angeles

Dear Michael,

I found this box in the trunk. It doesn't look like much to me, but you might be more attached to these tube socks, sketch pads, and pocket wrenches than I am. This should be the last of your stuff. It's funny how I haven't wanted to send it. As if all this junk were a part of you and this is another kind of good-bye.

I'm also sending you the mahogany clock from that weird antique store in Maine, because you always remembered to wind it (the key is taped to the bottom) and I'm tired of lugging it around. Yes, I had to move *again*. My previous benefactor, Mr. Lee Hassler, needed his office back, having suffered from the vicissitudes of the film industry himself, and I was lucky enough to be lunching with my friend Casey when he mentioned that he had moved into his new house in Malibu before his place in the Hills had sold and he was uneasy with it sitting empty. And here I sit in this Normandy mansion high above the flickering lights of Hollywood. It's a beautiful, comfortable place (they left the furniture) but not my own; every night I feel like an impostor walking into someone else's living room. It reminds me of the summer Mad and I cleaned out estates for my dad. First we'd collect anything sentimental — photos, wedding rings, letters — in case an heir was eventually located.

A dress could have sentimental value, Maddie said. How do you know what's important to the person?

The person died intestate, my father said. They gave up their vote.

In the stale, hot house I would rifle through some dead woman's closet, underwear drawer, every secret hiding place we could imagine. I felt bad doing it. Like a thief violating some lonely person's privacy. I imagined some stranger doing this to me one day, some lawyer's daughter rummaging through my rose-scented hosiery hoping to discover a velvet ring box or a creased envelope swollen with G.E. stocks. Maddie once found, in the pocket of a mink coat, a letter that solved a long-forgotten local murder.

I pitied the dead people for having no one who cared about them and their stuff, but what really killed me were the photo albums, painstakingly constructed with hundreds of black-and-white and color snapshots arranged and tucked into corners, the evidence of unique but totally ordinary lives of birthday parties, Christmases, and Hawaiian vacations that had once been photo worthy and that now meant nothing to no one. When I found one I'd sit in the closet under the row of clothes and flip the cardboard pages, trying to figure out which skier, which picnicker in Bermudas, which New Year's reveler was now dead in the morgue, and sometimes the only way I could tell would be by matching the tweed jacket or paisley polyester dress in the picture with the one hanging pointlessly above me. I kept a notebook called Dead People's Stuff and made up stories about these people based on what they'd left behind. One woman had a closet full of toilet paper, drawers of never-worn panty hose, and enough rolls of aluminum foil to make a spaceship, and not one single photograph anywhere; another Deceased, as my father called them, had a shoe box of dog-eared love letters from someone who was not his wife, and I made up a story about that, about where those two women were now, and why no one cared anymore about a love affair that once might have changed the lives they had left to live. Maybe one day some lawyer's daughter will read this letter and wonder what happened, where our lives took us, and why. On nights like this, writing to you from another stranger's desk, everything uncertain again, it does feel that way, that life takes us like a riptide, where one minute you're close to shore and the next you're not, you're way out, and the people on the beach are waving to you as they get smaller and farther away.

Olivia

❖

January 31, 1999
Hollywood Hills, California

Maddo,

Look at this place! You must come out soon. These pictures don't capture how HUGE and beautiful it is. So what it's not mine. There's a steam bath and a Jacuzzi in the master bathroom, and see that little waterfall into the pool? That's hot water overflowing from the hot tub above it on the hillside. There are flowers every-where — bougainvillea and roses and jasmine. The kitchen speaks for itself (Victory oven!!) and it's just begging to be used by some-one like you, who knows how. And how 'bout that BIG-SCREEN TV, huh??? Please come out soon — before you (and hopefully I) — go back to work.

Speaking of houses . . . I've already apologized to you and Bobby about Dad. I know I promised not to tell ANYone you wanted to buy that house on Monroe. He wasn't supposed to say anything to you, let alone Bobby! I told him not to about a hundred times. I can't help it if Dad and Bobby had a few drinks together and then Dad let it slip. I was only trying to see if, *in the event* that you and your husband decided you wanted to buy that place, we could help you with the down payment. Bobby should lighten up. How can he think he has "no choice now"? That now he has to go into debt to buy a house you can't afford? No one said he has to buy the house. Dad's just being generous. And he's getting enough flak from Mom for it, so tell Bobby to relax.

But I am sorry if it's caused you trouble at home. I was just trying to help.

Lots of love,
Livvie

P.S. I've got miles on United you and Bobby can use.

February 1, 1999
Hollywood Hills

Dear Tina,

I'm glad you vicariously enjoy my life as much as I enjoy yours — and I mean that. Sometimes when I'm eating my takeout alone, I jealously dream about your dinner routine: the family descends on the kitchen, frantic for food; the TV news is the soundtrack; you're heating Spaghetti-Os for Ryan, grabbing some melba toast for yourself because you're perpetually (and, may I say, needlessly) dieting; Stephen comes in, his tie loosened, and he grabs a fistful of your ass as he pinches a tiny meatball out of the pot, swearing when it burns his fingers. I want to be there. In that picture. Part of a family getting ready to eat together. Part of a family, I guess is what I'm starting to dream of. I was so eager to get out of my childhood family that I never imagined I'd want to make my own, but here I am, longing for that messy, joyful chaos. I know you might think, I'll trade! But you wouldn't, really, would you? Even tonight, when I went to the premiere of the new Harrison Ford movie. It sounds glamorous, but here's what it was really like . . .

I was there with this agent with dyed-black blown-dry hair and oily skin, named Russell. Men should not dye their hair, they should not not not. Maybe there's a way to do it well, but it usually looks like they washed their hair in black paint, which basically says, I'm vain and cheap — real attractive attributes. You may wonder why I was with this greasy-faced bad-dye-job. Well, I thought it was business. He thought it was pleasure. You know where this is going, don't you? Earlier that day I was in his colleague David Vekich's office, discussing other financing opportunities for *DQ* (another studio passed yesterday), when Russell dropped in. David brought Russell up to speed, and while he did I noticed Russell checking out my legs and then smiling at me coyly, boyishly, as if he'd been caught with his hand in his pants: *naughty Russ.* He had to run, but Russell had an idea for me. What about the Harrison Ford premiere tonight? You gonna be there? he asked.

I wasn't planning on it (I wasn't invited).

Well, come with me; we'll talk about it at the party.

If old *Quixote* wasn't on the critical list I might have said, No, a meeting in your office would be better. If I didn't need to remind people that I'm still in the business, I might have said no. But I didn't, so I can't blame anything but my own ambition for the pickle I got into later. But first I had to panic about what I'd wear, since I had just worn my last "casual chic" ensemble to the *Magnolia* premiere, and money was too tight to buy anything new. This party would be full of hip, successful, confident people casually wearing $3,000 worth of clothes (e.g., $200 white Helmut Lang T-shirts and $1,200 Dolce & Gabbana skirts) and most of these people would not know me, so my outfit would have to identify me: it had to say I'm hip and successful and confident, too, and above all it had to say I'm not from the Midwest and I'm not my mother, who shops at Talbot's. Clearly far too many things for any single outfit to say. I slipped on low-slung black pants, my only pair of good shoes, those Manolo Blahniks I bought four years ago, and a blue gray silk T-shirt.

The movie was godawful, but I said it was incredible because Russell represents the director. The minute we were outside he grabbed my elbow and pushed me like a lawn mower over to the Armand Hammer Museum, where the party was being held. A red carpet, taped down with silver duct tape, stretched from the door of the Westwood Theater three blocks to the museum. Inside there was the usual mix of stars and jumbo shrimp. I know I sound jaded, Tina, but after you do these things once a week for a few years, how can you *not* be? It's like going to the office Christmas party every week, only it's covered by *ET* and CNN because Ben Affleck and Susan Sarandon are going to be there. Even my first few times seemed odd to me: you get dressed up, sometimes in black tie, park in an underground lot, and walk into a mall to watch a movie, while news cameras follow you as if walking itself were a newsworthy event.

This one was pretty well attended: besides the stars from the movie, there were lots of A-list names walking around, like Brad and Jennifer, Jack, Warren, and Steve — yes, Tina, *that* Steve. As he walked by, he smiled at me and I smiled back. I still wonder what happened and what I was supposed to do. . . . Oh, well.

So tell me about this money you think you can get for *Don Quixote,* I said to Russell once we were seated in a banquette. Russell's hungry eyes searched the room. He downed his double vodka and signaled for another.

For what?

My movie, *Don Quixote.*

Please. He laughed.

Renée Zellweger walked in with a very cute guy. I felt Russell's hand on my thigh. As I removed it, he said, Radiant. It's like there's a fucking lightbulb up your ass.

Nice, huh? This was Russell's idea of seduction. I had to head him off before he believed that I had led him on and then rejected him, before he could knead my right breast and then call me a dick tease when I slapped him for it. I decided to tell him that I was in love. It doesn't always work — the married ones say, Perfect, so am I — but for those colleagues looking for wives it usually slows things down. They say being in love makes you radiant, I said, removing his hand from my *lower* shoulder.

You're in love?

Yeah.

What?

What?

That's not how you were sold to me.

What do you mean, sold to you?

Vek said you're available. Goddamn, that fucking asshole, I'll kill him. This was a setup.

No, he just misunderstood —

212

He set me up to look like a fool. You're in on it, too, aren't you?

I didn't want to cause trouble for Vekich — or this guy, who might still be the gatekeeper to $50 million — so I said, I'm in love with someone, but . . . he's not in love with me, which is probably why Vek was confused.

Oh, that's terrible. . . . That's so sad. You must be crushed. I know what that's like. I just went through the most hideous divorce. I was destroyed. You must feel terrible.

I'm managing, I said, removing his hand again.

I can see the pain in your eyes.

— Russell, let's talk about this money for *Quixote*. What company is it?

TLC is what you need, my lady.

TLC? Who are they?

Tender loving care? You've heard of it?

No —

TLC is what you need to get over this idiot who dumped you. TLC from me, you silly little vixen. It's the only thing that works. A new man. Then he roared. He roared, Tina, like a kid imitating a lion — roaarr! — and then he nuzzled my neck. I jerked away. You're so jumpy! He laughed.

Look, do you know someone who might want to make *Quixote* or not?

I'm trying to help you and all you want to talk about is work, work, work. I'm seducing you, for chrissake!

I'm flattered, Russell, but like I told you, it's just too soon; I'm still in love.

And I'm telling you, the only way to get over that asshole —

— is with another one?

Exactly, the lion roared again, this time pulling me into him. I got up, realizing I was the one who'd been set up. Russell followed saying, I can't wait, either, baby. He grabbed my elbow again, insisting on walking me to my car. I'm a gentleman, he said, giggling. This town isn't safe. This town is full of sharks! He was drunk, and right when I was thinking the night would end in criminal court, Renée and the cute guy appeared in our path. He turned out to be Ben Wilcox, the director of *Catherine the Great* and *Lies of Silence* (really good if you haven't seen them). He said, Hey, Russ, do you know Renée?

Russell dropped my elbow guiltily and redirected his ardor toward the star. Renée, you look gorgeous!

Later, I thanked Ben for rescuing me. He said — in one of those English accents that can melt a girl's heart in just two syllables — You looked like you needed it. He was cute, Tina: blue lashy eyes, brown hair, kind of a less nervous Hugh Grant. I think we flirted with each other, although, as you can see, in Hollywood flirting is a tool used for many purposes, so I didn't take his charm personally. We talked briefly about his jungle action pic; I'd heard they were having trouble finding the male lead, but Ben said they were in negotiations with a star. Too bad, I said. Warners was hoping you'd jump off that and onto *Don Quixote*. I nibbled some shrimp and said good-night, and walked the dark, empty streets of Westwood to my car, listening to my heels click against the concrete, the sound of a woman hurrying home, alone.

Love,
Olivia

Date: February 2, 1999
From: OliviaHunt@usol.com
To: David_Vekich@Williammorrisagency.com

Vek,

Couple things:

1. That was no Colombian *cable* company.
2. Tell your colleague Russell if he finds me that $50 million, I won't press charges. He'll know what I'm talking about. You probably do, too.

All the best,
Olivia Hunt

February 8, 1999
Los Angeles

Dear Mom,

I think Maddie's having a great time out here. (She is looking so good! I can't believe how thick her hair already is, and that short shag really suits her.) Today we went to my friend Casey's new place in Malibu, a stunning Frank Lloyd Wright on a bluff overlooking the sea, which somehow seems even bigger and bluer from the vantage of a $7 million estate.

It was a beautiful day. The beach house (not the main house) is a small white clapboard nestled under pines and palms tucked under the bluff, and the beach was all ours: no people, no other houses, we could have been on a desert island in the South Pacific. Casey's housekeeper laid out a big lunch for us: there were cut pineapples, mangoes, strawberries, all kinds of vegetables, and roast chicken and cheese. The wind was low and the air warm enough for Maddie to walk a few feet into the water with her cane, Bobby at her side. I watched from a striped chaise. I wish you could have seen her, Mom; she really looked good, just horsing around, splashing Bobby with her cane, teasing me. She made donuts in the sand with Casey's golf cart and looked happier than I've seen her in ages. I think this trip has been good for her; she seems to be getting stronger every day. We haven't done much besides take Jacuzzis and lie in the sun. She and Bobby seem a little tense with each other, but I guess that's understandable. She snaps at him and he's stormed off more than once. I haven't been able to get her to talk to me about it. Do you know what's going on?

Later that night I was changing for bed when from the upstairs window I saw them skinny-dipping in the pool. Maddie was floating on her back, and Bobby had his arms beneath her but he wasn't holding her, so she could feel the wonderful weightlessness of floating without the fear of sinking. I imagine flying must be like that. The moonlight shimmered on the water around Maddie's body like a silver halo, and I wished you were there to see it, Mom, because you'd have felt, if only for a moment like when a breeze passes through you, that everything is going to be fine.

Maddie is moving around downstairs. She wants to teach me how to make chicken cacciatore. Tomorrow we're doing Disneyland, which fills my heart with joy. Yes, I'll make sure she doesn't overdo it.

Love from Los Angeles,
Olivia

Tina,

Greetings from the Grand Canyon. A mad, mad, Mad idea. She put Bobby on a plane home, and we rented a red Mustang and promptly started fighting. It's been fun except for all the bad music she likes (still!). We finally agreed: whoever's driving controls the music. With only one arm, Mad drives like a drunk. She bobs and weaves onto the shoulder and makes these huge loopy rights. Already killed some cattle. Pulled over for going 90 mph. Flirted her way out of it. Yesterday we parked at the edge of the canyon and watched the sun go down, staring at eternity. She said, You have to believe in something, Olivia. I said, Erosion? She said, You don't fool me.

Getting our kicks,
Olivia

◆-◆-◆

2/12/99

Dear Jimbo,

How do you like this postcard? Mad's choice. She knows how wild you are about cactuses. I'm writing this for Madster, who's driving (really badly) across (what I hope is) northeastern Arizona. She wishes you were here because you're more fun than I am (and you always take her side when we fight, which we've been doing a fair bit of). Oh, she wants you to just guess what I'm always doing?

Talking on the phone. (Not always, how could I fight with her? Or help her drive? Or write this letter?) She knows I'm trying to produce a major motion picture, but it's always something, isn't it? (She's never happy, is she?) You see why we need you. Besides being good company.

Her Royal Madness said to write these words: we're going to Dixon because Michael and Olivia are going to get married. (Totally false. Michael doesn't even know we're coming. As he's now dating some photographer-slash-poet, this is more like an ambush.) Mad says don't listen to anything I say.

We hope you're not working too hard and that all your girls are fine. We miss you. Next summer we're all taking a Winnebago trip again; put it on your calendar.

Love to you & Sarah & Soph & Nell,

Madeline (and Olivia)

2/13/99

Dear Jim,

I'm <u>not</u> writing this for Maddie, because she's never speaking to me again. She's stuck to it for the last 200 miles, so it's finally nice and quiet in this car. Did you know that Mad believes in alien abductions? We were staying in a roadside motel outside Winslow, Arizona, and she said, This is the kind of place where it happens, where they take you, do experiments and stuff, then put you back in your bed. (She thinks this is what happened to Buster; remember when one day he started watching the five o'clock news? And he'd howl if you changed the channel? I couldn't come up with a better explanation myself.) In the morning I had a little red circle on my stomach and I acted scared, like maybe that's what had happened to me. Look, the window is open and we didn't leave it open, did we, Mad? She looked worried — and then I started laughing because I was only teasing. It's not like I let her believe it for more than thirty seconds. Anyway, just in case you didn't know this, never bring up alien abductions around her.

More from New Mexico,
Olivia

⬥⬥⬥

February something,1999
New Mexico

Dear Mom,

Maddie's napping, so I thought I'd send you a quick note from the Eagle Guest Ranch in Datil, New Mexico. After getting seriously lost for a few hours last night (our path swings as widely as and in accordance with her moods), we wound up within striking distance of a place called Pie Town, home of the Pie-O-Neer Café, which dates back to 1922 and whose motto is, "Life goes on and days go by. That's why you should stop for pie." So we did. Blueberry for her, peach for me. Maddie bought us red baseball caps with the motto on them, and the owner took our picture in front of his place. Mad said, See? Aren't you glad we got lost? I think she's having a good time. I'm trying to be agreeable as much as possible, but, man, she has some moods, doesn't she? I know some are medically induced (yes, she's taking all the pills) and some are reality induced. Yesterday, getting ready for bed, she had a hard time undoing her shirt and she broke down and cried. I started to help her and she slugged me. She lifted up her left arm, which hangs like a dead snake, and said, Look at this. They might as well cut it off. I can't have kids now.

Of course you can. Why can't you?

I can't even get out of my own fucking shirt.

Maddie, people with handicaps have kids, even quadra —

Shut up, Olivia. Just shut up.

That night I woke up and she had the windows open and the blankets off and she was wet with sweat. It's so hot in here, she said. I'm boiling.

Her left foot and hand seize up in spasms when she gets anxious. With her right hand she was uncurling the clenched fingers of her left fist, and her foot was shaking. Her eyes were dark and scared. I threw off my blankets and said I was hot, too. I filled the brown plastic ice bucket with water and got a washcloth. I wiped the sweat off her body and I thought of you, Mom, and all the times you did that for me when I was a kid sick with the flu or strep. The big yellow baking bowl filled with cool water and a few ice cubes floating in it. The turquoise-colored washcloth, and your tenderness.

We miss you,
Olivia & Maddo

February 14, 1999
Ojo Caliente Springs

Dear Dad,

Re: Our projected lottery winnings

The New Mexico state lottery is worth $83 million tomorrow. Maddo and I just spent the last three hours carving up $83 million, and you are going to make out so great if we win, Dad; we're going to shower you with yachts and cars and cool gadgets from Sharper Image, for all the times you would have spent your winnings on us. Tell Mom we have a few big-ticket items set aside for her, too.

We're having a most excellent trip, especially since the Mad One can't complain about my cell phone anymore. I was wheeling her out of Earl's Diner in Gallup last night when she made me stop to give a panhandler some money and guess what he did to thank us? Held us up! With a gun! It didn't look real, but we didn't risk it and I handed over my phone and our cash, which wasn't much. She was furious and she told him so. I thought he was going to shoot her just to shut her up. I said, See? See what happens when you try to help everybody?

We're going to stay here for a couple days and soak in the mineral springs and Mad is going to have many milagro wraps (don't ask; they're just supposed to be miraculous). It's one of the oldest spas in the country, built sometime in the twenties, and the only place in North America where five different types of hot springs come together in one place. The Anasazi believed that the waters were given to them by their gods after they wept many tears. A

Spanish explorer in 1535 said, "From the effect of the waters upon my men, I am inclined to believe that the waters will do many things that our doctors are not capable of doing." I am so inclined myself.

Last night Maddie fell asleep writing in her journal. As I put it away I couldn't resist peeking at what she'd written. I guess I was hoping to see she was having as good a time with me as I am having with her. But this is what I found:

There will be no leukemia! No fever! No infection!
There will be no leukemia! No fever! No infection!
There will be no leukemia! No fever! No infection!

Pages and pages, from every night, just these three declarations. She looks so good, and seems so herself, I guess I'd forgotten about all that. I hope that on this trip, now and then, she has, too.

Love,
Olivia

February 15, 1999

Eric Moriarty
President of Production
Warner Bros.

Via fax

Re: *Don Quixote*

Dear Eric :

Excuse my handwriting — I'm on the road without my laptop.

Good news: *Mrs. Doubtfire Returns* has been delayed again, so we have more time, but not much, since the weather in Spain gets too hot to shoot in August and we don't have three weeks' of interiors. Bad news: Zemeckis passed, so did Turteltaub, and Wilcox is still on the Fox movie. I'm out to Rob Reiner and Brett Ratner. Any other ideas are obviously welcome.

Don't worry about the Gilliam *Quixote*. I've heard the money isn't real yet, so I'm sure we can get started first.

I'm sorry my cell phone isn't working. I should be back in L.A. on Thursday, and until then messages can be left for me at Ojo Caliente Springs.

Yours,
Olivia Hunt

* * *

2/15/99

Dear Bobby,

Just thought you should know Maddie and I are alive, no thanks to her driving or civic spirit. Did you know you married an ecoterrorist? She saw a guy toss a McDonald's bag out his car window and gave chase, honking like crazy, eventually pulling up alongside him; despite my begging for my life, she screamed at him until he threw an empty beer bottle at her, which luckily shattered on the Mustang windshield instead of her head. We got his license plate number, so he hasn't heard the last from your wife (or the New Mexico state police) yet. I hate to think what she's like at home.

I'm putting her on a plane tomorrow. We can't wait for Michael any longer.

Your sister-in-law,
Olivia

February 16, 1999
Dixon

Dear Maddie,

Okay, things I'll remember from our trip. You better be on that plane working on your list. You can mail it from the airport when you get there.

1. Reading *Don Quixote* to you in the car. (I hope this is on your list, too.) Don't worry, the second half isn't nearly as good.
2. When you finally admitted that you stole my garnet earrings and lost them.
3. Painting your nails red on the edge of the Grand Canyon.
4. Coming over that crest outside Santa Fe and seeing the hillside covered with white windmills. (And yes, yes, we wouldn't have seen them if we hadn't gotten lost. Again.)
5. That Zen thing you told me about opening my fist to the world instead of punching it all the time.
6. Singing Hank Williams's "Jambalaya" one more time (47 times).
7. When you said to that mugger in Gallup, If I could stand up I'd kick your ass.

It's too bad you didn't get me all the way to the altar, but I never really expected that to happen, as much as maybe I secretly hoped it would. Even if Michael had been here, which I *did* expect. I was looking forward to the three of us hanging out a little. I'm going to wait one more day and then I have to head back, too. Especially now that I might have a director for *DQ*.

I hope you had as good a time as I did.

Love,
Livia

◆◆◆

February 16, 1999

Ben Wilcox
c/o Four Seasons Hotel
300 S. Doheny Dr.
Los Angeles, California 90048

<u>Via fax</u>

Dear Ben,

It was great talking to you today. Again, I'm sorry your movie fell apart. Seems to be going around. Luckily you weren't into preproduction yet — and luckily for me, you might now be able to revive *Don Quixote*, which I've asked CAA to send to you.

Warner's only problem with the script is the ending, which seems to have troubled readers since the seventeenth century. Some ideas are attached.

The other problem is (as ever) the budget. We could reduce the number of days if we cut the Sheep scene and Sancho's island sequence without, in my opinion, damaging the story. We need to shave another $750,000 before Lowenstein will green-light this. Some of my notes have that goal in mind.

I'll be back in L.A. this weekend if you want to talk before the meeting next week. I hope we're working together soon.

Sincerely,
Olivia Hunt

◦─◦─◦

February 19, 1999
High above Arizona

Madster,

I'm flying back to L.A. Michael finally called. He was away, winter camping with Willow. They caught some two-foot trout on the San Juan. I said, Gosh, that's wonderful. (I have one word for winter camping: *why?*)

As we slid into a booth at Dan's Café he said, I can't believe you did this. It's not like you. We met there because he wanted to be sure we really talked. We usually forget to do that — or agree not to. Who doesn't prefer pleasure over pain? For example, making love is much nicer than hearing about what a lousy girlfriend I turned into, always working or always tired from working, avoiding true intimacy (will someone tell me what *is* "true intimacy" for godsake?), unwilling to commit, or submit, whatever. Eating a good dinner, watching a movie, going for a walk, all these things are so much more pleasurable than hearing Michael say I changed into someone he wasn't sure he loved anymore.

He said, I never felt that important to you. I was about to say, Then why'd you stick around? when I remembered your counsel,

Maddie: don't be defensive or argumentative. Be open. *Open my fist. Open my fist.* I said, I'm sorry. You were always important. And that was true.

He had a lot to get off his chest. The diner did not serve alcohol, so there was no softening the blows. I swirled cold french fries in ketchup as he reviewed my first big fuckup, that stupid affair, and then ordered another diet Coke to get me through my second, my refusal to talk about it, and I ate a slice of double chocolate cake à la mode to help me bear the account of life in L.A. with Olivia: how for the last year he felt like I'd put him on hold, and then when I didn't come out for Christmas that feeling came back rather sharply. Just as I braced for some nasty pièce de résistance or possibly the butter knife between my ribs, Michael said, But I love you, Livia. And maybe we both just screwed up back then. But the only way to know if that was just a bad patch is to spend time together again. To live together. Here. Now. Not forever. But now.

Here? What about *Don Quixote*?

There'll always be a movie or another company with fifty million, another job around the corner, another meeting with —

Michael, I only have another few weeks and then we lose Robin.

Then it'll be Eddie Murphy.

Make Sancho black?

He didn't laugh. I want to make at least one movie, I said. I've put this much time into it, I can't walk away now —

Then you'll want to build on that. They'll throw more money at you.

We could divide time; lots of people do that.

We did that. It didn't work, remember?

He was referring to the affair. He didn't go further. I thought about what he was asking me to do. Okay, I said. I move here. What do I do all day?

You could write; you've always wanted to —

Oh, please. Who doesn't? Everyone's writing a screenplay; that waiter probably has a stack at home.

Look at your letters. No one even *writes* letters anymore.

I changed the subject to Willow.

I told you. She's a friend. Who's here. I want to be with someone, Livia. I want to have a family. He sighed and then looked at me. We'll figure it out. You can't know everything is going to be perfect before you commit to it. Sometimes you just have to have a little faith. You just jump. You'll be okay.

The light was unflattering in that diner. I wondered how I looked to him. You can never really know how you look to someone, can you? I hoped he was having as hard a time staying away from my lips as I was staying away from his. He looked to me like he always did, beautiful and wild. I still liked just looking at him. Which made all this talking feel pointless. In my subverbal heart it was all simply decided by the way he looked. I couldn't speak.

That's it? Nothing more to say?

Give me a minute.

I'm gonna take a leak.

I hate that expression.

Really? He laughed and walked away, and I noticed his jeans were looser than usual. When he came back I didn't say much. I tried to remember what you told me to say, but I had that muddle-headed sadness that comes over me like a flu in these situations. In the parking lot the sun stabbed my hot eyes. He put his arm around me and I smelled him — piney turpentine, tobacco, soap, sweat — and I wanted him. At my car he lifted my chin and kissed me, hard, as if it were the punctuation mark to this summit meeting, an exclamation point ! It was urgent, laced with the melancholy of a kiss that we knew could be our last, the desperation of a soldier's parting embrace.

Which is why we ended up back at my motel: it wasn't the *very* last kiss, not yet, anyway. We spent the afternoon in bed, skin against skin, talking and listening to the blizzard blow outside. Later he said he wanted to sketch me. He never has before, you know. I hated the idea, but I heard you saying, Don't be defensive, Livvie. I posed however he asked (and, no, I won't tell you how). Eventually I fell asleep and when I woke up he was curled around me, sleeping.

But come on, what am I going to do in Dixon? You saw this town. Sure, it's adorable. For a few days. For longer if you're a potter or a squirrel, maybe. Sure, I'd like to arise to the sounds of birds singing, make the coffee, walk our two young children to school while Michael works in his sun-drenched studio. I'd like to but. But *then* what?

You're saying give it a chance, Dixon's not forever. But Mad, once you choose to leave Hollywood, they don't let you back in. It's rude, like refusing to taste your hostess's homemade hors d'oeuvres. *We let you on the lot and you don't like it? You want to leave? What are you, nuts?* There is a very short list of approved reasons to leave the business, which (besides death) includes detox, children, and prison time, and the only hope of resurrecting oneself after some such imposed exile is to have made a big enough name for yourself before, so that you can't be forgotten in the six weeks you're gone. (A longer absence and even the mightiest perish.) My career is not what my own mother could call unforgettable. Leaving now means leaving for good. I told Michael I'd give him my answer in a week.

Love you,
Olivia

• • •

February 22, 1999
Los Angeles

Dear Tina,

I'm writing this from my new office. The commute is nothing and the view changes, so I'll never get bored with it. These are just two of the benefits of working out of your car. There are others. No rent. No fluorescent lights. None of that cog-in-a-wheel malaise caused by a maze of offices or gray felt partitioned cubicles. I'm currently parked in the Ralph's lot in Burbank. It's not beautiful — you see the local animal life procuring its next high-caloric meal (the face-lifted and buff-bodied shop at Gelson's and Whole Earth) — but it's convenient. I have a meeting. No, not for the cashier job advertised in the window (though you know what a sucker I am for uniforms) but at Warner Bros., only it's not for another hour, and I needed to roll some calls (is it "rolling" if you're placing the calls yourself?). WB is pretty serious about the movie now that Ben Wilcox wants to direct it. Yes, that English guy who rescued me from the bad dye job; I told you Hollywood is a tiny world. Turns out he, like many directors before him, has always wanted to make *Don Quixote*. If this meeting goes well, I'll be back in Spain next week. From all indications, Warners is going to make the movie, but, as you know, I've been here — and further — before. I'm not sure why it's so hard for me to say it's happening till it actually is. Most people in town don't seem to suffer from — what is this? Pride? Superstition? Pessimism? Producers and directors are constantly saying they're making a movie when they don't even have a script, or that Brad Pitt loves it when he hasn't even read it, etc. They don't seem to be afraid of being found out or disappointed; they're not afraid to look foolish for having believed. Is it gullibility or optimism? Do they truly believe their own hype or is their confidence a form of hype, too, part of what makes the hype become real? Perhaps it's Pascal's wager for producers — I might as well believe — which seems like a hedge to me. It's not honestly believing, it's choosing belief over nonbelief in a game of odds; it's *pretending* you believe, isn't it? Maddie said something about this on our trip, which surprised me. She said being faithful requires choosing what you'll be faithful *to*, what you have faith in; that there is choice involved. Not everyone grows up with faith or wakes up with it one morning. It's how you choose to see things.

Well, applying Maddie's philosophy, then, I choose to be happy you're pregnant (!!!), even though you don't want me to say it yet, not till you're in the safer second trimester; I'm happy now and can't wait till then. Then we'll be happy about that, about the third trimester and fourth and fifth (how many are there?), but now let's be happy about this, that you're pregnant at last! As Maddie said, believing that being happy about something before it's absolutely real will jinx the thing is a recipe for a lot of unhappiness, because something could always go wrong. And you miss out on enjoying the good thing you actually do have. You are pregnant, right now, and after years of trying to be pregnant there's a baby growing inside you, Tina. That's reason enough for joy, for today.

Love,
Olivia

◆◆◆

February 27, 1999
Hollywood Hills

Dear Michael,

This letter is not a stall tactic. It's a way to work out my answer. Maybe I won't even send it. I'll throw it away and just call you once I'm done.

I love you, and I have for so long that my fingertips, my heart, my mind, the marrow of my bones, are suffused with you. You are my first and last thought of every day. While sitting in traffic I wonder where you are. When I see something — a funny headline, a painting, a mountain bike — I think, Michael would love that. When I walk into a hotel room, you walk in behind me and pull me to the bed, and we roll across the quilted satin cover. When I slide a sliver of soap against my calves I remember your long hands on them. When I see a wedding. When my father called to tell me Maddie had leukemia.

You said you never felt important to me. It was hard to hear that. How could you not know? How could you not feel it? Could I have been that bad at loving you? Or could no one love you enough?

I agree the only way to begin again is to be together. But your insistence on Dixon feels wrong. For one thing, it doesn't seem like you. Since we met I've been ambitious and driven, and you've always encouraged me; you've wanted me to thrive. In this way I haven't changed — but maybe what you want has. You might now want something easier, a woman who doesn't work so hard, who lives where you live, a woman for whom *you* are the center of gravity. I could understand that. Yet you said you want me. . . . You know I couldn't be happy there, Michael. Which makes me wonder if there's something else behind your demand.

In Dixon you pressed me for details about that affair; it seems the more it has faded in my memory the bigger it looms in yours. I truly don't remember much, and any explanation will only sound like an excuse, a defense, and there isn't one. I remember I was lonely, needy, craving attention; you hated L.A., how the business had taken over our life and marginalized yours; you weren't working, you weren't happy, and then you weren't even there, long before you actually started going away. The director was someone whose films I'd admired for years. I was a freshman, he was the Brilliant Director, asking me to dinner, asking me to his suite, sending me flowers, asking me to come with him to Paris on the studio jet. I was flattered, I suppose; I didn't feel so insecure anymore. His attention felt like an affirmation of me, a kind of affirmation I was desperate for. But how could I do it to you? I felt terrible about that, so I quickly found a way to justify it, to rationalize what I knew had been weak, what had simply been wrong. I wrapped it in the flag of feminism: I can sleep with a man if I want, no man will tell me not to, no man will ever own me, I like sex as much as any man, it doesn't have to be love and marriage. I told myself it was no one's business, not even yours. It wasn't love, so it had nothing to do with you. When you said it was okay and we didn't talk more about it, I took it as your unspoken forgiveness.

But then you started leaving again and finally didn't come back, because you didn't forgive me and even now, years later, you still haven't. It's easier to blame all this on geography, but I can feel your unburied resentment and I think it's what is behind your insistence on Dixon. It's a test of my devotion, a penance, a sacrifice. I will always regret that affair and the way I treated you, Michael. Although I can't believe that once trust is broken the body of love cannot be healed, I do know the first step is forgiveness, and as long as your pride is more important, we can't start again, and it doesn't matter where.

Maybe I'm way off here. Maybe you just want a quiet life there in New Mexico, with a woman who is happy to follow you. Either way, I don't see how I can move to Dixon. To ask me to give up making movies is to ask me to give up what I do, and if you loved me, and not some idea of me, you wouldn't ask that. I don't want to walk away from this work now, especially not into the arms of a man whose demand feels not out of love, but pride.

I'm going to mail this before I call you and change my mind. As bad as I feel, I think this is right. It must be. You can love someone and not want to share his life with him. Or be able to.

Love,
Olivia

Dear Maddie,

We are so busy that it feels like there's a huge snowball rolling down a hill behind me, getting bigger and bigger and rolling faster and faster, and sometimes I'm in front of it trying to outrun it and sometimes I'm behind it trying to catch up with it before it flattens someone else. I can't believe I've been in Madrid for four weeks already. We've been hiring crew and actors, securing locations, building sets and costumes, reworking the shooting schedule, and still trying to find places to save money. I literally run between my office and Ben's; we wolf down cheese sandwiches in the SUVs, and lately find ourselves working till midnight, at which point I usually have a conference call with Warner Bros. about — what else? — the budget.

So I'll cut to the chase here. Mom said you and Bobby are fighting about buying that house. I read somewhere that buying a house together is even more stressful than getting married. Demanding a divorce before the closing is not a sign of failure, it means you're right on track. And you guys can't even really fight: he can't get mad at you because you're sick, and you can't get mad at him because you depend on him so much. Your trapped fury grows. So I understand all that. This is why you need to play him differently. I think this isn't just about money. It's about control. He doesn't have a lot these days, and you have even less, I know, so you're both trying to feel some, to feel some power over something. Michael once explained retail therapy to me: sometimes you have to buy something that you've been wanting for a long time — in my case, usually a pair of shoes — just to experience the fulfillment of a desire and the expression of control over something. I bet if you let him have all the control, he'll come to the right decision himself, he'll decide to buy that house because as a man, as your husband, he'll want to provide, protect, and make you happy. Let him think it's *his* idea, then he'll like it. This is a maneuver I've learned working with directors. Tina used to tell me to do this with Michael, but I was too proud, "too busy to play those games," and look what happened. It's only now, as I write this, that I realize what an idiot I was at Christmas, when I called Michael and just announced I wasn't coming to New Mexico. Even when he pointed out that I might have talked to him about it first, I basically said, What for? No wonder I'm a single working girl and you're the happily married one. . . . So do as I say, Madeline Anne, not as I do. Try this out on Bobby. Let him say no, we can't afford that house, and no, I do not want your father helping us, either. Then wait. I bet he'll announce his change of heart one morning over breakfast.

Gotta run. Lunch is over and there are five sheep wranglers waiting for me and Cully to interview them. How am I supposed to know a good sheep wrangler from a bad one? I don't even know what questions to ask. Yesterday it was horse wranglers. At least those guys had movie credits, which, combined with their personalities, made it pretty simple.

Love,

Liv

April 6, 1999

Eric Moriarty
President of Production
Warner Bros.

<u>Via fax</u>

Re: Soundtrack; end-titles song

Eric,

As discussed, attached is a list of composers (and their credits) whom we're interested in having do the score. Ben loves Ry Cooder, Eric, but he just doesn't think he's right for this movie.

I also talked to him again last night about Jennifer Lopez, but since she's not playing Dulcinea, Ben really doesn't think she's the best choice for the end-titles song. We'd still like to approach Bob Dylan. I know you asked for a *list* of alternatives to J. Lo, but, as discussed several times now, Bob Dylan seems to be the only name on Ben's list. I know how much you love J. Lo and her current success, and how much you hate Bob Dylan, so this could be another impossible dream of ours, but I bet tonight if you have a beer or a glass of wine in your hot tub and listen to *Blonde on Blonde* or *Blood on the Tracks* you, too, will see why Bob Dylan is considered one of the greatest singer-songwriters of all time and a *brilliant* choice for an end-titles song for this movie.

But in case you're *still* not convinced, you might play some Van Morrison, because — and here I am speaking only for myself and not Ben — I think he'd be an excellent second choice.

I don't need to tell you that time is of the essence here.

Sincerely,
Olivia Hunt

OH:rr
dictated but not read

April 16, 1999
Ritz Hotel, Madrid

Dear Dad,

Re: The money

Just a quick note to say I think it's great what you did for Maddie. I know how long you've been dreaming about that $35 grand and what a comfort it was to know it was there in the backyard, your private stash for private dreams. Like knowing where the nearest exit is. I still can't believe that it was *Mom's* idea. I *swear* I never told her about that money. She must have just seen you out there once. She does know you pretty well, Dad. Jim told me that she was digging it all up when you came home from work! For a minute were you worried that she was going to run off with it?

Maddie's thrilled. As early as I knew I would leave Shawnee Falls, she knew she would stay, and it's great you guys helped her buy her dream house. It is a beauty. And only a block away. It'll be easy to drop in uninvited anytime. Maddie said you've been having lunch with her every day and sometimes, when the weather is mild, pushing her to the park in the wheelchair. She told me it's her favorite time of day. I thought you should know, because she probably hasn't told you herself. It's great she's going back to work next week. I've ordered a good headset for the phone for her. It should arrive at her office on Wednesday.

Love,
Olivia

April 18, 1999
Ritz Hotel, Madrid

Dear Tina,

I just called you, but you're picking Ryan up from catechism. We are so time-zone impaired. At night when you can talk, I'm asleep, and when I can talk, you're at work. Good thing I like writing letters. What do you think of this new blue stationery? I'm having my coffee and croissant in the hotel's grand lobby this morning, in a cordovan leather chair underneath a king palm. Sometimes I do love hotel life. The staff become your friends, only you can ask them to bring you things and clean things and they always say, With pleasure, Senora Hunt. The sheets are always crisp and fresh. There's always people-watching to do in the lobby. Living with all these other strangers makes me feel less lonely, because we're all in the same boat, and here at the Ritz, anyway, it's a pretty nice one. I can't believe I've already been here nearly two months.

I'm sorry this pregnancy is so hard on you. I remember with Ryan you said you just felt bigger and happier every month. It usually gets better after the first few months, doesn't it? I hope so. I'm glad now that Stephen takes Ryan to school you can sleep in a little longer. Too bad he wants extra credit for it, but I think that's as normal as morning sickness. Speaking of men . . .

. . . I was calling to talk to you about Ben. For the last few weeks, from six till seven A.M. I have a morning workout with my hair: I curl it, flatten it, twist it, pull it out, put it up, brush it down, beat it — and then weep and gnash my teeth. You recognize this, don't you? Question is, what do I *do* with all this lust I feel for him? We're working together. He has to respect me. The crew has to respect me. The studio has to trust me. I'd be jeopardizing all that if Ben and I took off all our clothes and rubbed our naked bodies against each other for a few mind-blowing hours. As much as I'd like to do that, and I think he might, too. But I suspect my motives, don't you? My desire might be impure. I might just be getting back at Michael for Willow. I might just be using Ben till Michael comes to his senses. Or using him to get over Michael. Or letting off a little preproduction stress. Or simply because for six weeks we've been sitting close to each other in the back of an SUV and in restaurants and on the couch in his hotel suite, which is just down the hall from mine, and he's handsome and funny and smells good and, you know, I think I'm going to do it, Tina.

Don't.

Why not?

Wait till the movie's over. If you still like each other then, it'll be even better. Now you'll just be ruining your career for what could turn out to be a location romance.

Why is it that if a woman has sex at work she's fucking her way to the top and if a man does he's just fucking?

I don't have time for one of your feminist frenzies, Olivia, and neither do you. Don't martyr yourself for a dying movement.

But why can't I —

Wait? Yeah, why can't you? This is just another unavailable man obsession —

That's enough out of you.

Thanks for the talk,
Olivia

May 3, 1999
From a field in Spain

My Maddo,

I'm on the set in my director's chair. It's a beautiful spring day, a juniper breeze blows the umbrella flap up, and the sun blinds me. Everyone's eating lunch off the chrome catering truck. We started shooting five hours ago, just after dawn. The trucks, seventeen including our trailers, rolled out of base in the dark morning light and like a circus caravan parked on this grassy field behind a tiny hamlet called Villatobas an hour outside of Madrid. I remember standing on this field in January, wondering if we'd really be back shooting one day. Robin and John Cleese took their positions, and the background actors started moving the wheelbarrows and farm animals, and Ben shouted, Action! and the camera rolled toward them slowly on the dolly, and all the ups and downs and starts and stops and confusion and sleeplessness and anxiety and shouting all welled up in my chest and throat as the first few feet of film were exposed, as Robin said, *Senor Quesada, where are you going?* and John Cleese turned around in his handmade armor and said, *To right wrongs and honor the beauty of Dulcinea. To adventure, Sancho!*

I imagined you here with me, and if my cell phone worked out here I'd have called you. After we got the shot Ben hugged me. And we're off, he said, laughing, still stunned himself that he's in Spain shooting *Don Quixote* and not in New Zealand on his untitled jungle epic. I'm really glad we haven't weakened and fallen into bed with each other. It would change work; it would change everything. Although the idea continues to grow in my mind and, well, body. At night it can get a little lonely here. When his driver takes us to the hotel at night, and we're alone in the backseat, I feel the urge to lean against him, that's all, just to lean for a minute, to rest there for a quiet, wordless minute, to feel his warm body against mine. Sometimes, the way he looks at me, I think he's longing for the same thing. He's never made a pass, thank god. Or at least I don't think he has. I like him, Maddie. He's witty, and sweet, and easygoing — especially for a director. Maybe one day . . . But this isn't it. I still think about Michael more than I'd like to. I have a feeling this Willow thing is serious. I'm fine with it. It's fine. There comes a point, right? When you have to accept that people change and life goes on. We'll always love each other, but it was just too hard. Love should be easy. Life is hard enough.

Lunch is over. The camera crew is back, moving the equipment for the next shot. Tomorrow's weather report has just come in and it's not good: there's a 53 percent chance of rain. We were planning to shoot two exterior scenes. One where Quixote asks Sancho to record their adventures because *"a knight errant always had a chronicler write his outstanding tales."* And the second, the galley slaves scene. Do we take those odds, which, read another way, mean a 47 percent chance of clear skies, or make a run for an interior location, a "cover" set? We have so few of those, we hate to use them up unnecessarily. It's all a gamble. As Q says, *"War is subject to perpetual change."*

Love you,
Olivia

◆◆◆

May 5, 1999

Eric Moriarty
President of Production
Warner Bros.

<u>Via fax</u>

Re: Your notes on the dailies

Dear Eric,

1. In the seventeenth century men didn't wear long pants, which is why Sancho is wearing green socks stretched up to his knees.
2. We'll age Cleese a little less, but remember, the character of Don Quixote has not seen the far side of seventeen, or even fifty, in a very long time, so he has to have a few wise lines.
3. Richard Harris is absolutely fine. I don't know who told you he was drinking again, because he isn't. He's been a dream.
4. Cleese is against the idea of doing a "silly walk" in the movie and Ben agrees. I'll bring it up again, but they both seem pretty dead set against it.
5. We want Robin to feel it's okay to ad lib, because some of his most brilliant stuff happens that way, which is why Ben just

let the camera roll that day. Don't worry, it won't happen every day. We know we can't afford the time.

6. I'm glad you liked what you saw, except for these minor points. You're going to like today's dailies even more.

— Olivia

- - -

May 9, 1999
Café in the Prado

Hey Klein,

You would love this museum. The building itself, the paintings, the Spaniards. I hope you'll come one day, because you'll love it, and you'll wish you'd come over when your old girl Olivia invited you.

It was good to hear from you, even though you're now living with Willow, which seems a bit quick to me; it was only a few months ago you were asking me to give up my career and move there, but okay, you said you wanted to get on with your life, I guess you meant instantaneously. Still, it seems a bit quick to me. A bit quick. Okay, she's there, she's hot, whatever, keep it to yourself. I am happy for you.

Your letter confused me a little, though, because you seemed to be asking me if I was sure, in my heart, that this is the right thing for me. You said you weren't asking for your sake but for mine, that I should understand the reason I gave up and that it was worth what I lost. So I don't look back and regret it. That I wasn't being honest with myself, that I wasn't facing something.

It's a Sunday afternoon in spring. I'm sitting here in this grand café, listening to the pianist play a Schumann piece I used to know, and to the Spanish children laughing at the next table; a square of sunshine warms the back of my hand on this, my first day off in nine weeks. I love living in this old, bustling city. The movie is a monster. Every day there's a new crisis, but we're making it, we're making it, and that is unbelievably exciting. I think you and I are happiest when we're most engaged — in work or in love. I'm not ready to accept that I can't have both. But Tina might be right about us being too much alike; maybe we *both* can't have both, together.

So my answer is yes, I made the right decision when I didn't come to Dixon. But I know it's not without a cost. I feel envious of Mad and Bobby's devotion, I want that kind of love, and Dixon was my moment to reach for it — and I didn't. I couldn't. Maybe someone in the business would make it easier for me to jump, someone who shared or liked my work, and my life, enough to become a part of it, who wouldn't need me to sacrifice it. Like Willow is for you — someone who would make it easy. Or maybe you were right when you said this is who I am and I'll never be able to make that jump, for anyone.

One thing I know, Michael. I couldn't love anyone more than I loved you. I'm sorry you didn't know it then and, for myself, I'm sorry that it wasn't enough for me to choose differently.

Your old girl,

O.

Robert Connor
LaRoche Marketing and Sales
4560 Seneca Blvd.
Shawnee Falls, Ohio 45200

Dear Bobby,

What makes everyone think Maddie listens to me? If she won't listen to you about this — particularly about this — she sure won't listen to me. I totally trust your judgment, so if you say there's no time for her to freeze her eggs before the late-intensification chemo, then I'm sure there isn't. You've been a great advocate, helping her through this war that's been waged on her. Of course, she's always wanted to have a baby, and if her chances of doing that will be further diminished by this next round, then I understand how urgently she'd want to protect them. I'll do anything I can to help, but from the description of that fight you guys had, it sounds like the idea of using *my* eggs one day was even more upsetting to her. I think it's too soon to talk about those kinds of alternatives. As I said on the phone, she hasn't mentioned any of this to me, which makes it hard for me to bring it up without her knowing we spoke. She's dreading going back for more heavy chemo, especially since she feels fine. I don't know what to tell you, Bobby. I went online and read that ovarian-tissue freezing works only about 20 percent of the time anyway — have you told her this? And women don't always lose their fertility after this type of chemo, so she might be okay. I wish there was more time, even to consider the alternatives, so she wouldn't feel so rushed about something so important.

On a brighter note, I'm glad you guys are enjoying your great new house. Eleanor told me you've got the living room painted and that they're currently poring over wallpaper books for the bathroom and bedroom. Mad moves fast for a sick girl, doesn't she? I can't wait to see it. Things are going smoothly here, so I hope to surprise her with a visit in a couple weeks.

Until then, love,
Olivia

May 15, 1999
A bad road in Spain

Maddie,

I hope you can read my writing. I'm in the Range Rover and it's pretty bumpy. You know how I like to put things in writing. Well, this is important. Just because I was going over the pros and cons doesn't mean I'm not on your side, Maddie. I'm glad you've decided to freeze your eggs. I'm excited for you. The doctors are just covering their asses; everyone's so afraid of malpractice suits they can't encourage any risks, especially for something down the line that doesn't concern them, and which is not your life but new life. But I'm with you. As long as you keep doing the weekly blood draws and keep your biopsy appointment next week, I'm all for it, and I'm hoping with all my heart it works. It feels good just having this possibility. I'm happy you're doing it, Mad.

We're about an hour outside of Madrid. Today we're trying *again* to get the galley slave scene where Q comes upon a bunch of shackled slaves and, outraged by their oppression, attacks the guards and with a lot of courage and a little luck, succeeds in freeing them. Or not so luckily, because the freed slaves then turn on him when he insists they pay tribute to Dulcinea; they stone him and make a run for it and later one of them steals Sancho's mule. Last week we got rained out; yesterday the Steadicam didn't work. It took a couple hours to get a new one from Madrid. Ben changed the shot list, but there was still a lot of waiting around, which really irritates Robin, and he's already irritated with the DP, who is so slow and meticulous and humorless I'm getting irritated myself. He stands around with a little blue glass rectangle on his nose, some kind of light filter, waiting for a cloud to pass. His lighting and composition are beautiful, Ben and the studio are very happy with his work, but yesterday Robin summoned me to his trailer to ask me what I was going to do about him. I sat down in the dinette and tried to act comfortable, although some stars are so huge, I guess, so otherworldly, that you can't stop staring at them like they're an exotic animal. It's the confusion of being with someone who looks as familiar to you as your neighbor, but who in fact is a total stranger. I reassured Robin as much as I could — but I think he wanted to hear that I was going to fire the guy, which I'm not ready to do. On my way back to my trailer — it's our own KOA Kampground out there on the plains of Spain, with six trailers clustered next to one another under a big blue-domed sky — Cully Davis pulled me aside and told me Rocinante, Don Quixote's horse, was having some intestinal trouble that wouldn't be nice on camera. What about his double? (There's always two of everything just for situations like this.) Same problem, Cully said. Same bad oats, I guess.

Well, you asked for a chronicle of my days in Spain, Mad. Each one begins and ends with a dodged or undodged bullet. It's not all bad, of course. Last night at dinner John Cleese and Robin were so funny I got the hiccups, which Ben found even funnier, and I thought: these are the hours I'll remember. After dinner Ben and I were walking down the long hallway at the Ritz to our rooms when he stopped in front of his and asked, Can you come in for a minute? I thought, Oh, no. Another problem. Or — a pass. I'm not sure which I feared most. At the marble fireplace, near the couch, he poured two glasses of wine and handed me one. Thank you, he said, raising his glass. I didn't know what to say — what was he talking about?

He laughed. You look scared.

You want to change the ending again, don't you?

I just wanted to tell you you're doing a great job —

I can't get money for a reshoot, Ben, don't even —

You're so cynical, Olivia. I've been wanting to tell you how much I like working with you and there hasn't been the right moment. So I just decided that this was it. You're great at your job and you're a lot of fun to be with, too. You keep me going. So, thank you.

Oh. Well, thanks. I must have looked confused, because I was. Was this some kind of seduction — or did I just want it to be? He was a little drunk. He was grinning at me the way a man can when —

What's wrong? What are you thinking? he asked.

About what it'd feel like to be underneath you on that gigantic bed over there. No, of course I didn't say that, Madster; I was running through the logic one more time of why we shouldn't, just to make sure I hadn't done my calculations incorrectly and there was a way we could. Like, immediately. Right, think, quick, *why* not?

I'm so tired I'm not thinking. I'm just spacing out.

Well, go to bed, darling. (I love the way he says *dahling*. He only says it when we're alone or he's worried about something, and it sounds like half Cary Grant, half Mom.) I'll see you in a few hours. He walked me to the door. He kissed my cheek and I smelled some intoxicating aftershave and felt his warm sandpaper skin and I didn't want to leave. But I did.

We're nearly at the set now and the heavens are clear, thank god. I've never watched the skies so much in my life. I'm watching them for you, too. I hope this egg business works, Maddie. My fingers are crossed. (Legs, too.)

Your sister,
Olivia

May 17, 1999
Ritz Hotel, Madrid

Dear Tina,

Didn't you have a friend who froze her eggs? Maddie's in the process of doing it and I thought she might like to talk to your friend about it. She's taking the hormones and she'll have the surgery in a few weeks. Her oncologists objected (they wanted her to start reinduction chemo this month), but she's feeling so good she decided to make a run for it. Between this and the new house she sounds happier than she has in ages, and that's good itself. God, it'd be great if at the end of all this, there was a baby for her. . . .

. . . speaking of being pregnant. I'm glad you're feeling better. Being pregnant looks so painful to me I can't really wrap my head around the idea of it being wonderful. I imagine you feel stuffed, like when you eat too much and you wish you could open a valve in your stomach and let out a little pressure. I know it's not like that. But it looks like that.

And one more thing — you sounded a little defensive about Stephen's possible promotion. As if I wouldn't be happy for you guys. Of course I would be. I'm sorry it's a mixed thing for you, but how could it not be? You pass up your promotion (possibly) so he can get his — it doesn't feel fair. But as you've told me more than once, not everything is about fairness. He'll be happier, and you'll have more money, right? Maybe after this baby's born you'll want to take a few years off anyway. Too bad society thinks it's taking time off! Little do they know. Before I plunge into another feminist fury I'll sign off and get back to work myself.

Love,
Olivia

P.S. If you can fly in late August, I should be in New York then, if you want to rendezvous there. It'd be nice to know I'm going to see you soon. Or we could wait till after the baby's born and the movie's over, and I'll come out there. Think about it.

Ben Wilcox
c/o Ritz Hotel, Madrid

<u>Via fax</u>

Dear Ben,

I'm sorry about last night. I hope you understand why I ran out of your room at that precise moment. It was the last thing I wanted to do. Maybe you could tell. But it's what I had to do; you understand that, don't you? I really wanted to stay, Ben. But we simply can't have a nonprofessional relationship while we're having a professional one; it could cause all kinds of hell. Look — I'm already worried that you're going to be totally weird when I get back from Ohio. I know you were just offering me your shoulder to cry on last night, and until we kissed it was very comforting; thank you for being there, for being such a good friend, and for the joint, too, but from now on we just can't even *think* about doing anything like that again (as nice as it was), or, god forbid, *more,* until the movie's in theaters, don't you agree?

Now. In thinking about our scheduling problem, I came up with the following idea. Could we fold Sc. 32 into Sc. 21? Let's say Q and Sancho are already on the road together (Sc. 32) when Q sees the "travelers" and insists that they confess that Dulcinea is the fairest maiden in the world (Sc. 21). They demand to see her first. He replies: *"If I were to show her to you, what merit would there be in your confessing a truth so self-evident? The important thing is for you, without seeing her, to believe, confess, affirm, swear, and defend that truth. Otherwise, arrogant creatures that you are, you shall do battle with me.*" (I agree, *arrogant* is the right word here.) They refuse. Q attacks them and ends up on his ass. This could happen with Sancho, and after they've been roughed up and are back on the road together, Sancho could be moved to say his bravery line from Sc. 32 here instead: *"I would wager that in all the days of my life I have never served a more courageous master than Your Grace."* I think this edit works thematically and it would save us having to go back to that location: we could drop Sc. 32 altogether.

I think the rest of the line changes you made are great. May John and Robin agree, please, god. I'll call you from Ohio. And be back soon.

Your *producer,*
Olivia

◆ ◆ ◆

May 29, 1999

Dr. Robert Smith
Director, Sisters of Mercy Hospital of Shawnee Falls
11367 Adams Road
Shawnee Falls, Ohio 45200

Re: Dr. Johnson

Dear Dr. Smith,

My sister, Madeline Hunt Connor, has been treated by a lot of doctors, but no one as arrogant AND incompetent as the above-mentioned boob. What is with you people? I've never encountered

such a bunch of self-impressed, ignorant idiots under one roof —
and I've worked in Hollywood. But your hospital, wow, it just
takes my breath away. These "doctors" are so unpleasant they must
be castoffs from Staples or the Department of Motor Vehicles. They
must have been raised by wolves.

I wasn't always like this. I used to be a nice Midwestern girl
who respected authority and never raised her voice. See what your
hospital has done to me? I asked nicely the first fifteen times.
Then, after watching my sister writhe in agony for days, I had to
pitch psychotic fit #34 to get her bone scan done. You'd think getting the results wouldn't have required all this drama *again,* but
sure enough, it took psychotic fit #35 to get the results. This brings
us to the aforementioned boob, who breezed in Tuesday afternoon and announced that, uh, the cancer's spread to the bones,
and then started to walk out.

Hold on, hold on. Who are you? What do you mean it's spread
to her bones?

Her ribs are full of it. There's nothing to do once it metasta-
sizes. We can give morphine for the pain, but that's about it.

But she's got leukemia. Leukemia doesn't metastasize.

The shoulders on the Boob rose and fell as he expelled some
seriously exasperated air at me. Are you a doctor? he said, squinting at me.

Just the question I was about to ask him! No, I said politely,
but leukemia doesn't metastasize.

Well, her bones have cancer in them, lady —

— They do not! They do not! Stop saying that. Stop it!

He said, Whatever, and walked out.

I'm sure I don't have to tell *you* this, but being a cancer of the
blood, leukemia can't "spread" anywhere because it already *is*

everywhere; the guy was wrong. I tried to reassure my sister that in this case I really *did* know more than that white-suited total stranger who had just lobbed a grenade into her room, but she is still deluded about doctors, she's as trusting as a child, and she spent the next three days, which is how long it took to get a *correct* reading of the scan, thinking they were nearly her last.

Okay, okay, people make mistakes; contrary to what they believe themselves, even doctors are only human. That's not what's driven me to such rudeness here. It's the way the guy walked in, tossed off what he thought was really, *really* bad news, and then just split. Am I wrong to think he should have introduced himself, sat down, talked about his findings, one human being to another, and explained that her oncologist would discuss them with her in greater detail? Is this really asking too much?

Seething,
Olivia Hunt

May 31, 1999
Shawnee Falls

Dear Tina,

I'm in the tree fort. It's such a warm night I couldn't stay in the house. I've got a flashlight and a sleeping bag and a flask of wine. Just like old times. The only thing missing is you, or Tony and his bong. This tree has seen a lot. Our first crime (underage smoking). Our first fight (when you called me bossy). Among other firsts.

Sorry I didn't get a chance to call you back today. Eleanor said you called. She told me Stephen did get that promotion, which is great news. I assume she told you ours. Relapse. Bone marrow transplant. My mother. My mother. Why does she torment me so? Why can't my feelings for her be uncomplicated? Half the time I want to slap her and the other half I want to hold her and the other half to be held by her. I know that's three halves. I said it was complicated. We've been at each other's throats this week about the bone marrow transplant Maddie is considering. Eleanor doesn't want her to do it. She thinks the odds are not worth the pain and suffering. She doesn't believe it will work.

You never believe anything will work, I said. We were on the couch in the family room. It wasn't dark when I set the flowered teapot on the coffee table, but as we talked the light drained from the room.

You never face reality, Olivia.

How do you know what reality is, Mom?

Olivia (*oh, how can a mother explain?*) . . . I just don't want her to suffer anymore.

What if it gives her her life back?

She looked at me with pity and dread, as if I were a child who'd just demanded the truth about a beloved but now dead pet. You don't know! I said, sick of her certainty.

Honey, have you read all the —

— I gave you that stuff; of course I've read it —

Then why can't you see?

Why can't she be one of the good numbers? The odds aren't zero, are they? They're twenty-four percent. Twenty-four percent succeed and are cancer free. There are always amazing cases, too. How do you know she won't be one?

Relapse within fifteen months, Olivia. It said. Well. It's only been eight.

From the beginning her doubt has been an unmoveable wall of marble that I feel compelled to hurl myself at like a dumb sparrow against a kitchen window. Twenty-four percent isn't a great number, and we're all afraid, even I am now, Tina, but it seems to me our only choice in this has always been how we respond to those ever-changing numbers. Eleanor's response seems to say, Forget it, what's the point? I'm smart enough to recognize defeat. Let's just get it over with; at least I'll have the dignity of end-running this, at least I can say to the cruel or at best indifferent universe and to the rest of you suckers who believed in that 24 percent, Hah! I knew it! *I* wasn't fooled! I read the literature. I was right! *I'm* not surprised things ended this way, and if my brilliance isn't exactly consolation, my mind-blowing grief is eased somewhat by my own crafty foresight, and, in the incredibly unlikely event that my daughter receives an eleventh-hour miracle pardon, the indignity of being wrong will be ameliorated by the very good news that my daughter is alive. Eleanor's response offers a way to avoid what, unlike Tennyson, she must fear most, which is to have loved and lost. I say "loved," not "believed," because I think there is a causal relationship: when you love truly you must truly believe. I don't know how you can put your own need for protection from pain above your daughter's need for maternal strength and courage and truly love her at the same time. I seethed and sipped my weak tea in the dying light. We listened to the traffic on Hamilton Road, other lives driving home, to the movies, to the mall, and possibly to the same hospital where on the seventh floor Maddie was lying in a bed talking to her husband about the choice she would have to make tomorrow. Eleanor set her teacup down and asked me: What do I tell her? I can't tell her to do it when I don't think it'll work. I'd feel like I was fooling her into doing more suffering. And then there's Bobby.

If Maddie listens to anyone Tina, it's Bobby. Her husband, who believes Jesus will come through for them. Eleanor is intellectually underwhelmed by this, of course, and it's caused some tension between them. I've seen her look at Bobby with what can only be called a withering patience, but she always backs off; like Maddie, Eleanor doesn't believe in God, but she believes in Bobby, in his strength and devotion and resilience, which has inspired Mad, and in the sanctity of her daughter's marriage, even if it's only a year old, and even if it's to a man who puts his faith in the Lord more than in science. Yet how can she sit by and watch her daughter make what she believes is a fatally dangerous move?

What can I do? she continued. I can't lie to her and say You're going to get better, when I don't believe that, but I can't say Stop, give up, or she'll think I'm being negative. But it's not that, Olivia. It's how she should spend what time she —. Why spend it being tortured and suffering in a hospital for —? She could travel, or just relax in her new home for however long she —. Who knows? But if I say don't do the transplant she'll think it's because *I* don't want to go through all this, when —

Guilt, fear, and love seized her and her small body collapsed into itself and her hands flew up to hide her face. I suddenly saw through my rage something really obvious: Eleanor is her mother. Maddie is her baby girl. Eleanor is supposed to protect her from the world and she can't. She didn't. A mother's only wish must be to see her child thrive. This is a different agony for her. And Eleanor was confiding in me, her other daughter. She was asking me to love her enough to understand that she simply doesn't know how to do this, that although I don't want her to be, and she's not supposed to be, she's afraid. I set my cup down and pulled her to me.

We heard my dad's car wheels on the gravel, then the Caddy's door shut, then his feet on the back steps and the kitchen door creak open and close and his voice saying, Eleanor? Honey? She exhaled and said, We're in here, Ed. He followed her voice and stood in the doorway and said, What're you doing in the dark?

Crying, I said.

Oh, Jesus, he said, and walked away.

He can't stand it when I'm upset, she said.

Still? After all his practice.

A few minutes later he came back and said softly, Maybe we should go to the Club for dinner?

Love,
Olivia

May 31, 1999

Eric Moriarty
President of Production
Warner Bros.

Via fax

Re: The yellow in the Duke and Duchess's costumes

Dear Eric,

I'm sorry you still have problems with the shade of yellow in the aforementioned costumes.

Our research department has assured me that this color is historically accurate and the art department assures me that it's beautiful and the director and the stars like the color a lot, so I really think we should stick with it. But thanks for your suggestion.

Sincerely,
Olivia Hunt

rr: OH
dictated but not read

+ + +

May 31, 1999

To: Costume Department
From: Olivia Hunt

Re: Duke and Duchess's costumes

I have talked to WB about their color issues and everything is fine. Carry on with the yellow.

cc: Ben Wilcox
    Cully Davis

rr: OH
dictated but not read

Dear Tina,

I need your advice. I was at Maddie's today, helping her plant the vegetable garden and pack for the hospital. We finished the tomato and pepper plants and went inside. She went upstairs to pack and I started fixing dinner. Bobby was still at work. I turned on the clock radio to listen to "All Things Considered." I was chopping the onions when I heard something crash above me. I ran upstairs and as I did, I heard more things breaking and a low, painful moan. There, in the spare room, which for the previous owners had been their little boy's room and which was still wallpapered with squat tugboats and cheery teddy bears, was Maddie, surrounded by broken lamps and dishes and holding a paintbrush dripping with blue paint and walls that were splattered and covered with her rage: FUCK YOU FUCK YOU FUCK

I didn't move. I watched her back and shoulders shudder as she dropped the brush and shrank down into a ball on the floor. All I could do was put my arm around her, but she flung me away. At dinner I struggled and failed to get her to talk — or smile. Then we watched *Wheel of Fortune* and later I went back to my parents' house.

I don't want her to be angry, Tina. I want to lead her out of that hard place. Maybe this is selfish. Maybe I know she has good reason to be angry and the reason includes me, because like billions of people — billions! — I'm healthy and she's not and there's no goddamn reason. (Which I still can't believe: is there *really* no reason?) Although she's never said it, how can she not resent me and my life? So it's hard for me to say anything, but I want to try. I thought you might have an idea. Of even how to begin. The only thing you can't say is trust in God, because Maddie never has, and I don't think she'll be more inclined to now.

Love,
Olivia

◆◆◆

June 4, 1999
Cincinnati

Dear Michael,

I'm writing this in room 842 at the University of Ohio Medical Center. It's a good-sized room, with two narrow beds, two TV sets opposite them, and a big window that overlooks the arboretum. Maddie is in the bed near the window, sleeping. I'm in the other bed because no one requires it at the moment, there is a vacancy at Hotel Hell, there is some happy girl out there who doesn't yet know this bed has her name on it. The nurses don't like me stretching out here, it's against policy, but Maddie is so nice to them, especially for someone with recurrent acute lymphocytic leukemia, that they can't refuse her. It's three A.M. and I thought I'd get some sleep. Hopefully writing this letter will relax me. I will grab the words that are bouncing like pinball marbles in my head — *thrombocytopenia blasts Dulcinea ducal castle Michael reinduction allogenic La Mancha marrow Willow costume overun* — I'll collect them all and line them into neat sentences and tuck them into bed.

Maddie relapsed. I hate to put it that way; it suggests responsibility, that she did it, she relapsed, when it's the cancer that did it. There is a continual balancing act between acceptance and defiance, between being the victim and being the attacker. As a fighter, she just lost, which implies weakness, ineptitude, a lack of some crucial talent, and suggests some other fighter would not have lost; a smarter strategy, greater strength, and this defeat would have been, could have been, a victory. You can't say, well, this enemy is just too strong for any fighter, because she is the enemy, too; the cancer is a part of her, as much as her will to conquer it is. However you look at it, this round was won by cancer.

Which explains my current location at the University of Ohio Medical Center, this megalopolis of medicine perched on the highest hilltop in Cincinnati, a kingdom of science separated from the town of mortals below by an encircling moat of asphalt cleverly called Medical Center Drive, a thirty-building yellow-brick compound as impenetrable and formidable as a medieval fortress without the charming Arthurian turrets and within which are bridges and subterranean secret passageways connecting a labyrinth of linoleum hall floors so buffed, so shiny, so smooth, so slick as to resemble ice and which in turn connect villages Hematology to Oncology to Radiology to Urology to Morphology to Burger King. Yes, there is a Burger King not only within these kingdom walls but inside this very building, which could be considered the castle, since it's the biggest and tallest building and it houses that granddaddy of medicine, the Cancer Center. This Burger King is not merely a concession stand, it's a full-blown restaurant conveniently situated adjacent to the shitty cafeteria, complete with baskets of fries cooking in vats of boiling animal fat, hockey-puck hamburgers sizzling on the grill, sullen servers just daring you to tell them what you'd like, lines of humans in seam-stretched pants waiting for more mounds of salty, greasy, addictive, delicious junk. I find it puzzling and morally inconsistent — well, it's just not *fair* — that they allow this artery killer in here and yet a girl can't light up a cigarette anywhere. (I have mostly quit, by the way. It's just around hospitals I really get the urge these days.)

When we first saw the great walled city, as Bobby, Maddie, and I drove up the hill two days ago and followed the signs to the Cancer Center, Maddie said, It's scary-looking, isn't it? Hell, yes, I thought. I pretended I felt differently and said, No. To me, it says Power. Science. The best technology. The best.

Earlier that morning we had breakfast at her kitchen table. I watched a blue jay on the feeder split black seeds in its beak. I wondered what the life expectancy of a blue jay was. Bobby was packing Mad's things in the car. It was quiet, in an awful way, and then Maddie looked at me and said, You think it'll work, Liv?

She was looking right at me. I said, Yeah. It'll work. Jim's marrow is a perfect match.

Her eyes held mine, checking for cracks in my confidence.

It'll work, Maddie.

Then she said, Yeah. I think so, too.

To prepare for a transplant, she must first get into remission. Tomorrow she'll choose between Door Number 1, the high-intensity chemo, and Door Number 2, the low-. She has a better chance of getting into remission with Door Number 1, but Door Number 2 is far less dangerous. In other words, if the high-intensity doesn't kill her, she'll have a better chance of living; it's another one of those devious, vertiginous little medical brain teasers. Rates of short-term survival against rates of remission against rates of long-term survival — it's a kaleidoscope of numbers, of shifting odds, and the gamble she takes could prolong or end her life. I studied these numbers, and I almost wish I hadn't, because what good are they, really? Forty-two percent this, sixty-one percent that. They get in the way of what Bobby has, which is total faith. It's just like Ed and the lottery. If my father followed the odds, he'd never play, which would deprive him of the pleasure of dreaming about what he'd do with the $27 or $113 million purse. I was arguing with my mother about false hope the other day. I said hope is neither false nor true but a kind of happiness itself, a fuel that carries us toward our dreams. You feel better when you're knee-deep in hope for something, whether it's for the love of someone, for a promotion, for a baby, for a clean bill of health — or, in your case, Michael, for a successful show. I'm sorry to hear you've had to delay it. But it sounds like it's worth it, if Barbara is so excited about this new work. Your dealer is never excited about anything, so these pieces must be really good. After being stuck for so long you must feel great to be working again, in the throes of it. You didn't tell me what you're doing, only that you scrapped the urbanscapes and that Barbara thinks these new paintings are possibly "the most exciting new work of any artist in years." Congratulations! Barbara isn't a gusher, so you must really be onto something. Perhaps your new muse is responsible? Send me a picture; I'd love to see what you're doing.

Out the window I can see the white smile of the moon. You might be looking at it, too, from your back porch, where it's hanging over the dark blue mountains. I don't know why I like that idea. I guess it would be a connection; you, me, and the moon would make a celestial triangle, a new consolation in the night sky.

Love,
Olivia

June 14, 1999
Cincinnati

Ben Wilcox
c/o Ritz Hotel, Madrid

<u>Via fax</u>

Dear Ben,

Please excuse my handwriting. My PowerBook broke down last night. I'm at an outdoor concrete table in the hospital courtyard. It's a clear, fine spring day and I had to feel it for a minute, to just breathe in the sweet magnolia scent of a June day in the Ohio Valley. One of the worst things about being confined to the hospital must be no fresh air. I would have liked to wheel Maddie out here with me, but she's neutropenic, which means her immune system is so compromised that she can't even have fresh flowers in the room for risk of airborne bacteria causing an infectious holy hell. This is normal; it's what the chemotherapy is supposed to do. I love how they call it *therapy*. It tricks you into believing it's good for you, like one of the many enchantments Quixote suffers from. When Maddie told the doctor that she'd chosen the high-intensity protocol he squeezed her shoulder and said, Good. You're making the right decision. I felt déjà vu and I couldn't trace it and then I remembered that it's in a draft of the script. The draft we like and that Warners doesn't. When Quixote agrees to the duel with the Knight of the Moon, the Duke squeezes his shoulder and says, Good. It's what a knight errant must do, Don Quixote. Heh, heh, heh. He smiles, knowing that the duel is just make-believe and that Q is doomed to lose it. . . .

. . . or so it is in the pages you faxed me, which at this point will never see the light of the big screen, Ben. I know you only agreed to Warner's version (contractually, remember!), where Q wins this duel and walks off into the sunset with Sancho, because you believed we'd have time to convince them that Cervantes' choices (and yours) were better. That you can't just slap on a happy ending, because the end is in the beginning and like an arrow once released from the bow it can only complete its trajectory, it can't end up somewhere else, it can't suddenly hang a sharp right. I understand and I agree. But I don't think these pages will persuade the studio. Q's defeat is too bitter, too agonizing after all the struggle he's been through. Dulcinea's kiss isn't enough to off-set the ridicule of the crowds laughing at him; Hollywood demands more than symbolism. And no, Ben, you know we can't possibly shoot both versions and then test them; it'd take another three days, which we don't have. I promise you Moriarty and possibly even Irving will be on set to make sure we shoot the duel — and the ending — the way we've contractually agreed to. But I have an idea that might satisfy everyone. It goes like this:

Q loses the duel. He says he knew he would. How could he possibly win against the notorious Knight of the Moon? Sancho says, Then why'd you agree to the duel if you knew you'd lose? And Dulcinea steps in with the answer, because she recognizes what Quixote's done and who he is: Because Don Quixote is a knight, she says, and a knight is courageous, even in the face of certain death. In this way Q is victorious. Sancho, as literal-minded as a comb, says, But I don't get it. Q says, Sancho, I had to try, didn't I?

These aren't the words, of course, just the meaning. I think WB might go for this because it shows Q was brave, not a madman playing dress-up, which is hard for people to get behind. It gives you the "renouncement" you wanted on the deathbed, or close to it, and it gives Q Dulcinea's approval, or love, which has been what he's wanted. I'd like the end to be at the tournament rather than back in Q's bed, which I find depressing and anticlimactic as hell; it echoes the it-was-only-a-dream end in the *Wizard of Oz,* which infuriated me as a kid. The grandeur, the flapping flags, the crowds cheering — that's a good setting for an ending. How 'bout this: he walks (okay, limps) off the field with Sancho and says, *I'm tired, let's go home,* and Sancho says, *But Your Grace, there are so many more adventures ahead for us.*

Something like that. Or is that too corny for you? I think the studio might accept it. More likely than Q dying and saying you're right, I was a fool, which is just not going to fly with them. I'll fax this now and call you later tonight to see what you think.

Olivia

◦ — ◦

Date: June 16, 1999
From: OliviaHunt@usol.com
To: JamesEHunt@usol.com

Dear Jim,

I'm sorry I called you a coward. You're not. I know you wish you could be here. I was just upset about what happened to Maddie and maybe a little jealous, too, that you have a family that demands your time. Of course you should be with Sophie on her fifth birthday. And I know with a boss like yours you can't take much time off. I was just out of my head with dread, and who better to share it with than my big brother?

But what did you mean by Maddie being easier for me to love now that she's sick? Do you mean it's pity I feel, not love? Because that's not true, Jim. Or that it's easier since she has no control, or I don't? It's true that our differences aren't as important now, but that's good, isn't it? And in other ways, nothing has changed.

Yesterday was a beautiful day. When I got to the hospital she was dressed in her sweats and she said, Get my chair, I'm going outside.

You can't.

She gave me that *Oh, please* look that we love so much. Jaw out, eyes lowered; a pro too tired to prove it. Olivia, get my chair.

Maddie, don't put me in this position —

Do you really think sitting outside for ten minutes is going to hurt me more than all that chemo? Come on.

I wheeled her out the door. We sat in the courtyard under a maple tree and talked about that Oscar video program she's trying to launch, how her vegetable garden was doing, how much weight Bobby has lost again, and then we were quiet for a few minutes. I wanted to talk to her. To tell her something important. It seemed like a moment when something important should be said. Something about the meaning of life. Something about love. You know what I mean? I was going back to Spain in the morning and I had to say something. I said, Maddie, I'm sorry about all this.

It's not your fault.

You're going to get into remission —

I know.

Do you want to talk about —

I just want to sit here. I don't want to hear anything but the wind.

So we just sat there, Maddie in her wheelchair, the white paper mask covering her nose and mouth, me on the bench next to her, not talking, the lime green leaves of the sugar maple rippling in the breeze.

See you in a couple weeks, Jim.

Love,
Olivia

— • —

6/17/99

Maddie,

Since you hate the way I say good-bye (acting like I'll be back in ten minutes) and I hate the way *you* say good-bye (acting like you'll never see me again), I decided to skip all that turmoil and just leave you this poem, which I found last night in a collection in the basement. It's from an opera libretto Auden wrote.

> *But once in a while the odd thing happens,*
> *Once in a while the dream comes true,*
> *And the whole pattern of life is altered,*
> *Once in a while the moon turns blue.*

Remember that,
and see you soon,
Olivia

June 18, 1999
Ritz Hotel, Madrid

Dear Tina,

After all that. After all those minutes and days and months; the meetings, the dinners, the glances and deflected glances, after sitting next to each other in planes, limos, and SUVs, our elbows, arms, fingers touching accidentally and not, his scent making me think about sex and the tension like a pacing animal always there; after all my willpower and self-control and virtuous restraint, and after all my goddamned hair trauma, when I got back to Madrid last night and Ben opened his hotel room door, I kissed him. He didn't say a word and neither did I. His hands pulled me against him and his foot kicked the door shut and we moved to the bed like a single body, a single utterly and ecstatically *mindless* body, and we stayed there for hours devouring each other, finally freeing that pacing animal, finally feeling the warm skin and mouth we'd been craving for months, his smooth body touching every inch of mine, falling into sweet oblivion as his weight pressed into me, kissing and fucking and holding on to each for dear life till the light of dawn and *my god,* I needed that.

But now what?

Olivia

Eric Moriarty
President of Production
Warner Bros.

<u>Via fax</u>

Dear Eric,

Okay, so you don't like the new ending. You made that clear. It's still not "up" enough. But if I may, I'd like to call your attention to a few things.

1. *Q is triumphant.* He wins the glory of Dulcinea recognizing his courage, which has been the whole point of his quest! It wasn't to defeat some fake knight, it was to prove his valor to her, and when she says she sees that — precisely because he *didn't* have a chance in hell of winning — it's his greatest, shining moment.

2. Dulcinea can only be beautiful in his eyes or Q isn't chivalric, he's just a regular guy. It's common to want to win the love of some babelicious, but it's uncommon, it's heroic, to see a babe in a beast. See?

3. He can't go off with her, he's an old man (and there's the fact that she's hideous). Besides, I refer you to the following films, in which, after the hero has achieved his goal, he goes off into the sunset (metaphorically sometimes) — he never goes off with the girl, Eric, this isn't a romantic comedy, it's an epic. Consider these: *Butch Cassidy and the Sundance Kid, Braveheart, Saving Private Ryan.* The hero dies. It's part of

what makes him a hero: he's willing to die; he's lived a life worth dying for. That's not a downer, that's inspiring. (Look at that greatest story ever told: if Jesus had lived, would half the world be Christian?) And don't forget, when Sancho turns to his wife and says, I was made governor of an island, you know that Quixote has won by "infecting" Sancho with his optimistic lunacy, too.

You're absolutely right about Penelope's heaving cleavage; we'll be sure to capture it. And we'll make the tag line funnier. We're going to keep tweaking, Eric, but please reconsider and approve these pages.

Sincerely,
Olivia

June 22, 1999
On set in Spain

Maddie,

I miss you. And the clicks of the IV and the middle-of-the-night beeps (which I still hear in my dreams). The swish of the nurses' thighs in their white nylon pants, the squeak of the orderlies' sneakers on that glazed linoleum, the gurney wheels humming past your door, the doctors' muffled voices, the buffing machine in the hallway at six and midnight. (Why must the floor be buffed? Another imponderable.) I miss watching the treetops rustle in the arboretum as I wait for the microwave to sanitize your food. I miss the ratshit coffee and Burger King fries and I miss feeding you ice chips, watching them melt on your burgundy lips. I miss being with you. Taking care of you. I just called, but Dad said you were sleeping, which must be better than being awake these days. I wish I could do something for you. I should be there. Not that I could do much. But all I'm doing here is watch John Cleese crawl in and out of a cage. We're shooting the aptly named Caging scene, where he's bound and put in a cage on an oxcart and wheeled home. It's terrible the things the world does to Don Q, and through it all he remains as trustful as a child. John Cleese is really good. I can't wait for you to see this movie, Mad. He's funny and poignant; he embodies the baffled elegance of this Knight of the Sad Countenance. Right now he's just sitting in the cage, head in hands, looking miserable — I think for real, because the DP is taking FOREVER this morning (I probably should have fired him). So far there's been more waiting than shooting. For me this is the hard part of producing: the set time. If you're good at the earlier part, when you have to pull all the pieces together, the script, the money, the director, the schedule, etc., then you can't be good at this waiting-and-watching part. With all our recent minicatastrophes, this quiet time only makes me nervous that another doozy is on its way. Yesterday was the best one so far. We were shooting the third and last day of the famous Sheep scene, where Quixote charges into a flock of sheep (always seemed stupid to me, but Ben, like Johnny, insisted on doing it). The morning went beautifully; we had only two fairly tricky shots left. After lunch, the sheep wrangler went AWOL. I dispatched a few PAs to the local *hostelerias* to find him, because José was the only one who knew how to get two hundred sheep to do what we needed them to do. Ben and I were in my trailer trying to come up with a new plan when the trailer started shaking and we heard a rumbling . . . We opened the door and there were our two hundred sheep, charging around the trailer like a river around a stone, stupidly following their leader sheep across the road and over a ridge into a deep ravine. Ben started laughing, thank god. It's one of the things I like about him — he's as quick to laugh as he is eager to make people laugh. It's weird to pretend all day that we're not sleeping together, and it's probably fooling no one. I don't regret it, Maddie. I really like him. He's irresistibly charming but not deliberately, more like a kid who knows he's so cute he can get away with anything — and does. He's gone out with a lot of actresses, which makes me wildly insecure, but I'm trying not to get ahead of myself here.

Well, the ravine was too steep for the sheep to climb out. Even after José stumbled back two hours later, he had to herd them about a mile away to where the bank was manageable. We picked up a couple other shots, but that sheep fiasco cost us a day — which, when added to the other three we lost to rain, puts us over budget by more than I can face. Goddamn sheep. I bet we end up cutting the scene in the editing room.

Cleese has just come over to wait it out with me. We're going to play backgammon while the camera problem gets solved. He sends you his very best.

Love,
Olivia

June 29, 1999
Ritz Hotel, Madrid

Tina,

What do you make of this:

After that first crazy night, Ben and I spent the next six nights together. You know what it's like: you think all you need is to let the horse go, all you need is to know something you don't, like what it would be like to kiss him, all you need is a *taste,* and you'll be able to get back in your box, when in fact, usually once you get what you want, what you then want is *more.* So we had more. And while you're having more you're feeling like you will burst with happiness and that you've discovered something no one else has ever known before, which is the harmonic convergence not of a bunch of far-off planets but the physical, mental, and spiritual spheres within you merging with someone else's, for a few hours, during one week in late June. Some call it falling in love. Others call it transportingly good sex. People like me say, Maybe it's both?

Our workdays are so long we hardly have time to talk. We fall into bed and six hours later we're on set again. And then last week, Ben stopped in the hallway of the hotel and said, Uh, I think I better just get some sleep tonight, Liv.

Oh. Okay. That's fine.

I'm just exhausted.

I know. . . . Me, too.

Don't take this the wrong way, okay?

I won't.

That was almost a week ago. We have six weeks of shooting left. What do you think? Is that a brush-off? Did I move too fast, did he feel trapped? Or did he just get what he wanted and now he's sated? God, would I feel like an idiot. I can't believe either is the case. But why wouldn't he at least want to sleep together, I mean, without having sex? Okay, maybe it's too early for that, maybe there's an intimacy in just holding each other that he doesn't feel or want — or is terrified of. But we haven't even eaten alone together since then. I hate to ask him what's up; that could appear needy, cloying, perhaps the very thing that was scaring him off, and of course I'm the producer, I'm supposed to be cool.

I shouldn't tell you this — you'll use it against me — but I have to admit, whenever we were just resting in each other's arms, Michael came into the room. He was there, just — there, standing in a corner, my phantom lover. I wonder if I'm in the room when he's with Willow. It's slightly disturbing that I can desire Ben as much as I do and miss Michael at the same time. Part of me stays in Ben's arms, and the other part joins ghost-Michael, standing in the corner like a witness. I read somewhere that for every year in a relationship, it can take two to get over it. So that means I'm single till the year 2009?

I am getting ready for this movie to be over. It's depleting, getting up at six and being on set for fourteen hours, outdoors, wind blowing, sun or rain coming down, people asking questions every five minutes, and then for the last few nights we've had very stressful dinners with the studio, in the form of Moriarty and Irving, who were in town making sure we don't blow their $50 million by shooting an ending they don't like. Finally, after a lot of shouting, we reached a compromise in which Q loses the duel but doesn't die in his bed or renounce his dream (as it is in the book). In the movie, he and Sancho will walk off into the sunset, making some hopefully hysterical wisecracks about their days and nights of adventure. Robin helped a lot with the studio, because fortunately we agree about what should be done. After one particularly difficult meeting, he gave me a ride back to the hotel in his car and said, Chief (he calls everybody that), you're only given a little spark of madness. Don't lose it. Why do you think he said that?

We're doing nights this week, where we work from four P.M. till four A.M., so I'll try to call you from the set, since for once the time difference will work to our advantage.

Your friend,
Olivia

July 4, 1999
Ritz Hotel, Madrid

Dear Maddie,

It's early Sunday morning and I just got back from our night shoot. The church bells of Madrid are tolling, calling believers to worship. Last night during lunch (which occurs at midnight when you shoot nights) I wandered into the ruin of a moss-covered stone chapel. There was no roof, no ceiling, only the star-filled sky. I sat against a wall and stared at it. Infinity. The simple fact of infinity is enough to make me very open-minded about the mystery of life. Isn't finite the opposite of infinite? How can we ever know anything definitively when the universe is infinite and expanding? The answer is always over that next hill, and the next, and next. When I look at the night sky and consider my relationship to it — one puny organism, out of billions of puny organisms, just sitting in the remains of an ancient chapel, breathing in and out, watching for shooting stars, trying to pick out the constellations, still — this moment both grounds me in the tactile reality of dirt, air, and skin and also lifts me up to believe that there must be someone, something up there, there must be. While floods and famine and cancer certainly suggest the universe is pure chaos and randomness, the beauty in the elaborate and connected natural order of things — of the veins of a leaf, of a river, of a bolt of lightning, to the veins in my hand — suggest there is purpose and meaning and, yes, maybe even something bigger and better than us. And more than the incredible natural order of the universe, there is love: how can love be the product of anything short of divine? Or is it simply our capacity to perceive and feel all this that is divine? Is divinity not some abstract unknowable "force" named God but our uniquely human ability to experience it? What do you think, Maddie? I realized last night that I don't really know what you believe. When we watched the sunset over the Grand Canyon you said, You gotta believe in something. But what? And how? Do you think you can only feel faith — you can only believe in God, in a meaningful universe — if you were brainwashed with Bible stories, the Talmud, Zen koans as a kid? You know how envious I am of Catholics and Jews, whose faith seems to become a part of their very blood and remain with them long after their educated brains have rejected it. But maybe our journey of doubt is a journey of faith, too.

I saw a shooting star and made a wish for you.

Love,
Olivia

Dear Michael,

I'm back in Ohio. I thought you'd want to know that Maddie had the bone marrow transplant and she's doing fine. (She said to say thanks for your letter and the painting, which is hanging opposite her bed. Very thoughtful to do a winterscape for her. Is this your new work? I thought you said it was figurative.) The high-intensity chemo got her into remission, and now she's had another round, which I guess destroyed all of her bone marrow to make room for Jim's. Besides waiting for the horrible side effects to begin, we watch her counts — the numbers of platelets and red blood cells and other vital things we the healthy take for granted. First we watched them dive down to zero — which meant it was time to tranfuse her with Jim's marrow — and now we're waiting for them to rise again, which will mean engrafting is taking place, that her body is accepting the transplant. Every morning at five a nurse opens one of those nozzles in her chest and fills a vial red, and a few hours later the paper equivalent arrives, rows of hieroglyphs, RBC, WBC, Neutro, and numbers that I have learned to decipher and on which we hang our daily hopes. So far she's doing so well the doctors are dragging in their friends to show her off; she's a medical wonder. She doesn't look any different than the rest of the poor fuckers on this ward, pale and paper thin, totally hairless again, this time her eyebrows are gone, too, but I guess inside things are moving along as planned. They still insist she'll be in here till late August, but they don't know Maddie, do they?

I hope I can make your show in September. We'll be in post by then, cutting the movie in New York, where I'll move as soon as we're done shooting. The movie is looking so good, Michael. Cleese and Robin are heartbreakingly funny together, and the cinematography is beautiful. I think even you might like this one, and for some reason, that's still important to me. In fact, I think it might have a lot to do with why I did it. As ironic as that is.

I'll be here till the engrafting takes place, then head back to Spain for the rest of the shoot. I miss you, even though, well — I'll leave it at that. It'd be nice to hear your voice sometime.

Love,
Olivia

July 25, 1999
Cincinnati

Dear Tina,

It's four o'clock in the morning on the BMT wing at U of O. I went for a walk through this monolithic maze of medicine, a late-night stroll through Hematology, Nephrology, Radiology; I even swung by the Pediatric unit to look at the tiny pink froglike preemies, hoping it would tire me out. This is an amazing place. The things medicine can do, all the lives it prolongs and improves and saves; it's as awesome to me as the greatest art, music, and natural wonders of the world. Doctors aren't the friendliest people I've ever met, but what they do is often quite close to miraculous.

From the pay phone I called Spain to see how things are going there. (Fine.) Ben is being wonderful again, by the way. He said sometimes he just needs nights alone, and I must never take it personally; it's just the way he is. I understand. These are not the best conditions for a new romance. Given that I'm always worried about Maddie and he's directing a movie, it's a sign of our compatibility that we can enjoy each other as much as we do. Hopefully when we're done shooting and Mad's home we'll be able to focus on each other and just see how it goes under more normal conditions. I am so ready for normal conditions, Tina. I really like him. I know it's early. But I feel kind of excited about what this could be. Before I left we had dinner in his room and he suggested we think about starting a company together. He said it so casually I wasn't sure he meant it. But I'd love that. It'd be perfect. To be partners that way. I'd never have to be alone on the road again.

Maddie just stirred. I untangled the IV line before it set off the alarm. The doctors say she's doing great, but, Tina, she's as fragile as charred paper. I'm afraid one day when the door opens the draft will blow her away. The only sign of life is the pain she's in. Heating pads would help, but heating pads are forbidden by the hospital insurance company. The nurses have taught us how to make them. In the hallway you find a supply cart full of towels, sheets, and diapers. You wet a towel and wrap a plastic adult-sized diaper around it, tape it shut, and cook it on high in the microwave for two minutes. Then you wrap the now hot diaper in another hand towel and rest it on your sister's blue-spotted belly, which relieves her pain and makes you feel infinitesimally less worthless. The blue freckles are actually bruises from injections. You know that mound of fat just below your belly button that even the super-ab workouts never flatten? Well, that's the only remaining bit of fat on her, so it's perfect for injections, and it's now covered with purply-blue dots, so many that if connected they'd create a whole barnyard of farm animals. I thought she'd think it was funny. I thought it'd be a laugh, a nice surprise. So while she was sleeping I connected the dots into Maddie Slays a Windmill, and when she woke I showed her my drawing and she hated it. It wasn't my best work, but that wasn't what upset her. She said, How could you do that?

What? I thought it'd make you laugh.

It doesn't. Wipe it off.

But you said it was a funny idea —

— Yeah, an idea. I have enough people poking me all day, Olivia, I don't need you doing it for a joke.

I then remembered that in the winter after the stroke I'd sent her a masseuse at the hospital and Maddie sent her away, saying the same thing. How stupid of me. I wiped it off and as I did she giggled because it tickled.

Do you want to write on me in revenge? Connect the freckles on my nose to the ones on my jaw?

She scowled. Those aren't freckles, those are age spots, sweetie.

Like a dueling pistol, I offered her the blue felt tip. She gave me a handlebar mustache. We got into laughing fits just waiting for various nurses and doctors to notice, or not. (Most didn't; this is an unbearably serious ward.) What I've read about laughter therapy makes about as much sense as chemo and radiation therapy, so since the fall I've tried to keep the laughs coming, and I've forced her to watch every comic I could find at the local video store: the Marx Brothers, the Three Stooges, Buster Keaton, Woody Allen, Richard Pryor, Monty Python, Eddie Murphy, and about fifty Hollywood comedies from *Austin Powers* to *Groundhog Day*. (Tina, any personal favorites you can recommend?)

I've offered to read to her, poetry or philosophy or trashy novels, but as when she was young she prefers custom-made stories, new installments of *The True and Outstanding Adventures of the Hunt Sisters.* I think she must enjoy seeing me work, because it's hard to make up a story on your feet. When she had fevers I placed the sisters on ski slopes and arctic tundras so I could describe ice and snow and cold wind. The stories are ridiculous, fantastic and illogical, and they never really end.

We also do laps. The nurses say laps are important, and didn't Aristotle say life is movement? Every day around one o'clock I drag her out of bed even if she begs me not to. She swings her long sticks to the floor and when I squat to slide on her slippers she hears my knees crack like a fire and says, Livvie, what's wrong with your knees? I place the BMT mask, a white paper disc with a special killer filter in the center, against her steroid-swollen face and as I gently pull the elastic thread over her smooth head I remember shoving her striped woolen cap on her six-year-old brown-haired head in the winter, and then she places her good hand on my shoulder and pulls herself up and out of bed and we're off, out the door and racing to the toboggan, both calling, I get front, and *whooosh,* down we go, down the fresh-fallen snow on the hill, tumbling off at the bottom, starting a snowball fight with Jim or making angels or, in this case, shuffling very slowly down the wide corridor of the BMT wing, and sometimes there is another poor skeletal fuck, tuna fish colored, too, shuffling down the promenade in his baggy bathrobe with his IV pole on his arm like a loving dance partner, and we decide to overtake him, that miserable old man, that miserable old woman, you can't tell the difference, everyone is old and miserable here, but she's not, she's not, she's eighteen, getting ready for the prom and hissing at me to do her hair right.

In the patients' kitchen I often bump into an older man microwaving some food for his daughter, who is in the room next to Maddie's. She's been in there for five months. Nonstop, not even an hour pass to the courtyard. One hundred fifty days in solitary. She's on her *second* transplant. Quarantined. Fifty-three years old. Her father, Len, is a tall seventy-five-year-old man with a kind, relaxed face. Reminds me of Jimmy Stewart in *Harvey*. Especially when he tells me he's not worried or afraid because he knows that the good ol' Lord knows what he's doing, that his daughter, like all five billion of us, is in the good Lord's really huge hands, which Len knows are loving. Loving? You call this *loving?* I don't say that to Len, though I sure think it; I don't say anything negative because I don't want him to clam up, I want to bask in the music of his faith, I want him to keep talking, keep telling me how it works, Len, how even your daughter, who hasn't been out of that room in five months, is doing fine because she also knows that the Lord is at the helm of this sinking ship, and I listen to these words, my mouth open wide, hungry for the host, hungry for that feeling I still don't have, hungry to believe he's right, hungry to believe there is reason enough to believe.

Love to you all,
Olivia

July 26, 1999
Cincinnati

Ben Wilcox
c/o Ritz Hotel, Madrid

<u>Via fax</u>

Dear Ben,

There is a blueberry patch on a high granite bluff overlooking Basswood Lake in Canada. It is a bushy low bench of dark green leaves with bouquets of berries, shiny black beads of sweet fruit: a bonanza, my uncle Walter would call it, and my sister and I are sitting in the middle of it, empty Maxwell House cans in our laps, picking and eating as we go. Our aunt Louise is preparing pie dough in her cabin on the clear lake below. A virgin pine forest surrounds us. In short, it's heaven.

We're all geared up: socks pulled over our pants to keep the bugs out, faded cotton hats to keep the sun out. Uncle Walter drove us up the grassy path in his immaculate navy blue pickup, whistling "You're the Top" and "The Anniversary Waltz." I am secretly in love with him because he is handsome, he is quick to laugh, he doesn't drink. Should be good up on the rock, he says, there's been enough rain this year. He leaves us at our bonanza and goes to find his own.

I'm going to pick more than you, Maddie taunts.

But I'm going to eat less, so I'll end up with more.

She considers this and doesn't bite the blueberry that's

between her front teeth. I snap her picture. She's daring me, always, but to do what? More, I hear her voice say. Just more.

She drops the berry in the empty can. Picks another handful. I'm going to make tarts, she says. I have a new recipe I want to try. She's nine years old.

Auntie won't let you. You know she's the boss.

She has to let me try it. They're my blueberries.

Whatever.

We keep picking. Look how many I have already. She tilts the can and I see it's half full. When the twigs are bare she moves toward the outer reach of the patch. Livvie! Look!

There's a red bird lying in the patch. A cardinal. Don't touch it, I say.

We have to take it home.

What for?

To help it get better. Maybe it has a broken wing or something.

Leave it alone. We can't do anything.

I'm taking it home. She quickly tipped out all the berries and gently placed the small bird in her can. I thought of telling her it was no use, but I knew Uncle Walter would do that for me. He was a man with many rules. I was sure taking home wild animals had to be against one of them. But later when we met up by the truck he surprised me. We'll see what we can do for it, he said gently.

Aunt Louise found some old eyedrops and gave the black rubber–topped dropper to Maddie, who fed the bird sugar water with it. We dug up some worms and placed them in the shoe box hospital we'd made. Maddie wanted to keep the box near her bed, but Uncle Walter said No animals in the house, so the bird slept in the toolshed near the beach. In the morning I went to check on it and found it dead. I buried it in the soft black earth near some ferns. Maddie woke up later and saw the box was empty and screamed.

You fixed it, I said. It flew away. Back to the blueberry patch.

How could it? she said accusingly.

I pointed to the window, where one pane was missing. See?

She looked at me closely and long, gauging whether that was a lie or the truth, and then in her nine-year-old eyes I saw she knew I was lying, and then she let me. Okay, she said. I'm glad it flew home.

I'm not sure if this is what you had in mind, Ben. You said describe her in a single scene, like the first time you meet a character in a movie. I don't know what made me think of that. It doesn't capture everything Maddie is — she's stubborn and beautiful and intolerant and loyal — but you said one scene. I enjoyed remembering it, so thanks for suggesting it. I can't wait for you to meet her. And I can't wait to see you. I miss you.

Love,
Olivia

• • •

July 28, 1999

Dear Maddie,

It's time for me to go. But you're sleeping. I just want to say that for all the times I called you a bitch or a brat, defiant, contrary, stubborn, demanding, domineering, etc., I just want to say: I was right. Looking at you now as peaceful and sweet as a sleeping baby, it's hard to believe there's all that in you, all that majesty, but I've seen it since that afternoon last August when a stranger said leukemia and took away the life you knew, for a little while, and your innocence, forever. You're a force, a glory, you're my invincible little sister.

Uhck, I sound like a Hallmark card. But there are things as your older sister I have to say to you, and even though we've spent all these nights and days together I have failed to say them, largely because I'm not sure what they are. But I feel them. An urge to find and express some meaning in this madness and medicine and suffering. (I'm also stalling, hoping you'll wake up before the taxi arrives. I know you'll be mad if I don't wake you up, but you need your rest.)

When you were diagnosed, I wasn't worried, because I thought, Hey, cancer is curable these days; you see the stories everywhere. You'll do some chemo, your hair will fall out and grow back, and then, if not in several months then in a couple years, you'll be back to normal, back on track before thirty. I've always known that you're going to be okay, and this week I realized that the reason I know that is you: you've shown me it's what you believe and maybe even how to believe. Even when the numbers weren't as good anymore.

But that doesn't mean you haven't been afraid, and that's where I feel like I've failed. It doesn't mean this isn't serious, and sometimes I feel like the jester, the fool, breezing in with a few laughs, never making the moment right for you to talk, to be afraid with me. I wish I had been better at that. I hope this hasn't made you feel more alone. I can't say that you're not alone, because that too would be trivializing this, but, Maddie, I am closer to you biologically than anyone else in the world (even though I wasn't an HLA match) and I want you to feel emotionally close, too; I guess I want you to know that I'm with you always, I'm holding you, I love you.

So now I really do have to go. You'll be so pissed, but, well, I'm going to slip away here and you can read this letter when you wake up and I'll call you from Madrid. I read somewhere that in Chechnya they never say good-bye, only see you tomorrow. I think it's a good custom, don't you?

See you tomorrow,
Olivia

August 2, 1999
A field somewhere in Spain

Dear Dad,

Re: Parking fiascos

It's pouring down sounds like nails on the roof of my trailer. This is the rainiest summer Spain has had in fifty years; what luck. Hopefully it's just a fast-moving squall and we might still get a few hours of shooting in. We're in the middle of La Mancha on a wide-open plain, shooting a scene where Quixote tells Sancho that if he ever finds him cut in two pieces, say, after a great duel, he's got this special balm in his breast pocket that should fix him right up. It doesn't sound like much, but they're plodding along the open plain and it can't be raining or it won't match what we shot last week. We've already lost two days because of this weather, and yesterday the crew refused to work overtime, which set us back another half day. The studio calls nightly: What is your contingency plan? Why don't you have more cover sets? Cully, our line producer, takes the brunt of this, but they like to terrorize me, too, just to make sure I know they're watching every hundred grand I blow through. I can't control the goddamned weather, can I?

So I've got a minute (or perhaps a hundred) and wanted to talk to you about Mom. When she called you from the U of O parking garage and said, Ed, I can't find the car, it wasn't very helpful when you said, Well, where did you park it? *Needless to say,* if she knew the answer to that she wouldn't have spent two hours shuffling up and down all five dark floors looking for it. "Disappointing" best describes your next response, when Mom asked you to come and help her and you said, Well, I don't know where you parked the goddamned car, how can I help? It was considerate of you to have told her, at least a hundred times, to write down the parking space location — G75 Pink Floor, D42 Blue Floor, etc. — but it was less so to wonder, at that precise moment, why she hadn't. I know, I know, this is all ancient history now, she did find the car after a third hour of looking, so why am I taking the time and taking the trouble to write about this from my trailer in the Spanish countryside? Because I know you love Mom and you want to be a good husband — yes, yes, of course you have already been one, in many ways, and for many years, but here's another way you might be, just in case one day Mom can't find the car again. In the interest of being perfectly clear, I've written the scene the way I think Mom would like it to go.

Mom: (*crying; confused and worn out from wandering the five-story medical center parking garage and the previous four hours at the bedside of her retching, critically ill daughter*) Ed, I can't find the damn car.

Dad: (*stressed, from a problem at work, from his secretary's infernal incompetence, from seeing his vivacious, buxom daughter shrivel into an old woman and being unable to stop it, again!*) Oh, that's terrible, Eleanor. Do you want me to come and help you look for it?

Mom: *(grateful for that tiny, tiny gesture of benevolence from the heretofore angry universe)* Oh, would you, honey?

Dad: *(spirits lifted; buoyed up by the long-lost feeling of accomplishment, of actually being able to do something)* Of course I would. Go to the cafeteria and wait for me there. Buy a magazine. Have a cup of tea and a slice of Georgia peach pie. I'll be there soon and we'll look for the car together.

Yes, it's irrational, impractical, a waste of two people's time, but sometimes a woman just wants her man by her side, gently but firmly holding her up as she tries to find where the hell she parked the car.

Your daughter,
Olivia

＋＋＋

August 4, 1999
Madrid

Dear Tina,

This is what I was trying to say the other night. The more science can do, the more we expect it to do: the more problems science solves — from infertility to cancer — and answers it provides — from the origins of the planet to the human genome — the more faith we put in it to answer everything, when inevitably, like a computer, science can only provide information, never understanding. It can never answer the question *why?* Only we can find meaning in what science explains, and I'd still like to know that the meaning is not just make-believe, a dressing up of the facts to suit our childlike longing for a happy ending. I'd like a hint — a hint is all! — that we're not *making up* the meaning but in fact finding it. Which leads me to something you asked in your last letter: why do I like to visit churches when I don't believe in God?

When I walk into an old cathedral like they have on every corner here in Spain, I in fact feel as if I'm trespassing. I feel I've made a mistake, I've entered a secret club, that I shouldn't be there, especially if a service is in progress. If there's a gang of tourists following a lecturing guide, I don't feel awkward, because the church has been rendered a relic to be studied, like a museum, and loses its living, spooky power. But when it's empty I enter the ancient darkness and I smell the damp cement and the burning wax, and the statues of Jesus and the sad-eyed Virgin look down at me through the vaulted shadows, and I look at the marble tombs and sarcophagi and the magnificent frescoes of the glory and the agony of the lives of Jesus and the saints, as a pale robed priest or nun floats by on air, silent as a spirit, and I see the bowed heads of believers on their knees, and I hear the muffled whispers of their prayers, I feel alone and apart from them and that I don't belong in that place. I want to. I am in awe of it. But I'm outside. I envy those praying people. I want to feel what they feel. There is magic there, but I can only watch it, like an audience watches a ballet, never knowing what it feels like to pirouette on one toe, to sail through the air in a *grand jeté*. Perhaps the reason I go into churches is because I'm hoping that once, something will happen, one day I'll have a conversion experience: I'll hear a voice, or see an angel or maybe Jesus himself or the Virgin welcoming me; it may only be a fleeting feeling like the ripples on a still pond that tells me I now belong in that cathedral, in any cathedral, and I'll understand the world and life in a way that I now simply cannot.

The Iglesia de San Isidro is a few blocks from the hotel. A quiet square surrounds it. I go there early in the morning, about seven, on my way to the production office. The streets are still quiet. There might be a breeze in the leaves of the jacaranda trees, a newspaper vendor cranking open his iron kiosk, café tables being set out by a sleepy waiter. I walk inside the cathedral and I am blinded by the darkness. I wait until my eyes adjust and I see where I am. To the right there is a little shrine with a painted statue of the blue-draped Virgin on a pedestal around which are three rows of candles and often a few bouquets of red carnations or drooping daisies at her feet. At that time of day there might only be one or two candles lit, but I am always relieved to find that this shrine is never dark. Melted white wax coats the curved metal stand. I drop some pesos in the slotted worn brass box and take a taper and touch its wick to the flame of a lit candle, and then I push it into an empty hole and I think: *Heal her, please heal her.* I read somewhere that it's good to imagine the person bathed in a bright light and to imagine your love like the sun shining warmly on her, surrounding her in goodness. I look at the flame and think these thoughts. Sometimes I look at the blue-and-red stained-glass window and watch its colors dim or brighten as the sun is veiled or unveiled by a passing cloud. Then I find an empty pew in the back of the sanctuary and I wait. I breathe in the musty, mote-filled air, air heavy with centuries of hope and prayers, with wishes granted and denied, air that's filled the lungs of crying babies as they were christened with holy water and the lungs of mourning mothers, and now mine, as I say a prayer for Maddie, and wait.

Love,
Olivia

August 22, 1999
New York City

Dr. Louis Fontaine
University of Ohio Medical Center
3490 Medical Center Drive
Cincinnati, Ohio 45000

Dear Dr. Fontaine,

My sister, Madeline Hunt Connor, has been treated by a lot of doctors, but no one as kind and professional and gifted as you. From the first meeting, when you patiently explained everything and answered all of our questions, to the comfort in just seeing you every day, even when you weren't on call, knowing that you were tracking things very closely, you were a great advocate, doctor, and friend to her. I don't know a thing about medicine, but the fact that the BMT went smoothly and she went home early must have a lot to do with your good work. I can't thank you enough.

Sincerely,
Olivia Hunt

September 16, 1999
New York City

Dear Tina,

I've been meaning to write to you for weeks. Please note *another* new address! Another stranger's apartment, full of someone else's chairs and sheets and framed posters and red plates. I'll be in this one till Christmas, and I'm thinking that after that, I'll get my own place — here. I'm ready to call New York home. The longer I'm away from L.A. the more I know it's not for me, so I'll have to make it work from New York. Who knows, this may be my last film anyway. Although it looks good, Tina! Last night I saw the rough cut, and I think, I *think* it might be good. It's hard to tell, I'm so close to it. I've read or heard and now seen these lines and scenes a hundred times, so to me some of it is boring as hell, but I hope that's just my jaded perspective, and of course sound and music and the effects will make it much more magical. We show it to our first audience in ten days.

My apartment is on West Eighteenth Street, the top floor of a brownstone with wide-planked floors and windows overlooking a garden. It happens to be conveniently located only six blocks from Ben, who owns an apartment on West Twelfth. I don't remember how things were when I last wrote, but I'd guess they're about the same. We have a good time together and we work well together, but something's missing or hasn't developed yet. I can't put my finger on it. He's not a great listener, but he's so easy to be with, maybe that's not that important. I'd like him to turn off his cell phone when we're eating, but maybe it's too early to expect that. Or he's too ambitious. He has a lot of friends here, so we usually go out with them, which is fun; they're mostly other people in the business — actors and writers — so it's always lively, and we all know who we're talking about, what we're talking about. He still pulls a disappearing act now and then. Last week we were in the cutting room all day together, and at night he just left. After four mysterious nights he appeared at my door early Sunday morning with the *Times* and bagels. I grumbled, but not that much. He's adorable in this way that makes it impossible to stay mad at him. We work so well together, and this life we share is easy and fun. I can imagine a future with Ben, so I'm trying not to blow it. We're going to Hawaii for Christmas, and maybe it'll be so romantic one of us will finally say the old *L* word. . . . You'd think two people who say it all day long — I love this scene, I love your work, I love that shot, I love him — would have got around to saying I love you by now.

Maddie's improving much quicker since she got home. How anyone gets well in a hospital is perhaps the only miracle that happens there. It's Day 65 for her; 35 to go and she'll be out of the woods, the transplant will be deemed a success. We count the days like apples in a basket, and each day that is added brings her closer to the life she used to know. Between her counts and these numbered days, and the movie's schedule, I've never been so aware of the enormous magnitude of a single day.

Please don't worry about coming to her birthday party. If your doctor says don't fly, you can't fly; you and the baby's health are more important than a party. Mad will understand, and I'll be so busy I wouldn't have much time to see you anyway. And I'll definitely come to Portland once the baby's born. You must be so ready for her to come out.

Love,
Olivia

◆ ◆ ◆

September 16, 1999
New York City

Dear Friend,

I'm writing to ask you a favor. As you may know, my sister, Madeline, has been very ill this year, and I'm organizing a surprise birthday party for her on October 3.

She is Bruce Springsteen's #1 fan; she has been since she bought *Born to Run* when she was ten years old. I'm hoping I can get him to call her on her birthday. If you know Bruce or know someone who does, could you pass this request on? My sister's name is Madeline, and the phone number to call on October 3 between 1 and 5 P.M. EST is listed below. I'm sending this letter to a bunch of people and maybe eventually this will reach the Boss himself.

Thanks in advance,
Olivia Hunt

September 22, 1999
New York City

Madster,

The minute I saw him I wanted him again. The minute I saw him I also felt like he was mine, still, and always would be. In some way. He was looking his best, of course. An open-collared white shirt showed off his New Mexican tan and white teeth. He looked great. I know you told me to bring Ben, but I didn't. I haven't seen Michael in six months; the first time shouldn't be with my new boyfriend — especially when I'm not even sure that's what Ben is. As much fun as we have together, Maddie, I can't shake this feeling that I'm replaceable, that if it wasn't me, he'd be as happy with some other girl. It's like the difference between being a star who can get a movie financed and just an actor who fills a part. You should feel like a star, right? Maybe it's just a matter of more time.

I arrived at the gallery late. The room was crowded and literally buzzing; you could feel the excitement. Michael was surrounded by people, but none who looked like a beautiful poet-photographer. As I searched the room for Willow, I saw them — the paintings. Huge, passionate, vibrant oils — of *me*. Well, a highly idealized version of me. From that day in the hotel in New Mexico, when he sketched me. Besides my thighs I recognized the TV set on the dresser, the multistriped curtains, the orange quilted bedspread, my open brown purse. The startling thing about the paintings (besides their subject) was how exuberant they were, how alive. "The colorful sensuality of Gauguin painted by a passionate, troubled heir to Munch," as the *Times* critic gushed this morning.

At the opening, the critic kept squinting at me and he asked Michael who was the girl in the painting? Michael answered, Someone I'd like to meet.

So it's not like they're *completely* representational, but close enough to feel pretty strange walking into the gallery last night. I thought about storming out — he could have at least warned me — but I couldn't leave without at least glimpsing his new girl. I watched Michael, a crowd of fawning fans hanging on his every word. He looked as shy as ever, uncomfortable with all the attention but happy, too, that he'd clearly succeeded in communicating something. There was a confidence about him. When he saw me he broke away from the group and crossed the room and said, Don't be mad, Liv. Please don't be mad.

Why didn't you tell me?

I thought you might not come. God, you look beautiful.

Yeah, so do you, I said resentfully. He hugged me and I cracked open inside. I was going to cry (why does he always do that to me?), but Barbara, his dealer, came over with some art world big shots in tow. While he talked to them she asked me what I thought of the show. I told her it was complicated. She said, It's brilliant. He's going to sell out tonight. He's incredible, Olivia. He's actually done something new; do you know how hard that is to do these days? It's unabashed art as beauty, beauty as art; it goes way beyond what anyone else is doing, it's so unselfconscious and *optimistic*. He's just wonderful. She stopped and looked at *Sunday afternoon #3* and said, But you've always known that, haven't you?

At the dinner after the show Michael told me he and Willow split up. I asked what happened. It didn't work out, he said. Later, when he added that she got too demanding, too needy, she couldn't stand how much he worked, I suppressed a smirk. I told him about Ben. He couldn't resist making a jab about my weakness for directors. Most of the night, sitting next to him felt perfectly normal, and even right, that I should be with him at this big life moment when everything was finally coming together. Some old friends were confused by my being there, others weren't; none dared ask. He was happy, Maddie. He asked about you. He drove to New York (he still avoids flying) and said he might drop in and see you on his way back to Dixon.

As soon as dessert was served he said, Let's get out of here. Barbara was annoyed, but he didn't care, he couldn't do another minute of schmoozing, even if it was all for him. It was one of the things I always admired about him; as good as I am at schmoozing, he can't do it to save his life.

It was warm last night, a September night, the streets crowded with people back from summer vacations eagerly reclaiming their city. As we walked up West Broadway he said, I didn't mean to do it, you know. When I sketched you that day in Dixon I just wanted to remember it, to remember you. Then I painted it. Barbara was out visiting and saw it and said it was better than what I was working on. I told her I couldn't do more — I knew you'd flip out. She said fine. But a few weeks later I found myself doing another one, and another one, and then I couldn't stop.

It's hard to be mad — his version of me is so spectacular no one recognized it as me last night. I should be honored to be his subject. Still, he should have warned me.

I'm sorry. I thought you'd be — I don't know — flattered.

Couldn't have done much for your relationship with Willow, I said unkindly.

I told her I was getting you out of my system.

But they're so . . . Well, like Barbara said: they're optimistic.

I guess I was happy when I was painting you. I wasn't thinking about anything, I was just doing it.

We walked and talked through Manhattan and at times it was as if we'd never left and this was a continuation of a walk we'd started after dinner one night years ago. Except some anxiousness is gone. I guess we don't want anything from each other anymore. I think that's what it is. We were just a man and a woman who've known each other for many years, who've loved each other, and hurt each other, who were walking up Fifth Avenue under a late-summer night sky, stopping for a drink, stopping for an ice cream, happy with that, which is maybe everything.

Outside his hotel on West Eighty-first, he said, I shouldn't have insisted on Dixon. You'd have gone nuts.

I couldn't believe what I heard. I looked at him and saw he meant it. He went on to say I was right, he had been angry, and had had reason to be. But that he didn't feel that way anymore.

A siren screamed by, piercing our silence. We were leaning against the building wall. Across the street the giant globe of the Hayden Planetarium sat unfinished, like the world cut in half. I wanted to go upstairs with him as badly as I knew we shouldn't. Then he looked at me as if he'd heard my thoughts and said, I'll always love you, Olivia. He stepped toward the door and added, I just wanted you to know that.

We kissed each other good-night (yes, Maddie, as more than just friends) and then once again as I got into the taxi. Later, as I watched the city lights streak by from the backseat, I realized that some love, no matter what happens, never ends, and there was as much comfort as sadness in knowing that I will always love Michael, even if we can't be together. When I got home, I finally had the cry I'd needed since he held me in the gallery.

Hey, are you ever going to write back? Don't give me that one-armed crap. It only takes one to hold a pen. And I need that chocolate chip oatmeal cookie recipe; the editing staff keeps begging for more.

Love,
Olivia

◦—◦—◦

September 28, 1999
Los Angeles

Dear Mom,

The French doors are open on my balcony here at the Four Seasons and I'm watching the sun slide behind the blue cylinders of Century City. The palm trees are dark against the evening sky and the streets are quiet. I can smell the sea on the humid breeze. I have a few minutes before dinner and I felt like writing to you. A letter is always a nice surprise, isn't it? In the stack of bills and solicitations an envelope with your name, pen-written, in a familiar hand gives you something to look forward to, like a hug when you get home from work. I'm sorry I don't write to you more often. I got into the habit with Maddie and Tina (who's due any minute).

We showed *Don Quixote* to our first audience and the studio last night: the much-feared preview. I've never been so anxious, or curious. After all these months with it, I just couldn't judge if the movie is good or not. The studios use a system to quantify that question and it becomes the basis of their entire release and marketing strategy; in short, these numbers tell them whether to get behind a movie or cut their losses and dump it. So if the preview doesn't go well, you might as well kiss a decent campaign good-bye. These numbers are determined by the answers the audience gives to two questions: Was the movie excellent, very good, good, fair, or poor? and, Would you recommend the movie? Definitely, probably, etc. If these "top two boxes" are good (over 80 percent), then the movie is deemed a hit and has a good chance of becoming one, since the studio will spend a lot advertising it. Once again I was watching the numbers; there are always numbers telling the story or predicting the future.

Ben was very nervous. I was, too. He gets quiet when he's nervous, so the limo ride from the Four Seasons in Beverly Hills to the Valley was long. At a stoplight I saw that old dump I was evicted from last year, and suddenly I felt fine. Because whatever the audience and the studio and the critics thought of *Don Quixote,* I'd gotten it made. I knew that; that was true. And there'd be more movies, some better and some worse; there'd be more tears and battles and goddamn rain, but it'd all be worth the feeling I had just then, as the light turned green and that apartment disappeared.

We sat in the back row of the multiplex theater so we could watch the audience reaction, and count the dreaded walkouts, which you hope are just bathroom runs. We had about ten walkouts, which isn't too bad. People laughed in the right places, but not very loudly. They cheered whenever Quixote won and seemed appropriately hushed when he lost the duel with the Knight of the Moon. And all this added up to 74 percent in the top two boxes. We had dinner with Moriarty and some other WB execs and discussed ways to get the number up. We're going to make some cuts (including that stupid Sheep scene!) and try Ben's ending at another preview in New York in a few days. Since we're not really done, I feel neither happy nor unhappy. We're still in the middle of it. I am relieved that it didn't go badly, but I can't really be happy till more of the audience is.

It was strange, Mom. When I got back to this room last night I felt emptied out. Not about the numbers — because they're good, and we'll make them better — but because it's over. I guess it's the emptiness that comes from letting go of something that's been yours for so long. Something that you've poured your hope into now doesn't need it, because it's done. You've given all your love, you've been hearing the hum of expectation for so long, and now it is suddenly quiet. Which made me think of these lines from a Yeats poem, and how a mother must feel:

> *I sigh that kiss you,*
> *For I must own*
> *That I shall miss you*
> *When you have grown.*

I love you, Mom,
Olivia

October 4, 1999
Somewhere over Ohio

Dear Tina,

Cincinnati–New York is only an hour and fifty minutes, so I can't get too long-winded here, but I wanted to tell you Maddie's birthday was a huge success. She thought she was going away with Bobby for the weekend, so I went shopping for lingerie and a new dress for her: I brought home ten of each and like a personal shopper laid them on the bed for her to choose. She is very thin, of course, a size two down from her usual ten, and her pelvic bones and shoulder blades jut out like Caddy fins, but one dress, a sleeveless red gauzy cotton with mother-of-pearl buttons, fit her well, and she chose a pale pink satin lingerie ensemble that she thought Bobby would like. Hopefully it will distract him from my chemo head, she said.

He loves your head. He's always stroking it.

Give me a break, Livvie. I'm bald. Did you get the Replens?

She was told by her discharging nurse that she'd need Replens, the feminine lubricant, if she wanted to have intercourse with her husband. Along this road, somewhere between Stroke, Relapse, and BMT, she went through a medically induced menopause, and although her body might need a little help these days, her libido doesn't: she said as tired as she's been, she still craves her husband's body and touch, and fortunately he still craves her. We even did it in the hospital a couple times, she said, and I thought, At last I know what I have in common with my sister: we're both a little hot-blooded.

The next day was the party. She thought she was going to the Inn on Lake Erie, where she met Bobby and where they honeymooned two years ago. When they dropped me off at Elmhurst on their way, the invited guests poured out of the garage holding the banner *Happy Birthday Maddie* and she gasped and said, Livvie, you bitch. More than a hundred people came. Her friends from as far away as California and Japan, and every member of our extended family, too, the happy cousins from Alabama, the unhappy ones from Dallas, all the people from work, including some constituents she's helped along the way. (And don't make me say it again: don't worry about not making it.) Eleanor had done a great job decorating; there were balloons and fairy lights and triangular colored flags flapping in the wind. Jim had set up a sound system, and Ed had an incredible spread of catered food covering a red-clothed banquet table. He gave a good speech, and then Maddie thanked everyone for coming and for helping her this year. She also had a poem memorized for Bobby. It was from a collection I'd given her for Christmas and about which we'd fought recently. I'd accused her of never cracking open a single book I'd ever given her.

She said, Livvie knows I'm not big on poems, and I sure never memorized one before, but I had some time on my hands lately and I liked this one called "A Birthday," by Christina Rossetti. It's how I felt when I met my husband and kind of how I feel today, too, so I'm going to give it a try:

> *My heart is like a singing bird*
> *   Whose nest is in a watered shoot:*
> *My heart is like an apple tree*
> *   Whose boughs are bent with thickset fruit;*

My heart is like a rainbow shell
That paddles in a halcyon sea;
My heart is gladder than all these
Because my love is come to me.

Raise me a dais of silk and down;
Hang it with vair and purple dyes;
Carve it in doves and pomegranates,
And peacocks with a hundred eyes;
Work it in gold and silver grapes,
In leaves and silver fleurs-de-lys;
Because the birthday of my life
Is come, my love is come to me.

She grinned and shot her hand up and said, Yes! Bobby kneeled down and put his arms around her. Later, as she was cutting a huge cake from Zaharuk's Bakery, the phone rang. It was Bruce Springsteen. Tina, even I got excited, especially watching Maddie's face as she realized, after drilling him, that it wasn't a prank, it wasn't a fake, it was the real true Boss of her dreams. She started laughing and crying, which triggered the same in all the women and some men, too. Later, Jim lit fireworks, and it wasn't till one A.M. that she went home. It's Day 83, Tina! Maddie said she feels good, so we're all breathing a little easier. She's coming with me to the premiere next month; we kept a second dress for that. We're using the premiere to raise money for the hospital Oscar video program that she started with my mom and a friend at work. Some studios are still holding out, but I think once more agree to do it, the others will, too, and this money will help finance the pilot program, which is for Ohio hospitals.

I can't believe we're already landing. Bye for now.

Love,
Olivia

✦✦✦

October 4, 1999
New York City

Mr. Bruce Springsteen
c/o John Landau Mgt.
11 Burtis Ave.
New Canaan, Connecticut 06840

Dear Mr. Springsteen,

Thank you so much for calling my sister, Madeline, on her birthday. It was unbelievably cool of you and she was so excited she couldn't stop laughing and crying — well, you know, you heard her. When you sang "Happy Birthday" to her she put you on the speakerphone so everyone could hear, and then for the rest of the party you were with us, *Born to Run* blasting from the speakers. She said it was hands down the best birthday of her life, and I can't thank you enough.

In case she forgot to tell you, you've gotten her through this year of hell: every morning she plays "No Surrender" — and she hasn't for a minute. My sister has always been your biggest fan, but now I'm one, too. Thanks again.

Sincerely yours,
Olivia Hunt

WESTERN UNION TELEGRAM

Date: October 27, 1999
To: Tina Burns
Mt. Sinai Hospital
Portland, Oregon

Congratulations stop Welcome to the world Madeline Grace all 7.2 lbs of you stop Love the name stop Will meet and greet you ASAP stop Love Olivia

November 15, 1999
Four Seasons Hotel, L.A.

Dear Tina,

I've booked a ticket to Portland for Thanksgiving because I have to see you (and meet my goddaughter) before another year rushes by. It'll be great to have three whole days together. It's been way too long.

As you probably read in the morning papers, *Don Quixote* didn't have a great opening weekend. Fifteen million is respectable, but not what the studio was hoping for. Maybe that Bob Dylan song didn't work. Maybe the ending wasn't up enough. Ben finally convinced Warners to go with his ending, where Quixote says, I'm not crazy. I know I'm not a knight, I knew those windmills weren't giants. Some people took this to be an apostasy, that he was renouncing his dream. But in fact he was proving how much he believed in it. He believed it *in the face of the facts;* that's what made him noble and brave, and, ultimately, that's what made him a knight. It's not a dream if you're just insane, is it? The critics got that and generally loved the movie (four stars in ten papers!), so we might have a chance at some Oscars. The high point of the premiere for me was when I introduced the movie and thanked all the people I was expected to thank, and then from the stage called Maddie on my cell phone. I asked the audience to give her a round of applause for pushing me to get it made and for launching the video program for hospitals (the premiere raised $100,000 for it). She was supposed to be up there with me, of course. I was so disappointed she wasn't. She's been doing so well I was surprised when she called last week to tell me she was too tired to make the trip. I know she would have if she could, so she must really be zonked. I think she's been overdoing it in the garden and decorating her new house.

I can't wait to meet your little Madeline. Her namesake is very proud that you honored her this way, and my mom was touched, too. Thanksgiving will have a lot of meaning for everyone this year. See you then.

Love,
Olivia

Dear Michael,

I don't know how to write this letter. I have been staring at this blank page for hours. The light from the sky has died. The trees are black. Maddie is gone.

You were the only person I wanted to call. I know you would have come. I called my mother's sister and brother for her. My aunt Louise screamed when she heard and dropped the phone on her kitchen floor. I called my father's partner. I wanted to call you, but I couldn't, because I knew telling you would break me apart. There was too much to do.

Last week when she was so tired, Bobby took her to see her doctors, who told her the leukemia was back. She could prepare for another transplant when she was stronger. She didn't tell anyone because she didn't want me to miss the premiere. Five days later she had trouble breathing and Bobby rushed her to Mercy.

From Tuesday till now I remember images as if from a dream where things happen, things fly at you, one minute you're in a dark hotel room in L.A. and the ringing phone scares you awake, then you're throwing clothes in a bag — nothing black, because that way she can't die, right? — the next you're running through the airport, and then you're holding her hand, asking her to squeeze it, *squeeze it,* and the next your high heels are sinking into the soft earth of the cemetery lawn, and like in a dream the images are contorted, surreal, impossible. I am walking toward a pale blue curtain in Mercy, hearing a loud gravelly rattle, the sound of Maddie gasping for air, for life, and then in ICU the vent stretching her lips wide open, the purple petechiae blooming like a garnet necklace around her swollen neck and her hand waving, waving — was it hello or good-bye? was it help or hold on? — we don't know because she couldn't say, she couldn't say a thing with the hose in her mouth, she couldn't speak or write, she couldn't talk to me, and now the doctors are asking what I want to do because she'd made me her advocate; me? why not you, Bobby? Because I couldn't do it; he is crying. The advance directive only states who will speak for the patient, not what the patient's wishes are, so should we resuscitate, Olivia? asks Dr. Fancyshoes, why him again, why is he part of the finale? Why can he live and —; no, don't, she wouldn't want to be a vegetable; no. And then her body heaving after her heart stopped, which was only moments before Mom and I are picking out her burial dress, fighting, of course, *No, not the jean jacket, for godsakes, Livia!* now picking out her plot at the cemetery where we rode bikes and where in the twelfth grade she got drunk and had sex with Danny O'Riley on some other sister's grave, and now as I'm dressing myself I realize, oh, no, I got the rule wrong: when you carry an umbrella it never rains. If you *bring* black she *won't* die. I'm shocked by this; I want to run screaming out of the house, but instead I quickly search the attic for something to wear. The only thing that fits is a pilgrim costume I wore for the senior-year production of *The Crucible*. A floor-length black pinafore with a high white collar. At the viewing six people are asking me not about the pinafore, as I look at the brass handles of the oak casket, but what Robin Williams is *really* like, what other stars do I know, and who isn't nice, who's really nasty? Six others telling me they have a great idea for a movie, and I might have bludgeoned each one of them, but then

I'm holding my father's dry hand or is he holding mine as we step toward the coffin to say good-bye to his daughter, to my sister, to Maddie.

Olivia

◄—►—►

November 24, 1999

Dear Bobby,

Here's $100 to get the window fixed. I'm sorry. When I saw that BELIEVE rock on her bedside table, the one she touched for good luck every morning, the one Sheryl bought for her in the Mercy gift shop, well, it just leaped into my hand and then it flew through the glass like a freed bird out of a cage. I don't remember throwing it. I hope this money will cover the costs. (The rock is still somewhere out there in the tomato patch if you want it.)

I hope I understood your instructions: I packed up all the clothes and toiletries, jewelry and medical supplies, and left only the kitchen and her desk untouched. I emptied the cedar hope chest.

I'm heading to Florida this afternoon. See you at Christmas?

Take care,
Olivia

November 27, 1999
Rome

Eleanor Hunt
7829 Southern Bay Drive
Naples, Florida 67845

Dear Mom,

I'm sorry I didn't make it there for Thanksgiving. You know I was planning to. But when I got to the airport I realized I just could not face a turkey dinner for three in the condo. I remembered the editor on the film had mentioned that his place in Rome was empty, and suddenly I knew that's where I had to go. I needed to be alone. I'm sorry.

It's a nice apartment, with high ceilings and fireplaces and windows that overlook the red-tiled rooftops of Trastevere, this neighborhood that feels like a little village itself, just beside the Tiber.

It wasn't packing up her things that did it. Bobby said he couldn't do it himself and he also couldn't look at her bathrobe hanging on the door another day or her "lucky" cap slung on the bedside lamp. He went up north with his family for Thanksgiving, so I had her house to myself. I liked being there again. I didn't want to leave. I liked smelling her. Seeing her things. Touching them. Her coffee cup, moisturizer, and opal earrings. A grocery list: frozen waffles, Kleenex, chocolate chips. I expected her things to be gone, like she is. What were they doing still there without her? It's illogical that her favorite shirt, her toothbrush, the blue jay in the backyard have outlived her. I slept on her side of the bed.

I buried my face in her clothes still hanging in the closet. In the morning, as I sorted through her things, I played her tape of fight songs — "No Surrender" and "I Believe I Can Fly." It was hard to throw anything away, even some of her graver fashion mistakes, like that Hawaiian shirt she wore for two years straight and those tight red toreador pants. I separated them into three piles: one for the Salvation Army, one for your attic, one for me. I brought her things with me. I like wearing her flannel shirts to bed, and the baseball cap from the Pie-O-Neer Café. Your stuff is in a box behind her trunk of school mementos and papers, under the right attic rafter.

Don't worry about me. I'm fine. I'll call soon.

Love to you both,
Olivia

- ◆ -

December 10, 1999
Rome

Dear Tina,

Thanks for your letter. I'm sorry I haven't called you back. I don't feel much like talking. Yes, I'm here alone. When Maddie died I didn't turn to Ben. I couldn't. Our love was too shallow, too new; his sympathy could only fall short. When I didn't ask him to the funeral, we both knew it was over. Timing is everything, I guess, and although I liked Ben a lot, I don't think I had enough time to love him before life events started happening. Under other circumstances, we might have made it. Under those normal conditions I keep looking for. He wasn't that upset. He didn't even seem surprised. He said he'd miss me and hoped I'd call him when I got back. That was it. Maybe I was just a location romance for him after all.

I did want Michael there, but I resisted. I'm not sure why.

I'm glad the baby is doing just fine; I can't wait to meet her. But I think it'll have to wait till after Christmas. Thanks for the offer, but I'm not ready to come home. I don't exactly have one yet, so apartment-sitting here suits me for now.

I'll call you soon. If we don't talk before this reaches you, have a Merry Christmas, Tina.

Love,
Olivia

December 11, 1999
Rome

Dear Michael,

It was good talking to you. As always. Thanks for tracking me down. (My mother swore she wouldn't give anyone this number; I told you she's always liked you.) I'm sorry I couldn't say much. I'm so hollowed out that I literally couldn't find the words. And if anyone could coax them out of me, it'd be you. Maybe this morning I'll be able to write a few.

You asked, what do I do all day here in Rome? Well, I go to the café for coffee in the morning and I read the *Herald Tribune*. I eat the words like raisins, a word at a time, remembering nothing. It's a pleasant ritual that gives me a sense of purpose and completion without burdening me with knowledge of things I can't do anything about: the Palestinians, the Republican presidential candidates. Then I walk the gray cobbled streets as the shopkeepers roll up their steel shutters and dogs zigzag ahead, pissing and sniffing and eating scraps of trash dropped by the garbagemen. I cross the Ponte Sisto, a narrow pedestrian bridge where there's a poor old guy hacking away at "Amazing Grace" on a tenor saxophone as beat-up as he is. It's the only song he plays. He's been trying to get it right for at least two weeks now, who knows how many weeks before that, and he can't find the high G, the "me" (as in, "wretch like *me*"), he just kills it, and then he goes right back to the beginning, as if that will lead him to the G correctly, as if he missed a turn back in the third measure, and one of these days I'm going to grab the poor instrument out of his grimy hands and blow that high G for him, even though I don't play the saxophone. I toss a few coins in his cap and he nods and I walk on.

I arrive at the Campo de Fiori, an open square that is the site of a daily market, and see what's being offered that morning. I've gotten to know a few of the leathery-faced vendors, which makes me feel like a part of this ancient corner of the world. I wander home a different route, over the Ponte Garibaldi, where the futuristic green tram whizzes by, thus escaping another round of un-"Amazing Grace." On the couch, or the terrace if it's warm enough, I read *The Decline and Fall of the Roman Empire* and go over my Italian exercises. I prepare lunch: a salad, some cheese, maybe some salami or prosciutto, with a glass or two of red wine. I take a nap. Then I wake up and go for a walk and have a Campari on the way home, maybe two, at the Calisto bar just off the Piazza de Santa Maria Trastevere, because it's cheap and quiet there and full of people who are worse off than me: junkies, janitors, the just-released. I watch all the people go by and think, Why not her? Why can they live and she couldn't? And what was all that struggle for if *not* to live? That's what I keep asking. That's what I think about when I walk through the marble ruins of the Forum and along the banks of the green Tiber: *What for?* The bone marrow biopsies, the spinal taps, the nausea, the fevers, the paralysis, the rehab, the abortion, those months in the hospital, all that just to die? You said I'm grieving, but no, I think I'm disbelieving. I'm stunned; I'm enraged at the cruelty, the big joke, and at myself for being blind to what was happening all along, all along. I was so sure everything was going to be fine. I kept referring to the facts as proof. I looked at those "facts" from my leukemia binder again, and right there, in the shadow of my pink highlighter, are facts that I simply and literally did not see: her prognosis was "dismal," the chance of survival after two years only ten percent. I thought remission meant cure, but of course I'd read a dozen times that remission only meant the cancer had been stalled; it didn't mean it had been killed, it didn't mean that she'd be the same again, it didn't mean that she'd live. I was a fool. And I fooled her into being one, too. I believed, she believed, we were a couple idiots, and my mother, as ever, was right. What the fuck was it for?

Olivia

Dear Bobby,

I found this poem in a collection of Pablo Neruda's poetry I bought yesterday. I thought of you, and of how much, and how well, you loved my sister:

> . . . *forgive me*
> *If you are not living*
> *if you, my beloved, my love*
> *if you*
> *have died,*
> *all the leaves will fall on my breast*
> *it will rain upon my soul night and day*
> *the snow will burn my heart,*
> *I shall walk with cold and fire and death and snow*
> *my feet will want to march toward where you sleep,*
> *but*
> *I shall go on living . . .*

All my love,
Olivia

Date: December 15, 1999
From: OliviaHunt@usol.com
To: JamesEHunt@usol.com

Dear Jim,

Thanks for calling the other night. I felt much better when we hung up. I'd forgotten how easy it is to talk to you. It'll be good to be living in the same city again. (I think I'll look in the Village, if you hear of anything.)

You were right: Maddie did push me to make the movie, so thanks for reminding me. I guess she didn't want me, or you, to move home. She wanted everything to be the same. And she never stopped believing she was going to get well; moving back home would have seemed like an admission of something that none of us could accept. Still, for my sake, for all the days I missed with her, I'll always wish I had.

Love,

O.

December 18, 1999
Rome

Dear Mom and Dad,

It's late here, a warm, starry night and I'm finally calm enough to write to you. Something amazing happened today. I was walking across a pedestrian bridge, a walk I take every day, and as I frisked myself for loose change for the street musician who is always there, struggling with "Amazing Grace," I felt some paper in the breast pocket of Maddie's jean jacket — you know, the one that she wouldn't take off all through high school, that to this day still holds the shape of her shoulders and her scent. I'd never worn it before, it's been too cold here, but today was like a new spring day. I unhooked the copper button of the pocket and pulled out a folded envelope and was confused to see it was addressed to me: *Livvie*, it said, in Maddie's hand. I ripped it open there on the bridge and sat down to read it. She must have written it the weekend before she died.

Dear Livvie,

I was going to dictate the recipes to you on the plane to the premiere, but I'll just write them down here myself. I owe you a few letters anyway. This might take a couple days — I'm so tired, you can't believe. Sorry about my handwriting. It's hard to hold on to the pen. I'm just so tired. I guess it's what they mean by dead tired, haha. It's weird to think when you read these words I won't be here. My hand is holding this paper and your hand will hold it, too.

I know you guys are going to be sad and I wish there was a way I could force you not to be. I don't want to make anyone sad. That's my last request, or demand more like it, and since you're bossy you have to tell everyone this for me: when you think of me, don't be sad. I want to be like a favorite song. The one you play to cheer you up and get you going again. And like a good song, sometimes I'll just pop into your head or you can play me whenever you want. Tell everyone that's my last wish, okay?

Livvie, you've got to help Bobby with the tomatoes. I'm sitting in the backyard looking at about two baskets' worth on the ground. You could make spaghetti sauce. I know you don't like gardening or canning, but he's going to need help and you know he's too proud to ask for it. God, I love him. And the way he loves me. Even the bald gimp me — if that's not true love, what is? That's what it should be like for you. I haven't met Ben and I admit I'm still rooting for Michael. Call me sentimental. But I think you two loved each other and work got in the way. And maybe your egos, too. And you were pretty screwed up back then for some reason. Maybe Hollywood got to you. I guess I got the looks and the brains. When you asked me would I go thru another transplant and I said yes, for more time with Bobby, you couldn't believe it, could you? Maybe because you never felt that way about somebody. You should be as happy as I've been, even through all this crap. Bobby loves me no matter what and we had such good times together in the boat or just driving around in the convertible or watching TV on the couch; I could never have enough of him, I guess that's why I want more, I do, just another day.

I knew I didn't have a chance in hell of making it, though. Dismal isn't exactly a good prognosis. But you can't just lie down, can you? And everybody's prognosis is dismal, isn't it? Right? You just forget about that and go for it anyway, not knowing when or how you're going to go one day, packing in as much as you can, just living it out, not waiting it out. That's what everybody does, and that's all I did. I'm still not giving up. I want to make you guys proud of me. And who knows. It's just that I'm so tired, Livvie, I feel like I could sleep forever, haha. Bet you never thought you'd hear me say I want to sleep, huh? But you never know. Maybe I'll hide this letter and I might find it one day when I'm cleaning out my closet and laugh. Or if it's meant to be, you'll find it. Like a message in a bottle.

I see why you like writing letters. It's kind of like being with the person. You think about them. See their face. Listen to what your

heart has to tell them. Like just now I thought of Dad. Tell him I'm
not mad at him. I know he's just a partyer like me. But don't let him
go off the deep end when I do (another dumb joke), tell him he's got
to be strong for Mom. And to quit smoking. And that I loved all those
lunches he brought me from my favorite restaurants and thanks
again for helping us buy the house. He used to wheel me down to the
park at lunch and every time I'd remember walking home from
school with you. It was only one year. I guess that's why it's so memo-
rable. The sun was behind us and made our shadows really long. I
would walk ahead of you in your shadow and make it taller or fatter
or sometimes just fit into it so you couldn't tell I was there.

I just dozed off. I should go inside and get the recipes, but I can't
move. I think I heard the phone ring. Mom, probably. I love her, tell
her that, okay? Even though we fought a lot. You should try not to.
She needs a friend, since that's what I was for her. You're going to
have to visit more often now, Livvie, and go shopping with her. Do
some gardening with her. It won't take that much out of you. She
tries so hard and she's been through a lot. You think she's negative,
but she's just a worrier. It was good to have someone worrying about
me. I could look at her and know she knew it wasn't good, she was
with me that way. She was just being Mom. I loved her cool soft hand
on my forehead. The way she hummed those folk songs whenever she
thought I was sleeping.

Jim is my bud and he knows that. Some people you don't have to
say anything to, there's just this understanding between you. He's my
big brother, it's like your first hero. That's how I always think of him.
Like he could do no wrong even when he does. I love Jim. Just thinking about him makes me smile.

I saved all your letters. I know you want to be a writer, you
always have, and you're just scared, which I don't get. Look at all

those stories you used to tell me when we were kids. Just write them down. Or take all the letters (they're in my bottom desk drawer) and write The True and Outstanding Adventures of the Hunt Sisters. Just don't be gloomy or snotty, nobody likes that. When you're stuck or writing something stupid I'll guide the pen, the way we did on the piano that day. Only this time, I'll be helping you. Think of me when you're stuck. Think: What would Maddie say about this? I can see you rolling your eyes. But hey, like I always say, you don't know everything, Olivia.

I wish I could write like you. I thought I had a lot to say to you and now all I can think of is, I love you, Livvie. People say it all the time, so it doesn't seem special enough for this kind of letter but it's what I feel. Love for you, and from you. You don't have a big sister so you don't know what it's like, but it's different than anyone else. It's like the best part of a mom and a best friend. Like you're always look-ing out for me. Bossing me around too much but you're my bud, too. I know you don't think you were good at it, but you were. Quit think-ing you weren't.

Okay, surfer squares, oatmeal chocolate chip cookies, chicken cacciatore, my salsa, spaghetti sauce — I think that was it. Those are the ones in my head. Everything else is in the blue recipe binder. Bobby might want that, but you can copy it. I wish I could make you some batches of stuff, but I think I'm just too tired out today.

I wish you were here. It's an amazing Indian summer day. The sky's so blue and it's not too hot and the maple tree is bright yellow. I love this day

Toward the end her writing is so faint, I hope you can read it. She knew I would find it. She knew I loved that jean jacket. I hope it makes you both feel a little better. I think it did me. I'm not superstitious; however, I can't help but notice I "received" the letter after an especially bad night, a night when I found myself thrashing and smashing the pillow with my fist and demanding a sign from her, asking the darkness, Where are you? where are you? possessed by a furious and acute sense of entitlement to a goddamned answer. In the morning it was bright and the weather had changed. The air was suddenly warm. I pulled the jacket out of the suitcase and slipped my arms into it. If that poor sax player had finally hit the high G of "Amazing Grace," then even I would have to believe that miracles don't happen only in the movies. But as I write this, I know that guy is still on the Ponte Sisto blowing F sharp. Maybe tomorrow he'll find his way there, his fingers and his lips and his breath together will hold and possess the G, and when they do the sound will be glorious because it will be full of the days before, the days when he was lost and only looking, playing happily in the Roman sun.

Love,

Olivia

Acknowledgments

The author would like to thank the following people for their invaluable assistance and support:

Thank you
Charlie D'Ambrosio, Patricia Zumhagen, Patricia Burke, Amy Fontaine, Terry Guzowski, Jo Human, Don Laventhall, and Julie Talen, for being great readers and true friends.

Thank you
Olivia Stewart, for loaning me your beautiful apartments in Rome and Venice.

Thank you
Everyone at Little, Brown: Michael Pietsch, Claire McKinney, Betsy Uhrig, and especially my editor, Judy Clain, for your incredible support and dedication.

Thank you
The Gernert Company and especially Betsy Lerner, my agent, for your warm wisdom, sharp critical judgment, and unflagging, good-humored patience.

Thank you
Anna and Ava Robinson, my wonderful nieces, for showing me the best sisters can be, and special thanks to my brother, Tom, and his wife, Audrey Matson, for always cheering me on, and usually over some really great food.

Thank you
Hal and Rosemary Robinson, my parents, for your enduring generosity and encouragement, and for teaching me to aim high, work hard, and to have a sense of humor about almost anything.